D1480471

PANHANDLE GUNMAN

PANHANDLE GUNMAN

A WESTERN DUO

RAY HOGAN

FIVE STAR
A part of Gale, Cengage Learning

Detroit • New York • San Francisco • New Haven, Conn • Waterville, Maine • London

GALE
CENGAGE Learning

Copyright © 2008 by Gwynn Hogan Henline.
Five Star Publishing, a part of Gale, Cengage Learning.

Set in 11 pt. Plantin.
Printed on permanent paper.

LIBRARY OF CONGRESS CATALOGING-IN-PUBLICATION DATA

Hogan, Ray, 1908–
    [Gun of a killer]
    Panhandle gunman : a western duo / by Ray Hogan. — 1st ed.
        p. cm.
    ISBN-13: 978-1-59414-623-7 (hardcover : alk. paper)
    ISBN-10: 1-59414-623-3 (hardcover : alk. paper)
    1. Western stories. I. Hogan, Ray, 1908– Gun of a killer. II. Title.
    PS3558.03473G785 2008
    813'.54—dc22   2008000693

First Edition. First Printing: June 2008.

Published in 2008 in conjunction with Golden West Literary Agency.

Printed in the United States of America
1 2 3 4 5 6 7 12 11 10 09 08

TABLE OF CONTENTS

★ ★ ★ ★ ★

GUN OF A KILLER

★ ★ ★ ★ ★

I

Luke Wade slouched against the wall of Red Hill's largest saloon, The Wagon Master, and stared moodily into the distance beyond the dusty street. So far it had been another wild-goose chase—and he was almost broke again. He stirred impatiently, frustration racking his mind and etching deep lines in his browned features. He guessed he would have to find himself a job, stick with it long enough to accumulate some cash—and then take up the search once more. A lean, gray-eyed, remote sort of young man, he pulled in his glance, allowed it to drift down the drab, narrow channel lying between the rows of weathered buildings. It was mid-morning and several persons moved along the plank walks, getting their business out of the way before the driving heat set in. According to the remarks he had heard since reaching Red Hill, it was unseemly hot for so early in the summer—what the hell, it was hot in summer everywhere, and every year.

His gaze halted on a buggy drawn up in front of Copp's General Store. A rancher, no doubt, who might possibly have room in his crew for another man. Two buckboards were in the wagon yard at the side of Marmon's Hay & Grain Company. Prospects, also.

Elsewhere along the street a few saddled horses dozed at hitch racks, and the town marshal, his star glinting in the sunlight, lounged in the open doorway of his office. The old lawman had watched him closely ever since he had arrived in

Red Hill, but that was always the pattern so far as Luke was concerned and he had grown accustomed to the cold, hard stare of lawmen during the past three years. Perhaps it was the grim, humorless set of his face, or maybe the flat depths of his eyes that drew their immediate suspicion, telegraphed to them that here walked trouble and sudden death. Or it could have been the heavy, ornate .45 worn low on his thigh. Regardless which, they would have guessed right—and Luke Wade reckoned he had good reason to be the sort of man he was.

It had begun three years ago, up in the lonely Chugwater country of Wyoming. There had been a ranch—a small one, to be sure, but one gaining ground as the months passed. He and his father Ben, who had been crippled in the war, had worked it alone. Things had looked promising, and Luke, on the very day he'd turned twenty, had ridden into Laramie to meet with a cattle buyer and arrange for the sale of their small herd.

It had taken longer than he'd expected, and by the time he'd had purchase details arranged and other matters settled, ten days had gone by. And then, when he'd finally returned home, he had found his father dead—murdered, their house burned to the ground, and the cattle gone.

Ben Wade had not died easily or quickly. Luke had found him near the well, two bullet wounds in his breast. Nearby had lain his old cavalry saber. With a faltering hand Luke's father had scrawled a message on the back of an envelope he had been carrying. Luke still carried the note.

So long son. Hate not seeing you but I reckon this is the way it was meant to be. Three men done it. Not Indians. Jumped me about dark same day you left. Strangers. Cut one with old Betsy. Nipple to hip. Not deep but he'll have a long scar. Big man. Then he shot me. Fancy gun. Wish I. . . .

There the painful, almost illegible scrawl had trailed off, leaving to Luke Wade a heritage of hate that had increased rather than diminished as the years had passed. He had little to go on—a big man with a long scar across his belly, and who had dropped his pistol during the encounter. Slashed by the saber, he had apparently shot Ben Wade, then staggered back clutching his wound. In the process he had lost his weapon and, not noticing, ridden on. Luke, hunting about for more evidence, had discovered it half buried in the sand, its blood-spattered, delicately carved handles with their silver inlays glinting in the sunlight.

So for three years Luke had been drifting back and forth across the frontier in a grim quest, always looking for a man with such a scar, and forever watching for reaction in a rider's eyes that would betray recognition of the ornate .45—the killer's gun.

That winter he had been in New Mexico's Seven Rivers country, near the Pecos. A tip from a drover had turned him west to Red Hill and an area known as the Mangus Valley—he had seen a man with a scar across his middle, the drover had said. There had been a saloon fight, and the man—a rancher, he thought he was—had stepped in to halt it, and gotten his shirt ripped for his efforts. The drover had been sure it had been in Red Hill . . . well, pretty sure. Man saw a lot of saloon brawls, knocking around the country.

But it was a lead, and Luke followed them all. He was hardened to disappointment after all this time, and he recognized the difficulty of locating the killer for whom he searched. Such a scar would always be hidden from casual glance—and a man could mask his surprise at seeing a weapon he had lost under the circumstances involved. Luke could have faced the killer a dozen times and never known it. But the search had become a grim, bitter way of life for him, and he wasn't going to give it up.

Now he was in the broad, gleaming southwestern corner of New Mexico, bordering on Arizona Territory. It was new country for Americans. Ranches had begun to spring up here in only the last three or four years, and possibilities, because of that fact, were good. It could mean nothing, or it could mean much. If the killer had been no more than a common rustler who'd taken the Wade herd for the immediate cash it would bring, he would be wasting time. However, if the murderer of Ben Wade were a ruthless man out to build up a ranch quickly for himself, he could very well be one of those newcomers who had settled in Mangus Valley. Chugwater was far away, and the time element was right. But the quest would have to grind to a halt, for now. A man had to eat, and to eat he had to work.

Luke reached into his pocket and brought forth the few coins he possessed. About $5, he saw, making a casual count. Enough to buy a drink or two and eat for a couple of days. By then he should have a job located. Ranchers were hiring this time of the year. He threw a glance at the buggy and saw that it was still unattended. He could talk to the owner later; meanwhile, he'd go inside and jaw with the bartender. Bartenders usually knew everything that was going on.

He wheeled, and came into hard collision with one of three men emerging from the saloon. The impact knocked the nearest of the trio, a squat, stubble-bearded rider, off balance and into his two companions, one a dark, swarthy Mexican, the other a redhead.

An oath ripped from the husky man's lips and anger rushed into his eyes. Wade, rocked to his heels, came up against the framing of the doorway. He caught himself, grinned tightly at the rider.

"Sorry," he murmured, and started to move on.

The bearded man lurched forward, threw out a thick arm, and checked him. He was not drunk, had consumed only enough of The Wagon Master's fiery liquor to turn him quarrel-some and belligerent.

"Sorry, hell!" he roared. "You think you can go shovin' me around, you got another think comin'!"

He placed himself squarely in front of Luke, huge beefy hands resting on his hips, head thrust forward. His two friends moved out onto the porch and circled softly in until they stood directly behind Wade.

Luke's eyes narrowed and the line of his jaw firmed, began to whiten. Back in the street he could hear the hollow beat of boot heels on the sun-baked earth. Beyond the squat cowpuncher, inside the smoky depths of the saloon, chairs scraped as men moved hastily out of the way.

"Said I was sorry," Wade stated in a low, controlled voice. "What do you want from me . . . my arm?"

"Come on, Del," the redhead said. "Forget it. He never done it a-purpose."

The husky rider hunched lower. He shook his head angrily. Sweat was glistening on his face and his eyes still burned.

"I want you, saddle bum," he said, glaring at Luke. "For maybe ten minutes. Aim to give you a learnin' about pushin' people around."

Anger was beginning to stir within Wade. The collision had been his fault—but it had been accidental and he had apolo-gized. As far as he was concerned, it ended there. But if this Del was looking for trouble, he had come to the right place. Luke Wade, while never courting trouble, never ran from it, either.

"Could be a bit of a chore," he said dryly, "even with your two swampers helping out."

Del's eyes flamed afresh. "You're mighty tough talkin'!" he snarled. "Now, I'm bettin' that fancy iron you got danglin' off your hip ain't nothin' but show. Pure damn' bluff. And I'm bettin' you're the biggest bluff of it all."

"Don't bet on it," Wade replied coldly. "Now, get out of my way. I'm going inside."

"No you ain't . . . not till I'm done with you!" Del shouted, and lunged, extended hands reaching.

"The hell with it," Luke muttered, and stepped quickly aside. He seized the rider by the shoulders, spun him about. Shoving hard, he sent him stumbling into the arms of his two friends.

"Get him away from me before I have to kill him," he snapped, and turned back to The Wagon Master's swinging doors.

"Hold on, damn you!" Del screamed. "Else I'll drill you from behind!"

II

Luke Wade froze. He hung there, poised, for several long seconds, and then wheeled slowly. He wanted no trouble, but Del simply wouldn't let it lie. Abruptly he was all out of patience.

The three men had backed off the porch, now faced him from the street. They had spread out slightly, a yard or so apart. Coolly Wade considered the disadvantage. Red Hill had fallen silent. He could see several white faces peering through store windows, their features taut and strained. The town marshal, who had pulled himself erect in the doorway of his office, watched narrowly. Across the way a big, fairly well-dressed man was helping a pretty girl into the buggy in front of Copp's, and the thought—*This is going to make me miss talking to him.*—passed through Luke's mind. And then he dismissed all vagrant subjects from his consciousness as Del's harsh voice came to him.

"I'm aimin' to see if you can use that there gun you're packin'."

Wade nodded. "Been a few others wondered about it." He

glanced toward the town's lawman. The marshal had not moved. Either he did not understand what was happening, or he was unwilling to step in. Luke's voice was loud in the tense hush. "You stack the odds real good for yourself," he said in a dry voice. He ducked his head at Del's companions. "They cutting a slice of this pie, too?"

"We're bunkies. They'll hang around, make real sure I get a fair shake. We sort of do that . . . look out for each other."

"I'll bet you do," Wade murmured.

Del laughed. "You gettin' cold feet, mister? Now, I'm a forgivin' man. All you have to do to get out of this is fall right down on your knees and crawl into that saloon. That's all . . . start crawlin'!"

Luke, his face a mask, kept his eyes fastened to those of Del. "Something I never did do . . . learn to crawl."

"About time you was learnin'!" the stocky rider yelled, and reached for his pistol.

With the smoothness of an uncoiling spring Luke Wade buckled, swerved to one side. His .45 smashed the silence of the street once, twice before he was prone on the worn boards of The Wagon Master's porch.

Out in the spread of the bright sunshine Del was staggering backward, having great difficulty staying on his feet. Abruptly his pistol fell to the dust. He clutched at his chest with both hands and a slackness settled over his face, displacing the astonishment that had gripped it. He began to sink slowly. Nearby the dark-skinned Mexican was on his knees, holding his left side. Blood oozed through his fingers.

Luke Wade saw this from the corner of his eye. His full gaze was on the third man, the redhead, who stared at him through a mixture of fear and amazement. His weapon was no more than half out of its holster. Wade had drawn and fired twice with deadly accuracy before the redhead could even pull his revolver.

"Your turn, Red!" Wade called through the coiling wisps of smoke.

The cowpuncher released the butt of his pistol, allowed it to drop into place. Fingers spread, he raised his arms slowly. "Not me," he muttered, shaking his head.

Wade did not stir. "Then get the hell out of here . . . fast!" he said in savage, biting tone.

Immediately the redhead wheeled to one of the horses at the rack. He swung to the saddle, wheeled about, and raced off down the street.

Instantly the town came alive. The marshal started toward the saloon at a fast walk. Men and women came through the doorways of several stores. The rancher, forsaking his daughter, now seated in the buggy, approached in long strides. Voices shouted questions, answers, and somewhere farther along a dog, aroused by the gunshots, barked in a quick, excited way.

Luke drew himself to his feet. He flicked a disdainful glance at the crowd gathering around Del and the Mexican, then, removing his wide-brimmed hat, he dusted the front of his worn Levi's and coarse shirt. Men began to pour from the interior of The Wagon Master, crowding by him and adding to the considerable assembly already in the street.

"Fastest thing I ever saw!" someone said in an awed voice. "He was through shootin' before any of them even cleared leather."

"Well, he sure didn't miss. Got that Del dead center. And the Mex . . . he's hurt bad."

"You see that other 'n' take out? Run like a scared rabbit."

Luke, the hard tension dribbling slowly from his body, turned heavily toward the doorway of the saloon. He needed a drink now worse than ever—maybe a couple of them. He took a half step into the broad, murky room, then halted as the marshal's voice caught him.

"Hold up there, you!"

Wearily Wade paused, then turned. He met the old lawman's burning hot gaze.

"Something bothering you, Marshal?"

"Bothering me!" the lawman raged. "You ride into my town, kill one man . . . maybe two . . . and then you've got the gall to ask me if something's bothering me! You're damn' right there is . . . you!"

Wade moved his shoulders slightly. "You saw what happened. There was no quarrel on my part. I tried to talk him out of it, but he wouldn't listen."

The lawman cocked his head to one side. He was an old man with a white, downcurving moustache. "Was you in his boots, would you? Way it looked to me, you didn't give him no choice."

"He had a choice," Wade cut in coldly. "He could have let it ride if he'd been of a mind. You figure to hold me for it?"

"He can't!" a man at the edge of the porch spoke up indignantly. "We all seen it. If ever a man was crowded into a shoot-out, it was you. The whole town'll testify to that."

The marshal half turned, gave the speaker a withering glance, then came back to Wade. "No, reckon there ain't no charges, but I'm serving notice on you now . . . keep moving. I don't want you around. Hardcase like you draws trouble, and I aim to dodge all of that I can."

Luke grinned wryly. "Man defends himself . . . and gets tagged a hardcase. Marshal, you got a funny way of figuring things."

"Maybe so, but I ain't standing for no killings in my town."

"You could've stopped it, Henry, if you'd wanted to," a voice broke in from the street. "Don't go passing your problems onto somebody else."

Wade shifted his eyes to the speaker. It was the well-dressed rancher with the pretty girl and the buggy. He was a big man with a bluff, firm way about him.

The lawman settled back on his heels, studying the rancher thoughtfully. "Mighty easy for folks to talk, Mister McMahon, but something like this works both ways. I wasn't so sure it was going to get past the arguing point. And if I'd stepped in then, I'd've had all you folks down my throat for being too strict. You'd've said I was butting in, and was running off the town's business."

"When a man wears a star long as you have, Henry, seems you ought to be able to spot the difference between a shoot-out and an argument," Mr. McMahon snapped. He turned his attention to Wade. "Who are you, mister?"

"Name's Wade. Luke Wade."

"Just riding through?"

"Maybe. Does it make a difference?"

"You bet he's riding right through," the lawman said in a hard voice. "I plain won't have him hanging around here, causing trouble. . . ."

The rancher glanced at Luke. "That suit you?"

Wade shrugged. "I'm not looking for trouble, Mister McMahon. I was just going into the saloon to ask the bartender if he knew where I might find a job for a spell. I'm about out of traveling money."

The rancher's eyes brightened. "You work cattle?"

"Yes, sir. From the Mexican border to Montana. Reckon I know as much as the next man about it."

The old lawman snorted. "Appears to me you know a damn' sight more about that hogleg hanging at your side."

Wade's smile was bleak. "I know about that, too."

"Could be just the man I'm looking for," McMahon said, ignoring the lawman. "If you're meaning that about wanting a job, follow me to my place . . . where's your horse?"

"Around the side," Luke replied. He glanced at the marshal.

"All right with you?"

The lawman turned his head and spat in disgust. "Can't see as I got anything to say about it. If he wants to hire you, ain't nothing I can do. But you sure better behave yourself if you come around here again!"

McMahon grinned briefly, the almost pained grimace of a man unaccustomed to displaying levity. "Don't fret over it, Henry. I aim to keep him busy." He nodded to Luke. "You ready to pull out?"

"Soon as I get my sorrel," Wade said, and started across the porch.

He stepped down into the street and headed for the side of the building where, in the shade of a low-spreading cottonwood, he had tied his horse. The words of a man standing with several others near the corner touched him.

"Now what the hell you figure Travis McMahon wants with a gunslinger?"

Luke Wade paused in stride, then continued on. *Hardcase . . . gunslinger.* He shook his head wryly. For a man trying to mind his own business he had acquired a tough reputation mighty fast in Red Hill.

III

As Luke Wade swung his horse in beside McMahon's buggy, he could feel the eyes of the girl, frankly curious, upon him. He turned to meet her gaze, and smiled. She swung her head back around.

She was around twenty, he guessed, with dark hair and eyes. Her skin was a light shade of healthy tan and from what he could tell she had a nicely developed figure that filled the white shirtwaist and skirt outfit she wore to perfection. She was even prettier at close range than he had expected, and he felt his interest brighten.

Women, ordinarily, held only minor attraction for him. Since he was never in one place for over two or three months at a time, most received only passing note from him. But there was something different about this girl, something that had captured his fancy instantly. He wondered who she was—McMahon's daughter, he had assumed—but he found himself wanting to know for certain.

As if reading his mind, Travis McMahon said: "Wade, I'd like to have you meet my daughter, Samantha. Samantha, this is Luke Wade."

The girl faced him, and nodded. Luke touched the brim of his hat with two fingers. "Pleased to know you, ma'am."

Her eyes sparked. "Don't call me ma'am!" she said stiffly. "I'm younger than you, I expect."

"Likely so, ma'am," Wade replied, some of the grim lines about his mouth softening.

McMahon laughed. "And don't go calling her Sam, either. Riles her something fierce."

She turned again to face Wade. "I'm happy to meet you," she murmured politely, her words almost lost in the steady *clop-clop* of the trotting horses. "Will you be working for us . . . for my father?"

Samantha was studying him intently, Luke realized—and realized, also, that it was a study based on curiosity rather than on personal interest. To her he was a gunfighter, a killer—he had just shot down one man, badly wounded another.

"For the association," McMahon said, answering the question for Wade.

Luke thought he saw a faint twinge of disappointment in her eyes, but he couldn't be sure. He shifted his glance to the rancher.

"Association?"

"A bunch of us ranchers . . . half a dozen or so, scattered up and down the Mangus Valley. We've got ourselves a problem, and after seeing you handle yourself back there in town, taking on those three bully boys, I figured we could use you."

"Doing what?"

McMahon shifted impatiently on the seat of the buggy, hooked the instep of his boot on the dashboard. "No use me chawing it over twice," he rumbled. "We're having a meeting at my place soon as I get there. You'll learn about it then."

The rancher paused, staring out over the long plains dotted with yellow-shaded creosote bush and pumpkin-shaped snakeweed. It was poor land, apparently unused by the ranchers. Their spreads would be farther on, beyond the low, black-edged rim of lava rock that lay ahead, Wade guessed.

Abruptly McMahon said: "Why? You particular about the kind of work you do?"

Wade shifted his shoulders. "Not me . . . only don't get any wrong ideas about me. I don't make it a habit of gunning men down."

"The way you handled that iron you're wearing, it seemed to come mighty easy."

"Man learns to take care of himself."

There was a long minute of silence, and then the girl hesitantly said: "Were . . . have there been . . . others?"

"Samantha!" McMahon exclaimed disapprovingly. "You know better than to ask a question like that!" Immediately then he further broke the tacit custom by adding: "Reckon I should have asked you before . . . are you running from the law?"

Wade said—"No."—and let it drop.

It was none of McMahon's business. He intended to keep it on that basis. The law actually was not looking for him, but to say he was unknown to a great number of sheriffs and town marshals would have been untrue. It was a tender subject, best left unexplored.

"I know I've got no right prying into a man's private affairs," the rancher said, his words a deep grumble. "Howsomever, I had to know. Could save us some explaining later."

Wade's glance at the rancher sharpened. "Does it make a difference if I was wanted by the law?"

McMahon shifted his bulk again on the seat. "Not 'specially, so long as you stand by the association and don't forget who's paying the bill."

Luke sighed. Some kind of a range war, he thought. A lousy damned range war. He'd been through one, and, when it had been over, he'd told himself he'd never get mixed up in another. He began to pull in the sorrel and draw to a halt. Now was the moment to back off—before he ever got in.

McMahon hauled his team to an abrupt stop, glaring at him. "What the hell's the matter?"

"Think maybe you picked the wrong man to hire," Wade answered.

"You said you were looking for a job. . . ."

"I am . . . but I don't aim to get myself tangled up in a war. Did once, and swore I wouldn't again."

"War?" McMahon echoed. "You mean a range war? Who said anything like that?"

Luke frowned. "Just figured that was what you had in mind."

"Well, it ain't," the rancher said bluntly. "Now, supposing you just keep your shirt on until you hear what we've got to offer. Then you can pull out if you've got the notion. Fair enough?"

Luke nodded. "Fair enough," he said, and touched the sorrel with his spurs.

They reached the rim of the *malpais* buttes, and swept down a narrow, gentle slope into a broad valley carpeted with purple-tasseled grass and dotted with young trees. Far to the left Wade could see the sparkling twist of a river, and beyond it a level horizon of dark-faced bluffs. To the right a low range of shadowy, timbered hills formed an opposing barrier. It was beautiful cattle country—ideal, in fact, Luke decided, and in his wanderings across the country he had seen some fine land.

"Thirty miles across and better'n a hundred long," McMahon said in a pride-filled voice as he allowed his gaze to roam the lush, green panorama. "Finest cattle raising country in the world. Someday there'll be ranches all over it."

Luke Wade's long-standing habit of careful, easy probing came to the fore. McMahon was one of the ranchers that were suspect. He had shown no interest in the killer's gun, but that was no sure indication of innocence.

"Wonder it's not already crowded," he observed. "Not many valleys like this left."

"Only opened up little over three years ago. No water until then."

Luke motioned toward the river. "Looks like plenty."

"Now, yes, but three, four years ago there wasn't any river. Then something happened up north of here. Earthquake, maybe it was. Whole mountain sort of shifted, they say. Next thing you know that river started running. Sure was the making of this part of the territory."

Three or four years ago . . . ? Wade was silent while he considered that. "How long have you been here?" he asked casually.

"Came in right after the river started flowing. Heard about it from a friend who happened to come through here. Got myself here fast as I could and filed me a claim. Dang' good thing I acted *pronto*. Half a dozen others were moving in, too."

"How much land have you got?" Luke asked, more to keep the conversation going than anything else while he mulled over the information. That McMahon had been one of those to start ranching just after the murder of Ben Wade and the rustling of their herd was of importance. And soon he would meet several of the others, the members of the association—all possibilities. A grim satisfaction settled over Luke. He was running in luck for a change.

McMahon's words broke into Wade's thoughts: "What with the free range, I reckon it's close to seventy thousand acres."

Luke had to connect the statement with the question he had asked—and almost forgotten. He nodded. "Man could fatten a lot of steers on that much grass. How big a herd you running?"

McMahon looked down. "It's going to surprise you, maybe, but all I've got is a hundred and fifty head or so. Same with all the others. We're all small, just getting started. None of us got enough stock to brag about . . . and we're all plenty shy of cash, mostly because of what happened last year."

"What was that?" Wade asked, angling the sorrel in closer to the buggy in order to hear better.

"You'll get the story at the meeting," the rancher said. He pointed to a small cluster of buildings grouped in the center of small cottonwoods that appeared suddenly on their left. A flat-faced butte lay to the south end; it had hidden the ranch from view until they were almost upon it.

"That's my place. Ain't much yet, but if things'll go right, it will be someday. Looks like the rest of the boys are already there. Reckon we better hurry it up a mite and get the meeting started."

Luke Wade touched the sorrel with his rowels as McMahon shook his team into a gallop. He was anxious, too; he wanted a good look at all the men of the association—men who had moved into the Mangus Valley country around three years ago.

IV

An older edition of Samantha McMahon stood in the doorway of the ranch house as they wheeled into the yard. Seven or eight men, all wearing the hard-finished garb of working ranchers, lounged in the shade of the wagon shed. McMahon, pausing long enough to allow his daughter to collect her parcels and dismount, moved on toward them.

Wade, a quietness possessing him at the thought that he might, at last, be coming face to face with the ruthless killer he had sought for so long, guided the sorrel to one of the pole corrals and swung down. Winding the leathers around one of the cross legs, he walked slowly to where McMahon and the others had gathered. The big rancher, out of his buggy, was speaking hurriedly and earnestly to the men. Evidently he was giving them an account of what had happened in Red Hill.

As Luke moved up, the group parted, spreading out to meet him. Most were smiling but there were a couple who regarded him soberly, almost with hostility.

"Just been telling the boys about your trouble in town," McMahon rumbled. "And how you handled yourself."

Wade merely waited, saying nothing. He reached into his shirt pocket, produced the makings, and began a cigarette. Face tipped down, he gave each rancher a close, hard scrutiny. Any one of them could be his man.

"Reckon the first thing we ought to do is make some introductions," McMahon said, leaning back against the hind wheel of a light wagon. He waved a hand at a graying, long-faced man. "This here's Charlie Peck, Luke. Owns the place west of mine."

Peck stepped forward. Wade watched his eyes intently. The rancher said—"Pleased to meet you."—and shook hands.

A tall, smiling man with lean, somewhat sharp features stood next to Peck. Not waiting for McMahon, he thrust out his arm, grasped Luke's hand in a firm grip.

"I'm Helm Stokes. . . . It's a pleasure. From what Travis told us, you must've made the town set up and take notice."

Wade smiled with his eyes, liking the rancher immediately.

McMahon motioned to a third man. "Otis Kline."

Kline ducked his head forward. He was one of the older ones, around fifty, Luke guessed, a husky, square-faced sort of individual. He did not offer his hand.

"How do," he said, then added: "Ain't so sure it's not a mistake, bringing you here. I don't hold with killing."

"Neither do I," Luke replied coolly. "Man does what he has to sometimes."

"There's other ways," Kline said.

From behind the rancher a boy, somewhere in his late teens, pushed forward, reached for Luke's hand. He was smiling broadly, plainly pleased to meet Wade.

"I'm Joe Dee Kline," he said. "You sure must be a wonder with that fancy gun you're packin'."

The squat rancher's son, Luke supposed, and started to say something, but McMahon cut in on his intentions: "Albert Dunn. Owns the Square D layout."

Dunn, like Peck, was older. He had a round face, and he showed evidences of once having been considerably heavier, but age and the dry, hard labor of ranch life had trimmed him down.

"A pleasure," the rancher said, and inclined his head.

"Will Johnson," McMahon continued, pointing to a slightly built, balding man. "And the last one there, with the mashed-in nose, is Hank Timmons. Hank lost an argument with a bronc' he was bustin'."

Both greeted Wade, and stepped back into the line. Luke, saying nothing, swept the ranchers with his intent glance once again. None had revealed any reaction to the gun he carried— none except Joe Dee Kline, and his was one of boyish admiration. And all, excluding the boy, of course, and possibly Johnson, fit the vague description of the killer left him by his father— particularly Travis McMahon, he realized with a start. The scar would be the only sure proof.

"We're getting together to talk about the drive we're starting tomorrow," McMahon said, looking directly at Luke. "But first I reckon we ought to fill you in some." He shifted his eyes to Stokes. "You lay it out for him, Helm."

Stokes squatted on his heels and drew a cigar from his pocket. He bit off the end, spat, and struck a match to the tip. He exhaled a cloud of blue smoke, considered it briefly, then began to speak.

"We've got us a little different sort of a problem up here in Mangus Valley. We're all new and just getting started. Means we ain't big enough to do things on our own so we all have to work together. And none of us has much stock, so what we have to do is pool what we want to sell and make a drive to the railhead. Town called Anson's Fork. East of here. Takes about five days to make the drive."

Luke vaguely recalled the settlement. He had passed through it once, perhaps twice in the course of his wandering. About all he could remember about it was the name itself. All towns eventually got to where they looked alike.

"Herd generally tots up to a couple hundred head. Not big, as herds go, but every steer means plenty to the man who owns him."

"Means the difference in making a go of our places, or winding up broke . . . if we lose them this time," Charlie Peck said.

"Losing them?" Wade said, his brows lifting.

Stokes nodded. "This'll be the third time we've made the drive. First year we got them through. Last year we wasn't so lucky."

The rancher paused, and scratched at the ground with a twig. Apparently what had happened that previous summer was a painful memory. Luke waited.

"Last year," McMahon finished in a savage, angry tone, "the god damn' rustlers hit us . . . got away with the whole herd!"

"About ruined me," Otis Kline said, wagging his head dolefully. "Forty of them critters was mine . . .—and they was worth sixteen dollars apiece. I was figuring strong on that cash. Had it in mind to do a right smart amount of fixing up around my place. Way it turned out, me and my family lived on beans and cornbread all winter."

"If it happens again," Albert Dunn murmured, "I'm through. I'm pulling out."

Wade's voice was incredulous. "You never found any trace of the herd? How could a couple hundred steers just drop out of sight?"

"Sounds plumb loco," Stokes agreed, "but that's the way it was. I ramrodded the drive, so I was there. You got to remember this. We didn't have any regular drovers. Was just me, one of my hired hands, and another fellow . . . rancher named Willson. He got killed by the rustlers. They jumped us about dark third day out. Some rough country between here and the railhead . . . brushy cañons and the like. Willson stopped a bullet while he was building a fire for night camp. My man was out tending the herd and they knocked him over the head, tied him up, and left him laying in the mesquite."

Stokes hesitated again, once more toying with the twig. His face was stiff, solemn.

"Helm tried to stop the rustlers by himself," McMahon said, taking up the account. "But they drove him back to some buttes and pinned him down with rifles. They kept him there for better'n a day. They'd have killed him sure, I reckon, if he'd showed his head."

Luke still found it hard to understand. "But two hundred steers . . . there'd be dust, tracks. Seems like a man could've followed, even a couple of days later."

"Grass country," Stokes said. "Not much dust. On top of that, it rained. First thing I did when I saw that the pair pinning me down had pulled out . . . that was a day and a night later . . . was to try and locate the stock. It was too late then."

"What about the railhead? Anybody ever show up there with your beef?"

"Never did. Oh, several herds came in, but they were from other ranches east and north of here. None of our stuff was ever seen."

For several moments Luke was silent, then he said: "Looks like the answer is for all of you to take a hand in the drive. Give yourself more protection."

"Sounds simple," McMahon agreed, "only it ain't. Ranching's a family affair with each one of us. I mean, we do our own work. None of us ever has enough ready cash to hire help, which means we have to stay pretty close to home. Only reason Stokes can get away is that he ain't married. He's not trying to do so much . . . like the rest of us."

"Main reason I volunteered to boss the drive," Stokes said. "Don't have but mighty little to lose. I can afford to take the time off. Rest of the ranchers, well, if they ain't home, the work just don't get done . . . and this is a mighty important time of the year around here."

Luke Wade understood the problem. It was the same everywhere. Building a ranch was a hard, grubbing life in the beginning. A man depended upon his wife and children for help in many ways, and got it, but the major portion of the work was of a nature that only he could handle. And he was realizing, too, the importance of a successful drive to them. Each gambled what stock he figured he could afford to sell for the sake of cash money. If the sale were completed, the family, and the ranch, could make it through the winter months fairly well. If the stock were lost, it was a hard, bitter blow that could shut a man down, end his hopes and dreams.

But he had his own problems, he reminded himself suddenly.

He couldn't afford to get too involved—only to the point of what it meant in terms of money to him.

"Where do I fit?" he asked then.

"You'll ride guard," McMahon said promptly. "Like a shotgun man on a stage. Only you'll be watching out for rustlers. Seeing you back there in town give me the idea. Stokes has agreed to boss the drive again. He'll take along one of his hands, and Kline's boy, Joe Dee, wants to go. Makes three to handle the herd. Not enough, I know, but it's the best we can do."

"With you along doing the outriding and keeping your eyes peeled," Stokes said, "I figure three'll be all we need. We'll be able to sort of bear down on the herd, keep it moving good."

A trail guard, outrider for a bunch of cows. He'd had worse jobs. Besides, it could put him one step closer to the man who'd murdered Ben Wade. "What's the pay?" he asked.

"Talked it over," McMahon said. "We're willing to pay you four bits a head for every steer that's tallied into the loading pens at the railhead. Figures up to a hundred dollars, more or less . . . for about a week's work."

"But only if you get through," Dunn warned. "If we don't make a sale, I couldn't scrape up enough cash to buy you a square meal."

"Me, neither," Peck added.

There was silence after that. It would be good pay, Luke realized, real good. More than he could make in three months at a regular ranch job. But worth more than all were the personal advantages that had already occurred to him. He could be getting close to his father's killer.

"You've got yourself a deal," he said.

McMahon smiled broadly. "Fine, fine. Glad it's all settled. Now, let's go up to the house. Expect the missus has got some coffee ready for us."

V

Mrs. McMahon, aided by Samantha, now in a simple gingham print, had coffee and a small wedge of dried apple pie laid out in neat rows on the kitchen table when the men entered the low-ceilinged house. Each helped himself, and then found a place in the front room or back porch to enjoy the light repast. The coffee was good, the pie excellent, and Luke Wade found himself hoping there might be seconds, but he would ask for none. From what he had heard in the wagon shed all of the Mangus Valley ranchers were on a shoestring footing and it wouldn't be right to take advantage of their hospitality.

He looked up after finishing off the pie and discovered Mrs. McMahon watching him from across the kitchen. Samantha favored her entirely and it was as though he were glancing at the girl twenty years from that moment.

Luke nodded politely. "It was fine pie, ma'am. I enjoyed it."

She gave him a restrained smile, and said: "We haven't been introduced, but I guess you are Mister Wade."

"Yes'm . . . Luke Wade," he replied. "I. . . ."

McMahon, overhearing partly, wheeled. "Oh, Molly, I forgot to. . . ."

"We've just met," she said, a faint thread of disapproval in her tone. "He enjoyed my pie."

"Man'd be crazy if he didn't," the rancher declared. "Luke's going to work for the association . . . leastwise long enough to see the herd through to the railhead."

Mrs. McMahon nodded. "I'm sure there'll be no trouble, then . . . not after what Samantha told me."

Something akin to anger stirred within Luke Wade. Molly McMahon disliked him, that was plain, and she was basing her opinions of him on the shoot-out at Red Hill. He started to say something, to explain and make her understand that he didn't while away his time shooting men to death—and then thought

31

better of it. The effort wasn't worth the end result, and it would be smart not to get too friendly with any of the ranchers and their families. It could complicate matters later.

"How about more coffee?" McMahon asked, trying to cover his wife's hostility.

Luke began a refusal, but hushed when the rancher re-filled his cup unheedingly. When it was full, he said—"Obliged to you."—and walked out onto the rear porch slowly. Molly Mc-Mahon said something in a sharp tone to her husband but Wade gave it no attention, preferring not to hear.

The remainder of the ranchers were scattered throughout the house, conversing in pairs and groups. Luke wondered what had become of Samantha. He hadn't noticed her for some time.

He halted on the porch, grateful for the faint breeze blowing in from the plains. On ahead, beyond McMahon's barn and lesser sheds, he could see a garden, green with half-grown stalks of corn, squat tomato plants, peppers, and other vegetables. All appeared to be thriving.

A small orchard had been planted, but the trees were yet too young to bear. Another couple of years, at least, Luke estimated. There was a fenced-in chicken yard where a dozen or more hens and a solitary rooster scuffled in the dust, and in the shade on the north side of the barn a cow munched contentedly on her cud.

Travis McMahon had a fine start—but it was easy to see the rancher trod a thin line. The slightest thing going wrong could mean disaster. And it would be the same with all the others in Mangus Valley—all but Helm Stokes, perhaps. He struck Luke as being a man who didn't particularly care whether the sun rose or not. Being unmarried made him that way, likely; he could weather adversity without feeling its brutal pinch.

At that moment Samantha, accompanied by Joe Dee Kline, emerged from the barn. Unaccountably Luke felt a slight twinge of resentment at seeing them together—and then he grinned wryly. What the hell was wrong with him? What right had he to have feelings of any sort about the girl? Anyway, Joe Dee was several years younger than she was.

He watched them approach the house, Samantha easy and graceful in her walk, the boy hovering anxiously nearby and talking rapidly. She made a fetching picture in the bright sunlight, her dark hair glinting, her skin soft and creamy-looking.

They reached the porch, entered, and halted before Luke. At once Joe Dee said: "Mister Wade's going with us on the drive tomorrow."

"Call me Luke," Wade said, feeling uncommonly old before the boy's enthusiasm.

"He's going with us," the boy repeated. "Be the guard. We'll get the herd through this time sure!"

Samantha studied Wade soberly. "I'm sure you will."

"Nobody'll try jumpin' us . . . not with him along. You can bet on that."

"Mister Wade's reputation should guarantee it," she said dryly.

From the interior of the house Otis Kline's deep voice sounded: "Joe Dee! Let's get started. Lot of work to be done around the place before you leave."

"Yes, Pa," the boy answered. He grinned slyly at the girl. "So long, Sam . . . see you when I get back."

She frowned, then made a face at him. "Good bye, Joe Dee. Take care."

"You bet," the boy said, then, grinning at Luke, added: "See you in the morning, Mister Wade."

Luke watched him turn and enter the kitchen and hurry on into the adjoining parlor. Others were leaving and he wondered, briefly, if he should hunt up Stokes and arrange to stay the night with him at his place so as to be on hand the following morning. He decided to let matters take their course. If Stokes wanted him, he'd sing out. Besides, it was pleasant being there with Samantha.

"I was showing Joe Dee our new colt," she said, the stiffness gone from her tone. "Foaled about a week ago. A real pretty little bay with four white stockings. Would you like to see him?"

Wade smiled. "You bet I would," he said, placing his empty cup on a close by shelf. "Always had a weakness for bays."

"So you ride a sorrel," she said mischievously.

"Just happens so," he said quietly, following her out into the yard. "Still like bays."

She half turned, and stared at him intently. "You mean that, don't you? I'm sorry . . . I didn't intend to josh you about it."

"Forget it," he said, feeling awkward about his actions. Samantha continued to study him. "I guess it's what you are that makes you so dead serious . . . so withdrawn, sort of. . . ."

"What I am? What's that?"

She shrugged her slight shoulders. "A gunman," she said frankly. "It makes you the way you are."

He laughed. "I'm no hired killer, if that's what you're thinking. I never shot it out with a man in my life unless I was forced into it . . . just like this morning. I expect every man goes through the same experience a few times in his life. Some back off and run away, and others stand their ground. I just happen to be one that doesn't believe in walking away."

Samantha was quiet for a time. Over in the orchard a meadowlark whistled cheerfully. She glanced in that direction, then said: "I think I know what you mean. But it isn't that . . . it's something else that makes you the sort you are. . . . What is it?"

Wade's jaw hardened. He was vaguely irritated and somewhat surprised by the girl's perception. He forced a smile, pointed at the open doorway leading into the barn immediately ahead.

"Is that where you've got the colt?"

She nodded, crossed in front of him, and led the way to one of the stalls arranged along the wall of the bulky structure. She halted, still not speaking.

A leggy colt, sleek and shining in the murky light, turned a narrow head to view them, then resumed his nuzzling of the mare beside him.

"A real fine bit of horseflesh," Luke said. "Going to make a good animal."

"You don't care to talk about it?" Samantha said.

He stood silently, for a moment put to a loss by the question. Then he realized she was still on the same subject.

"No," he said gruffly. "I don't care to talk about it."

Maybe he should—maybe he should ask her about her father, start out by inquiring as to whether he'd been in the war or not, gradually lead up to the scar—and if he had one. If so, where? And ask about the others—Stokes, Kline, Charlie Peck, all of them. They were all prospects for the business end of his killer's gun. Why not involve her in it, too?

Somehow he could not—not right then, anyway. Maybe later, after the drive, when they were better acquainted. It just wasn't the proper moment. Vaguely he wondered why he should feel this way. Never before had he permitted anything or anybody to hinder the quest—why now? Maybe he really didn't want to know; maybe he was afraid of the answers he would get from her. He pulled himself up short. That was crazy thinking. He'd find out soon enough, and, if it turned out to be Travis McMahon he wanted—well, so be it.

"I'm sorry," he heard her say as she turned toward the door. "Whatever it is, it must trouble you a lot."

He fell in behind her. "Didn't know it showed that much. But don't worry about it. I've lived with it a long time."

He halted, aware of someone standing in their path. It was

McMahon, his face stiff, almost angry. Beyond him, her expression dark as a thundercloud, Molly McMahon watched from the porch.

"I was showing Luke . . . Mister Wade the colt," Samantha said.

The rancher's eyes were sharp. "Your ma wants you, Samantha."

The girl sobered at his tone, gave him a disturbed look, and hurried away. McMahon jerked his thumb toward Luke's sorrel.

"Expect you'd better line out for Stokes's place," he said. "You'll be spending the night with him."

It was evident from the rancher's manner that plans had been changed. Likely McMahon had intended for him to stay the night under his roof and then join Stokes and the others in the morning. Something had altered that—something that had to do with Samantha, he guessed. Probably the McMahons didn't relish the idea of their daughter's getting too friendly with a gunslinger.

Wade sighed inwardly, and brushed aside the impatience that moved through him. Just as well. He recalled his previous determination not to get involved with any of the Mangus Valley people. And he guessed he couldn't blame the McMahons. Likely he would feel the same if he had a daughter.

"Whatever you say," he murmured. "How do I find Stokes?"

McMahon backed into the yard, pointed into the northwest. He settled his finger upon a triangular peak near the end of a distant mountain.

"Ride straight for that . . . the Stokes place lays about a third of the way. Can't miss it."

Wade nodded his thanks, and struck out across the hard pack for the sorrel. He heard the rancher say—"Good luck."—but he did not turn to voice a reply, simply lifted his hand and allowed it to fall.

Mounting, he wheeled about. Abreast of the house, he glanced toward the porch. Samantha had disappeared inside. Molly McMahon stood there, her expression of disapproval still holding. He touched the brim of his hat and continued on.

When he rode out of the yard moments later, he could still feel her gaze; it seemed to be pushing him, driving him as though she were determined to remove him from her family circle and life as quickly as possible.

It was just as well, he told himself again.

VI

Luke Wade took his time reaching the Stokes ranch. He circled wide, noting the fine rangeland across which he rode, enjoying occasional glimpses of blue quail, long-haired jack rabbits, and swift-winged doves. He paused once, enraptured by the sight of a great, golden eagle soaring high overhead. He watched, breathless, as the huge bird abruptly plummeted earthward, seized some luckless small animal in its talons, and rushed away. Apparently it had been a wet spring. Flowers splashed their color at every hand—clumps of goldenrod, patches of verbenas, blankets of fleabane and yellow-hearted asters, and entire slopes of red bee plant.

He rode into the Stokes's yard shortly after full dark. It was a much smaller ranch, insofar as structures went, than McMahon's. There appeared to be only the main house, a close by combination kitchen and bunkhouse, a privy, and a few small sheds, besides the corrals. There were cattle inside the enclosures. They constituted the herd, he assumed, that was to be driven to the railhead.

The main house was in darkness but a light glowed through the kitchen window, and, after stabling the sorrel and throwing down a quantity of feed for him, Luke made his way to that structure.

The cook, a gangling, elderly man in tattered overalls, glanced up sourly as he entered. The room was miserably hot, filled with the odor of fresh bread and frying meat. A platter stacked high with beef already cooked sat in the center of a wide table, along with several loaves of cooling bread. The man was preparing sandwiches for the drive.

"Who might you be?" he demanded, peering through bushy, gray brows.

"Wade. Grub sure smells good."

"Wade, eh? Stokes said you was stayin' the night with the McMahons. Didn't fix you no meal."

"Plans got changed. Don't go to any bother. A piece of that meat and some bread will do me. And coffee, if there's any left."

The cook shrugged and resumed his chore. "Help yourself. Cup there on the shelf."

Luke, after selecting some of the beef and bread and pouring himself a cup of the strong coffee, sat down at the table. He ate slowly, relishing the savory food.

"You'll be carryin' your own grub," the old man said. "Stokes ain't takin' no chuck wagon. Says there ain't enough men goin' for that."

"Expect he's right. Man won't have much time to eat anyway. . . . You know my name. Like to know yours."

"Friends call me Caleb. . . . Likely wastin' my time fixin' all these sandwiches, but if I don't, there'll be a lot of bellyachin'."

"I'll eat mine," Luke said. "Bread's sure just right. So's the meat."

Caleb looked up, clearly pleased. "Find yourself some fresh butter over there in the window box. Makes that bread some tastier."

Luke immediately helped himself to another thick slice of the bread, this time fortifying it with a large chunk of butter.

"You're welcome to come do my cookin' anytime you want," he said, resuming his chair.

Caleb grinned a toothy appreciation. "Obliged to you, but I reckon I'm set for a spell."

"How long've you been with Stokes?"

"A month, maybe two."

"You acquainted with this part of the country?"

The old cook continued to work with his sandwiches. "Been around, off and on, ten, twelve year."

Luke allowed that to ride. Unconsciously he had slipped into the old pattern of probing that had become second nature with him.

"This Stokes seems a right nice fellow. Only met him today. You know him long?"

"Not long."

"Hear he's been here about three years."

"Reckon so."

"Figure I'm going to like working with him. Was he in the war?"

Caleb laid down his knife. He cast a sideward glance at the window. "Must've been that there dang' butter," he muttered.

"Butter? What about it?"

"Makin' you fire all them questions at me . . . which I ain't answerin'."

Luke grinned. He'd been trapped before and he'd learned the best way out was to laugh it off.

"Sure, old-timer . . . was just wanting to know the man better."

"Well," Caleb drawled, "I don't know nothin' about Stokes and I reckon, if you're goin' to learn anything, best you ask him yourself."

"Just what I'll do," Luke said, rising. "Obliged to you for the meal. Was plenty good. Any idea where I can bed down?"

"Right through that there door," Caleb said, pointing with the knife to the wall behind Luke. "You'll find a bunk that ain't bein' slept in. Crawl right in."

"Rest of the boys already turned in?"

"Yep . . . Pete and Al Cobb and Jim Leggett. They're in there."

"That Stokes's whole crew?"

"Yep. That's all of them."

"Which one's going on the drive?"

Caleb sighed, dropped his knife onto the table. "Jim Leggett, so I hear. Stokes is leavin' the others and me to look after the place while he's gone. Why, I sure don't know. Ain't nothin' worth lookin' after. Now, dang it . . . you wantin' to know anything else?"

Wade grinned, and said: "No . . . guess you've said it all. Good night."

" 'Night," Caleb replied, and recovered his knife. "Don't be forgettin' your sack of vittles when you pull out, come mornin'. Be here on the table."

"I won't," Luke said, and, opening the door, he turned into the pitch dark, stuffy interior of the bunkroom.

VII

Helm Stokes was in the kitchen drinking black coffee when Wade entered shortly after 4:00 that next morning. The big rancher gave Luke a broad smile and offered his hand.

"Glad to see you, Wade. Sorry I wasn't up when you rode in last night."

"It's all right," Luke replied. "Caleb here took care of me fine. About ready to head out?"

"Soon as you can get some breakfast down. Leggett and the others are already shaping up the herd."

The cook set a plate of meat and potatoes before Luke and filled a tin cup to the brim with steaming coffee for him. Wade sat down and began to eat.

"You said something about your men getting the herd under way. Did you decide to take your whole crew?" he asked.

Stokes shook his head. "Only Leggett. Al and Pete will stay with us long enough to get things started." The rancher paused, glanced through the window at the sky. "Going to be another scorcher."

"Here's your vittles," Caleb broke in, pushing a bulging, string tied flour sack across the table at Luke. "Don't go trottin' off without 'em."

Luke smiled, and thanked the old man. They were still friends, he guessed. He finished his plate and rose, taking the provisions with him. Stokes was still looking out through the streaky glass of the window.

"Guess I'm ready . . . soon as I get my horse," Luke said.

Stokes wheeled, then hurriedly drained his cup. "Fine. Meet you outside."

The rancher, astride a tall, black gelding, was waiting when Luke swung into the yard. He pointed to a shifting, irregular mass on the mesa a quarter mile distant.

"Looks like the boys have got them moving."

They rode off the hard pack onto the grassy plain and angled toward the moving herd. A faint film of dust was rising, now hung like a transparent, dark-edged cloud against the gray flare of coming daylight. In only a few minutes they had caught up with the cattle.

Wade, having had his time with trail drives, gave the herd quick appraisal. It was ragged and far from being properly shaped up. But he guessed he was too critical; the drive was just getting under way. Give it another hour or so and matters should improve.

He could see young Joe Dee Kline riding swing, at their left, but as near as he could tell no one was at point yet, leading the cattle. Three riders loomed up in the half light to his right and loped toward Stokes. From habit, Luke eyed them speculatively.

"Got 'em movin'," a thin, balding man said, wiping at his face.

Stokes nodded. He waved a hand at Wade. "This here's Luke Wade, boys. He's the man that done all the hell-fire shooting in town yesterday. Hired him on to ride guard for us. . . . Luke, baldy there is Jim Leggett. Other two work for me. Al Cobb's the one on the buckskin . . . Pete Nogal's the one with the fancy saddle."

The three riders nodded unsmilingly. All were quiet-faced men, almost secretive. Luke acknowledged the introductions with a faint tip of his head.

Stokes said: "Al, you and Pete might as well drop back. We can handle it from here."

Immediately the two men whirled away and struck out at a lope for the ranch house. Stokes raised himself in his stirrups and considered the herd. After a few moments he turned to Leggett.

"Jim, you and the boy'll have to ride swing and look after the stragglers, too. Just keep whipping back and forth. I'll take the point." He paused, glancing at Luke. "You do what you figure best. I'd suggest you move out front, keep ahead of us. You can watch better from there."

Wade said: "That's what I had in mind. Want me to tell the boy when I go by?"

"Obliged to you if you would."

Luke spurred off, circled the loosely formed herd, beginning now to string out far too thinly, and galloped toward Joe Dee. The boy saw him coming, and drew to a halt. He grinned broadly through the dust and sweat already streaking his face.

" 'Mornin', Mister Wade!"

" 'Morning, Joe Dee," Luke answered. "Stokes says you're to work this side, and keep after the stragglers. Leggett's doing the same on the right."

"Sure," the boy said agreeably. He twisted about and looked to the rear. "Looks like I got me some stragglers right now. See you later!"

Joe Dee raced off and Luke continued on, forging out ahead of the cattle. Cresting a low hill, he studied the herd once more. If Stokes didn't hurry up and get the steers bunched, a hard day would lie ahead for the horses and their riders. But that was the rancher's problem. He had his own job to look out for. Removing his hat, he mopped at the sweat accumulation; as Stokes had observed, it was going to be hot. Good thing the cattle had watered before the drive had begun.

They were moving across a broad, grassy swale that lifted slightly toward the Sacramento Mountains to the east. The going would not be so easy once they reached the hills, Wade knew. And his own job would be more difficult. He would have to be doubly alert, for the wild cañons studded with rock and thick underbrush would be ideal for rustlers to lay their ambush.

Stokes would have his hands full, too, getting the herd through, and Luke didn't envy him the task. With only two drovers, inexperienced ones at that, he would be fortunate to make it without loss.

Again Luke brushed that worry aside; moving the stock was Helm Stokes's chore—his was to keep the rustlers at bay if any materialized along the trail. But deep inside he held a hope that the herd would make it through—and he was determined to uphold his bargain to that end. At first it had been only the money he would receive, and the opportunities to know better the ranchers of Mangus Valley, that had interested him; now another factor concerned him—if the drive failed as it had that previous year, all these ranchers would face a bleak future and possibly complete ruin. That should have no meaning for him, he told himself as the sorrel plodded slowly on, keeping pace with the flowing sea of brown, white, and tan now below. He should hold to his purpose—and so far he had accomplished little in determining who, if any, of the Mangus Valley ranchers might be the man he sought.

The need for a job had got in the way—the necessity for hard cash. If it hadn't been for that, he could, at that moment, have been prowling about, making inquiries and coming up, possibly, with helpful information. But everything had been sidetracked, and he was losing time.

He was overlooking Helm Stokes and Joe Dee Kline. While neither seemed likely to be the killer, they might be able to give him some ideas. When they bedded the herd at sundown and were all together again, he'd drop a few casual questions. He should take advantage of every moment.

The day wore on, hot and windy. By mid-afternoon both man and beast were suffering under the lash of the sun. Stokes had brought no extra horses, an indication of inexperience to Wade, and Luke knew trouble would face them the following day when they'd reach the rugged, sprawling Sacramentos.

They made an early night camp and Stokes upset Luke's plans by separating the riders, Luke included, and stationing them on the four sides of the herd. It was a wise precaution and Wade approved—but it did prevent his making the inquiries he had had in mind.

They were on the move again by 5:00 the next morning, and three hours later were entering the mountains through the narrow mouth of a steep-walled cañon. The heat, trapped by the rock walls, shielded from any breeze, was monstrous, equal almost to that of the blazing deserts of northern Mexico and lower Arizona. The horses tired quickly and the herd became unruly, started to break up, stall, and refuse to continue. Stokes, aided by young Kline and Jim Leggett, rushed ceaselessly back and forth through the milling animals, shouting, cursing, lashing the brutes with folded ropes. Several times Helm Stokes fired his pistol as he tried to regain control of the stubborn cattle.

Their efforts met with little success, and Luke, watching impatiently from a ledge 100 feet or so above the trail, saw that disaster was imminent unless something were done fast. He made a final sweep of the area with his glance, saw no horsemen that might be a threat, and rode down to give the cattleman a hand. The herd was in confusion; steers were plunging erratically off into the maze of rock and brush, bawling loudly. Some stood motionlessly, legs spraddled, refusing to move; others had turned about and were bucking the flow, trying to double back up the cañon. As he wheeled in beside Stokes, the rancher, his face caked with dust and sweat, flung him an exasperated look.

"For hell's sake quit fighting them!" Luke yelled above the tumult as he shook out his rope. "Let 'em go!"

"Heat's turned them loco!" the rancher shouted.

"I can see that . . . but they can't go anywhere but on down-cañon, or back. Walls are too steep for them to climb. You keep this up and you're going to lose some stock!"

An old, gray mossy-horn whirled suddenly, cut away from the others of his kind, and came charging straight for the two men. Instantly Wade spurred the sorrel forward, lash swinging from his hand. When only paces separated him from the heat-maddened steer, he swerved sharply left, brought the rope down with stinging force across the brute's bulging eyes and nose.

The steer bawled, veered right, and once again was moving with the herd. Wade cut back to where Stokes was fighting his horse, trying to keep him crowding the rumps of a small jag of stock.

"Like I said," Luke resumed, "they can't go nowhere but back or on. Let 'em scatter . . . the sides of the cañon will stop them. All we got to do is trail behind and see that none of them doubles back."

Stokes nodded his head in understanding. He brushed at his face and said: "I'll hail in Leggett and the boy. With the four of us riding abreast, like you say, we ought to get them down the cañon."

Luke watched him move ahead into the boiling dust cloud and disappear. A small knot of steers off to his left began to balk, stall, and try to turn about. Lifting his rope, Luke forced the sorrel in close, and hammered at the stubborn animals until they broke and moved on.

Stokes, with Leggett and Joe Dee, hove into view. The rancher was waving his arms, yelling his instructions above the noise of the herd. Luke joined them and together they dropped back and took up trailing positions across the floor of the cañon. Pushing steadily, they kept the herd moving in front of them. It was a dry, choking task that lasted almost until sundown, but finally the ragged, narrow slash in the mountains opened up and the herd spilled slowly out onto a broad saddle.

"River anywhere close?" Wade asked, curving in near to the rancher. With the thirst the cattle would have after the cañon passage, there would be no holding them if they got wind of water.

Stokes shook his head. "Not until tomorrow. Almost a full day from here."

"Expect they'll settle down then. They're plenty tired."

The rancher nodded, and said: "That goes for all of us . . . and the horses, too. Glad you come up with that idea of pushing them through. We'd be back there yet if you hadn't."

Wade said nothing. It had been no act of brilliance on his part—simply common trail-driving sense born of experience. He liked Helm Stokes as a man, but when they returned to Mangus Valley, he was going to tell Travis McMahon that the ranchers would be smart to hire a professional trail-herd boss the next time they planned a drive; it could prove cheaper in the long run. They were lucky there weren't a dozen or more dead and crippled steers back up in the rocks.

"You making camp on the flat?" he asked, looking up to the extreme tip of a rocky ledge a half mile to his left.

Stokes glanced at the herd moving slowly out onto the grassy plain. "Looks like a good spot."

Wade said: "For a fact. Think I'll have a look from that point over there, see if we've got any company. Meet you at camp."

"We'll have coffee boiling," the rancher said, and moved on.

Luke swung back across the saddle, tired but glad that the emergency was over. He reached the first rocky outcropping below the ledge and urged the worn sorrel up the steep trail. Coming to the shelf, he halted and dismounted. Leaving his horse, he crawled out to the point and pulled himself upright.

Seemingly far below he could see the herd trickling lazily into the center of the grassy hollow. His eyes picked up Kline and Leggett, cutting back toward Stokes, evidently seeking the rancher out to get further orders. Stokes apparently was somewhere in the line of brush to their left. Luke could not locate him. He could see no one else on the broad plain, and, turning back, he searched the rough slopes of the hills through which they had just passed. There were only the twisted shapes of the piñons and cedars, the stiff pines, the shadowy rocks now beginning to cool.

"So far so good," he murmured aloud, and took a half step toward the edge of the shelf below which the sorrel waited.

At that exact instant a powerful force slapped against his

head. It spun him half about as a shower of lights, accompanied by the hollow, flat sound of a gunshot, burst before his eyes.

He tried to collect his flagging wits, then staggered again as a second, shocking wallop rocked him and sent raging pain searing through his breast. He felt his knees buckle and more pain surged through him in an overpowering wave. And then all was darkness.

VIII

Luke Wade opened his eyes with considerable effort. At first everything was a gray, ragged blur and sickening pain hammered relentlessly at his head. He lay quietly and the blur gradually faded.

He was flat on his back on a ledge. A sharp-cornered stone was digging into his left kidney, but the pain it engendered in no way matched that in his head and left shoulder when he tried to move, so he simply endured it.

The low, velvet black of the star-studded sky was over him and the light from a quarter moon was pale, scarcely illuminating the cold surface of the ledge. He had been shot, he now realized. Twice. And he had to do something about it, or he would bleed to death. He stirred again, trying to sit up. The slogging pain paralyzed his muscles and he had no strength at all. He did succeed, finally, in squirming off the cruel edge of the rock.

He knew he had to rouse himself, shake off the deadly lethargy—do something about his wounds. He'd sure as hell bleed to death, he warned himself again. Mustering his strength, he tried to rise. Abruptly he was violently sick and retched deeply—and then everything became gray once more and he sank back.

It was cold. Wade became aware of that. His lids fluttered open. Night was still upon him, and the moon had moved considerably since he'd last seen it. But the terrible pain in his head and the throbbing in his shoulder and breast had not changed; they were as agonizing as before.

He thought again of his wounds and the necessity for doing something about them. He had already lost too much blood, and it was continuing to seep steadily from his body. He fought himself to a sitting position. Wave upon wave of nausea swept over him and he vomited uncontrollably. Finally that ceased, and he sat head down, shoulders slumped. He had no strength remaining—but at least he was still upright.

After a time he stirred. Gingerly he explored that portion of his throbbing head where he could feel a stinging sensation. His fingers encountered sticky moisture—a line of it that extended from a point above his temple to the back of his head. He managed a tight grin. The bullet had grazed him—close. A fraction of an inch more and he would have known nothing about it.

He slumped again, exhausted by his slight efforts. Minutes later he began to probe the wound in his shoulder. The graze along his head amounted to nothing; it was the shoulder that was serious. Only it wasn't the shoulder at all, he discovered. The pain had simply settled there. The wound was an inch or two below, actually high in his breast. It had bled freely, front and rear, and from that he knew the bullet had passed entirely through his body. He reckoned he was lucky to that extent.

Again worn out, he slumped forward, supporting himself by his stiffened right arm. The wound was still bleeding and needed attention—but it would have to wait a few more minutes until he could develop enough strength to rig up bandages of some sort.

He thought then of Stokes, of Leggett and Joe Dee Kline. They would be searching for him—at least, they would if they, too, weren't dead or badly shot up. They could be nearby. He raised his head and shouted: "Stokes! Leggett! Joe Dee!"

There was no reply, not even an echo from the dark, brooding Sacramento cañons. He realized then that his voice was too weak to carry any appreciable distance. His gun—he could fire it a couple of times. He dropped his hand to his holster. Disappointment and frustration surged through him. The leather was empty. He looked about on the ledge, straining his eyes in the half light. He could see no sign of the pistol. Then he realized he was not on the same ledge at all—that he was below. When shot, he had staggered, then fallen to the next lower shelf of rock. His weapon must be up above.

A brief wave of panic shocked him. The sorrel—where the hell was the sorrel? Without a horse, badly wounded, he was most certainly a dead man, even if he managed to patch himself up. He stared about anxiously, trying to see in the dimness. He could not locate the horse.

Cursing softly, he regained control of himself. Do things one at a time. Worry about the next problem when you face it. Keep your head.

He reached up and pulled loose the bandanna he wore about his neck. Holding one corner by his teeth, he ripped it across the center. He paused until his breathing returned to nearly normal, then folded each half of the cloth into square pads. Then, summoning his strength once more, he slid his right hand under his stiff, encrusted shirt and placed one of the pads upon the wound in his back. Blood accumulated there held it fairly secure. The second pad he pressed against the opening made by the bullet's entrance. Then, by grasping the folds of his shirt front tightly, he was able to exert pressure and hold the pads firmly in position. They should at least slow down the bleeding until help arrived. . . .

Help? Who could help him? He considered that question soberly. Likely Stokes was dead—along with young Kline and Jim Leggett. And if they were not, they probably were far from where he lay on the ledge by that hour.

He turned his head and looked out onto the mesa, hopefully seeking the small, red eye that would indicate a campfire. If one were visible, it would prove that Stokes and the others were in the area. Or that someone was, he thought grimly. Disappointment again washed over him. There was only the pale, silver glow of the stars and weak moonlight. The light was so inadequate that he could not even tell whether the herd was still there or not. Certainly it should be.

He yelled again, putting all his strength into it, and calling out the names of each of the three men. Once more there was only silence. They were all dead—or they had gone. He was certain his voice could have been heard that time.

He grew drowsy. For a time he fought against the thought of sleep, but finally he gave it up. There was nothing he could do, anyway. He was too weak to walk, and in such a state of exhaustion that, if he tried to crawl about on the ledge in the darkness, he could fall again. He doubted if his battered body could stand another physical shock. No . . . stay put . . . get some sleep. In that way he could perhaps rebuild his strength now that the bleeding had been checked. Time enough to think about getting off the ledge when daylight came. He lay back and was asleep almost immediately.

When he opened his eyes again, he could feel the sun's blast upon his face and body. Amazed, he realized it was hours past dawn.

Disturbed by that, he sat up, and felt a glow of satisfaction when the knowledge came to him that he had accomplished that simple act without too much effort and pain. The night's rest had helped considerably.

He turned his attention toward the flat and the grass-covered swale where Stokes had intended to bed the herd. It was empty.

Surprised, he lifted his glance. Far to the east there appeared to be a thin, yellowish cloud poised above the horizon. It looked like dust, but at such distance he could not be sure.

It was the herd, he concluded. It had to be. Either Stokes had managed to fight off the rustlers and had pushed on with the stock during the night—or the rancher and his two riders were dead and the cattle thieves were in charge.

Regardless, he had to catch up. First, however, he must find the sorrel. Painfully Wade got to his feet. A surge of dizziness rocked him momentarily, and he stood there, weaving unsteadily until it passed.

He moved then to the edge of the shelf, and glanced about. He could not see below because of a third jutting finger of rock, but there was grass beyond it, he recalled, and, if luck were with him, he would find the sorrel there—assuming the big red horse had not been stolen by the rustlers or had trailed along after the herd. He started to make his way along the rocky surface when he recalled his missing gun.

Wade halted, and looked upward. The ledge from which he had tumbled was little more than six feet above. Having little strength and but one usable arm and hand, he worked his way up the short incline to where he had stood. The pistol lay near center. Apparently when the first bullet of the ambusher had grooved across his head, instinct and pure reflex action had sent his hand reaching for the weapon. The impact of the second slug had caused him to drop it.

He recovered the .45, jammed it into its holster, and started back down the grade. He fell twice, gritting his teeth with pain each time, but finally he was on the floor of the cañon. Hope leaped high within him when he spotted the sorrel 100 feet farther on, placidly grazing in a small coulée.

He reached the horse, clawed at the canteen hanging from the saddle, and eased his burning thirst. The sorrel whickered anxiously at the smell of the water and he managed, with one hand, to get a few swallows down the beast's throat.

That done, he rested briefly, then, gathering his strength, he pulled himself onto the saddle. The effort cost him consciousness again and for several moments he simply sat there in the blistering sunlight, hand locked about the saddle horn, sucking for breath while his senses floundered in darkness.

Finally that, too, passed. He raised his red-rimmed eyes and looked to the east. The dust cloud he had seen—or thought he had seen—was no longer visible. But the herd had to be there somewhere, he was positive of that. And he had to overtake it. Urging the sorrel into motion, he moved out of the wash onto the mesa.

The sack of grub hanging from the horn caught his attention. Immediately he became aware of hunger. And food would help him to recover his strength. He leaned forward stiffly and unhooked the looped cord. His head swam and he caught himself. He was weaker than he had thought—but he'd be fine now. As long as he had his horse and could stick on the saddle, he'd be fine.

But that could be the problem. A warmness on his chest told him the wound had begun to bleed again.

IX

The thick slices of bread and beef tasted good, if somewhat hard and dry. Luke finished one, and eased the thirst it created with another pull at his canteen. He felt some better but he could not shake the leaden weariness that clung to him. He wouldn't, he knew, until he got those bullet holes cared for properly.

The morning, breathlessly hot, dragged into noon. Still he could see no dust, and that mystified as well as alarmed him and turned him impatient. Where the hell was the herd? No man could drive 200 steers across a flat and through low foothills without raising some dust. Granted, the land was rich sod, covered with grass—but there still should be a little dust.

His mind, wandering slightly and vaguely confused, decided there should have been other things, too—a search for him on the part of Helm Stokes when he hadn't shown up at camp, for one thing. The rancher knew where he had gone, knew exactly which point of rock he had intended to climb and make his check of the country. Why hadn't Stokes come for him—or at least sent Joe Dee or Leggett to see what the delay was?

A thread of reason crept into his brain. Maybe Stokes hadn't had the chance; maybe the rustlers had struck too fast and too hard for him to do anything. Maybe Helm Stokes was dead, but he reckoned the rustlers would have had a hard time doing that; they hadn't had much luck getting rid of the big cattleman the last time they'd tried.

He shook his head. Everything was getting fuzzy again. He was sweating freely. He mopped at his face with the back of his right hand, allowing the left to hang stiffly at his side. The damned wound was continuing to ooze. He tried to adjust the pads, but they were stuck tightly and he flinched when he sought to change them. He gave it up, swearing vividly in a low, ragged voice.

Still no dust cloud in sight—nor had he come upon a hoof-beaten trail. The latter he could understand and it did not particularly disturb him; he could be above or below the exact route the cattle had taken across the broad plain. By angling either right or left he could eventually intercept their tracks, but the effort wasn't worth it; he was headed east and he knew that was right.

The lack of dust was something else. There simply had to be a pall, unless—Luke Wade's faltering thoughts came to a full stop—unless the herd was much farther ahead than he had figured. On such solid land with a small bunch of cattle, it was conceivable the dust would not be seen at a long distance.

But he had been no more than a half mile behind the steers when they had been bedded down. True, that next morning he had overslept several hours; the herd could have gotten a good start on him, but hardly sufficient to move completely out of sight. That left one obvious answer. The herd had been pushed on during the night.

Wade grunted as that conclusion became clear to him. It would have been one hell of a chore, forcing the tired steers on through the darkness. Like most animals, when sundown came, cattle instinctively sought rest. It was their nature, and being contrary, stubborn brutes, they would balk at every attempt to keep them moving. But it could be done if there were enough drovers on hand to keep at them.

He guessed that was what had happened. The rustlers had taken over the herd, after getting rid of Stokes and Leggett and young Joe Dee Kline. They had figured he, as the guard, was already out of the picture. They had then pushed the stock on for perhaps three or four more hours, getting the herd as far as possible from the immediate vicinity. Knowing the country, they had likely halted in a deep swale where they had rested the cattle until daylight, and then resumed the drive.

That was the way of it, Luke felt sure, and all he need do was keep riding eastward until he caught up. Just what he could do then was unclear in his mind, but he would think of something. The rustlers would be. . . . Then he saw the body.

Through the shimmering heat waves it was a dark lump on the gray-green of the mesa. A horse waited patiently fifty yards below in the shadow of a twisted cedar tree. Luke eyed the crumpled shape with almost stupid interest for several moments, then roused himself and veered the sorrel to it. His faculties were lagging and somehow he couldn't seem to get himself organized and fully comprehend the meaning of the lifeless shape. But finally it dawned on him that he had found Helm Stokes.

Only it wasn't Stokes. When he had slid painfully from the saddle and crouched beside the dead man, he saw with a sickening shock that it was young Joe Dee Kline.

Luke sat back on his heels, mopped sweat from his face and stared down at Joe Dee's drawn features. The mark of pain lay there—and fear and hope. There were two bullet wounds in his chest. Neither would have killed him instantly. Evidently he had managed to stay on his horse for some time, although unconscious, before he had toppled from the saddle. The pony, naturally, would have continued to follow the herd until its rider fell from its back.

The discovery jolted some measure of reason into Luke Wade's waning senses. He swore deeply while a driving, seething hatred began to build within him, lend him strength and pyramid his determination. Damn a bunch of ruthless bastards who would kill a boy! They could have avoided cutting him down—they could have just wounded him, even scared him off. They hadn't had to murder him.

Stokes and Jim Leggett were something else. He could understand their deaths. They were grown men, capable of handling themselves and able to cope with renegade outlaws on even terms. But a boy like Joe Dee, a youngster . . . ?

Luke pulled himself to his feet. He would have to do something about the boy's body; he couldn't leave him lying there for the coyotes and buzzards to work over. He steadied himself against the sorrel and glanced around for something with which to dig a grave. There was nothing, not even a length of dry wood. And there were no rocks that could be used to erect a mound.

Sighing deeply as he recognized the task that lay before him,

Wade heaved himself onto his saddle, his shoulder screaming at the effort, and moved off toward Joe Dee's mount. He would have to get the boy onto his pony somehow and take him on in to the railhead.

An hour later, almost totally exhausted, sweat pouring off his sagging frame in rivulets, he had the youngster aboard his horse and tied to the saddle. The labor involved cost Luke every ounce of strength he had managed to store up, and he clung weakly to the sorrel, mouth flared, while his lungs gasped for wind.

When he was again able, he grasped the cantle of his hull with his right hand and, ignoring the murderous pain in his shoulder, hauled himself onto the red. Nausea claimed him once more but he rode it out, simply sat quietly, head down while his senses reeled.

A drink of water helped. To aid himself further, he removed his sweat-stained hat and poured a small quantity of the water onto his head. After that, he felt better, and, taking up the reins of Joe Dee's buckskin pony, he pushed on.

Mind clearing, he wondered if it wasn't likely he would encounter Helm Stokes's body, and Leggett's, too, somewhere ahead. If he did, there would be nothing he'd be able to do about them but let them lay where they had fallen. He knew he didn't have it in him to hoist even one more body onto a horse.

The heat began to break as the afternoon faded. Ahead he saw the low, dark ridges of another range of mountains, lying directly across his path. They were not tall hills, he noted, and that was some comfort.

Anson's Fork couldn't be too far ahead now. Traveling somewhat faster than a herd of cattle, he would make the trip in considerably less time. That again brought up the question of the lost beef. What had happened to the herd? By all that was normal he should have overtaken it, or at least brought it into sight by that hour. There was still no sign, no track. And no dust.

But the missing steers had sunk to secondary importance to him now. He thought only of reaching the railhead, turning the body of Joe Dee Kline over to the authorities, and then seeing to his own needs. He was rational enough now to know he could do nothing in his condition.

Maybe the answer would be waiting for him at Anson's Fork. Maybe the cattle would be there and he'd be able to retain consciousness long enough to notify the local lawman. Just how the herd could manage to beat him to the railhead he was not sure, and he had neither the will nor the strength to puzzle it out. But that would come. Later, after he had visited a doctor and got some hot food in his belly, he'd be in shape to put things right. All that counted now was getting there.

He reached the first outthrusting tongue of the mountains shortly after sunset. He was so near total collapse he was not aware of the deep rose flame that blazed a ribbon across the western horizon, was conscious only that sharp pointed heat lances no longer stabbed into his back and shoulders. The sorrel began to quicken his pace almost at once, and Luke allowed the horse to have his head. He was too far gone to hold him back anyway.

It was water that drew the sorrel—a wide, ankle-deep river that came from the floor of a broad, steep-walled cañon and flowed across the trail. It was a great temptation to drop from the saddle and sprawl full length in the shallow depths of the stream, but Wade resisted the urge, knowing that once off his horse he would be too weak to remount. So he waited.

When the two animals had satisfied their thirst, he goaded the sorrel with his spurs and sent him plodding on woodenly. Things were a little better now. The heat was gone and a faint breeze had sprung up, slipping quietly in from the southeast, fanning his face and relieving some of the fire that seemed to be running wildly in his body.

Hours later—he had no real conception of time—his feverish eyes caught sight of lights far in the distance. His pulse quickened and he struggled to sit straighter on the saddle. But he was too weak for even that, and he compromised by simply riding hunched forward, peering anxiously into the darkness from beneath the tipped brim of his hat.

The sorrel seemed to move with incredible, aggravating slowness, and for a time the small yellow dots hanging in the night stood still, and he could draw no nearer. Each rise the lagging sorrel mastered seemed to be only one of a thousand more that lay between him and his destination. Frequently he dozed, always unwillingly, exhausted in body and mind, and then finally he roused to discover that the sorrel had gained a crest of a hill and stopped. Below, at the foot of the slope, were the first of the lights.

A harsh croak burst from Luke Wade's burning throat. He dug his spurs deeply into the horse's flanks, cursing the animal unreasonably. At once the sorrel started down the gentle grade, moving at a tired trot.

They reached level ground and Luke aimed the horse at the nearest of the houses where a lamp shone softly through a window. He reached the gate, turned into the yard, and halted in the square of light flung out into the darkness.

Mustering the shreds of his strength, he called out: "Hello, the house . . . !"

He remembered the door swinging open, was aware of the sudden splash of more light—and that was all.

X

Oddly it was the familiar odor of a strong antiseptic that brought Luke to consciousness.

There had been a bottle of it at home. Introduced by surgeons near the close of the war, it had proved most effective. Upon discharge, Ben Wade had obtained a small quantity of the potent germ killer and taken it with him. He had kept it on the shelf with other medicines and remedies and Luke had used it often for cuts and abrasions sustained while working around the ranch.

Wade looked around. He lay on a narrow bed, covered by a clean, white sheet. It was a small room, skimpily furnished. A window in the wall opposite was open and a curtain waved gently in the fitful breeze. It was shortly after sundown, Luke guessed.

He stirred, trying to sit up. Pain raced through his body and his left shoulder and arm were rigid. He glanced down. A neatly applied bandage encircled his chest and extended onto his arm. He frowned, and lay back. Lifting his right hand, he touched his head. It, too, was bandaged.

At that moment the door opened. A man in a knee-length white coat paused there and looked down on him. He had a round face, dark hair combed tightly to his skull. A thin moustache covered his upper lip, an obvious attempt to create the illusion of greater age. He could be only a few years older than Wade, he guessed.

"I'm Doctor David," the man in the coat said. "Hope you're feeling better."

Luke said: "I am. Reckon I can thank you for that." He hesitated, frowning. "Can't seem to remember getting here."

David stepped forward briskly and made a few quick adjustments of the bandages. "One of the neighbors brought you. Said you rode into his yard, yelled, and fell off your horse. He and his boy carried you here to my office. You were in mighty bad shape."

"It was a long ride," Luke murmured. Then: "Did somebody

take care of the boy's body?"

"All looked after. Lucky you aren't lying in a pine box at the coroner's, too. Hungry?"

Wade shook his head, surprised at himself. "No, not much. Could use some coffee."

"Expect you'd better eat anyway. You lost a lot of blood, and steak and potatoes are the best way I know of to get it back." David drew back, turning toward the door. Halfway into the adjoining room he halted and looked over his shoulder. "Almost forgot. Marshal wants to talk to you. Said for me to call him when you regained consciousness. Feel up to it?"

Luke said: "Sure, why not? Expect he wants to know what happened . . . and I got plenty to tell him."

The physician disappeared into the shadows. Luke heard him say something to someone unseen, and then the outer door opened and closed. He turned his head to the side and stared through the window. Lamps were being lit along Anson's Fork's main street, and the night's activities were stirring into life. There was the faint smell of dust in the still warm air, and somewhere a jackass brayed in raucous discord.

A heaviness came over him. He had failed the Mangus Valley ranchers, he realized bitterly. Instead of getting their herd through, he had lost it—along with the lives of Joe Dee, Stokes, and Jim Leggett. A hell of a mess he had made of it. Right now those 200 steers should have been in Anson's Fork's cattle pens, and he and the others should have been celebrating and preparing for the return trip. Instead. . . .

The door opened again, and closed softly. The sound of boot heels crossing a barren floor followed, and then abruptly an elderly man wearing a star stood in the doorway. Dr. David was at his shoulder.

"Our town marshal, Amos Spilman," the physician said. "Never did find out your name."

"Wade . . . Luke Wade."

"Luke Wade, Amos. You've got about ten minutes. He's not up to much talking yet."

"Won't take me long," Spilman said in a quick, business-like way. He entered the room and stood at the end of the cot, a tall, wide-shouldered man with deep creases in his weathered face.

"Where you hail from, Wade?"

"Red Hill . . . the Mangus Valley country. I was bringing. . . ."

"Who was the dead man you brought in, and who shot him?"

"Name is Joe Dee Kline. Son of one of the ranchers. Rustlers got him . . . along with two other men making the drive. Came close to finishing me."

"Rustlers?" Spilman echoed, pulling his face into a frown. "Where'd they jump you?"

"This side of the Sacramentos."

"How many in the party?"

Wade shrugged, and winced at the pain the movement caused. "Don't know. Never did see them. I got bushwhacked right off the start."

Spilman's features were flat, expressionless. He strolled to the window, brushed the curtain aside, and stared into the street. Without turning, he said: "Those other two men . . . who were they? How come you didn't bring them in, too?"

"Didn't run across their bodies . . . and, if I had, I'd never have got them loaded on their horses. It was all I could do to bring in Joe Dee. Names were Stokes and Leggett."

The lawman turned. "Then you ain't sure they're dead . . . for certain, I mean."

"Pretty sure," Luke replied, anger beginning to lift within him. "They killed Joe Dee, tried their best to kill me, and ran off with our herd. They had to do something with Stokes and Leggett, didn't they?"

The marshal nodded absently. "Seems so," he said.

"Then I figure you're wasting time. How about getting up a posse and heading west toward the Sacramentos. You're bound to come across the herd out there somewhere . . . if they haven't already been driven here."

"Been no stock brought in for a week," the lawman said.

"Then they're still out there. You find the herd and you'll find the killers, too. And if you do a little looking, you ought to come across Stokes and Leggett. They'll be somewhere between. . . ."

Luke's words trailed off. Spilman was wagging his head in a slow, positive way.

"What's the matter?"

"Not much I can do about it," the lawman said. "I'm just the town marshal. Got no authority outside Anson's Fork."

"Then who the hell can I talk to?"

"Sheriff, I reckon."

"He here in town?"

"Nope. Office is in Lincoln."

"Lincoln," Luke repeated wearily. "That's more'n a hundred miles away."

"Afraid so. I'm real sorry, son, but it sure don't look like there's much I can do for you and that herd you say you lost."

"I lost it . . . along with three friends," Wade snapped. He sank back, suddenly exhausted. "Devil of a note," he muttered. "You've got law here . . . only you haven't."

Amos Spilman lifted his arms and allowed them to drop in a gesture of resignation. "Like I said, I've got no authority, 'cepting here in town. Now, you get them rustlers and bring them in to me, and I'll sure as hell jail them for you."

"Be a little hard to do, me lying here in bed," Wade said sarcastically. He shifted his glance to David. "How long before I can get out of here, Doc?"

The physician pursed his lips. "Expect you've already tried to sit up . . . and you got your answer right then. You're plenty weak. Ought to stay where you are a couple more days at least. Three wouldn't hurt. Even then you'll have to take it slow."

"Wish there was something I could do," Spilman said lamely. "I. . . ."

"It's real important I get moving," Luke said, ignoring the lawman. "Fix me up, Doc. I can't hang around here no later than morning."

David cocked his head to one side. "I'll sure do what I can, but I won't guarantee much. However, you're a pretty healthy specimen in spite of what you've been through. Let's get some good food in your belly and see how you feel tomorrow."

"By then I'll be fine," Luke said.

Spilman edged toward the door. "What do you want me to do about the dead man?"

"Hold the body. His folks'll probably want to bury him on their ranch."

Spilman groaned. "Ain't hardly got no place. . . ."

"Use Hardyman's ice house," David broke in. "They just hauled in some ice from the cave."

"Reckon I could do that," the marshal said, moving on. He halted in the doorway. "Sure sorry there ain't nothing I can do for you, Wade."

"You might just take yourself a ride out west, sort of passing the time," Luke suggested. "Could be you'd come across the bodies of my friends. Don't think that'd be jumping your authority, would it?"

Spilman gave him a quiet look, shrugged, and left the room. David crossed to the window and peered out.

"It's taking them long enough to bring that meal," he grumbled. "Going to get myself a woman one of these days just so I can get my cooking done here at home. Think I'll trot over and see if I can hurry it up."

The doctor wheeled and disappeared into the other part of the house. Wade lay motionlessly, mulling over his conversation with Spilman. He would get no help there; that was clear to him now. What was to be done would have to be done on his own—and soon.

One thing was sure. The herd was still back on the flats somewhere. It couldn't just have been swallowed up. And Helm Stokes and Leggett, he'd have to find their bodies, too. It wasn't decent to let them lay out there in the sun, bloating, to become food for the carrion eaters.

He pulled himself to a sitting position despite the waves of pain that slugged him. David said he might be in shape to get up that next morning. Luke clamped his jaw shut; it was up to him to make it possible.

Resting his back against the wood panels of the bed's headboard, he tried to move his left arm. The muscles were stiff, seemed frozen into place. Pain racked him at each attempt to move it, but he weathered each onslaught and kept doggedly at it. After a few moments he was able to raise the arm slightly.

Encouraged, he began to flex the muscles, twist and work his wrist. Then the elbow. Gradually his arm began to loosen, but now his shoulder was flaming with pain. He heard David enter the house, and paused. The physician came into the room bearing a tray upon which was a plate heaped with steak, potatoes, fried eggs, hot biscuits and butter. A small granite coffee pot, steaming and full, and with a cup, were alongside. There was also a water tumbler half filled with raw whiskey. David gave Luke a swift scrutiny.

"I see you're already at it," he said, and placed the tray on Wade's lap. "That's fine . . . just don't overdo it."

He picked up the knife and fork and cut the meat into small squares. That done, he stepped back.

"Get that down first," he said, pointing at the liquor. "Then eat. I've been pouring gruel down you ever since you got here, but you need something solid that'll stick to your ribs. I'll look in on you later . . . and, when I do, I want to see that plate licked clean. Understand?"

Luke grinned. "Sure . . . I understand."

David bobbed his head, and again pursed his lips. "Maybe, just maybe, we'll have you on your feet by daylight."

XI

It must have been the whiskey that put the starch back into his muscles, Luke Wade decided that next morning when he arose, somewhat shakily, and began to pull on his clothing. The good food and the expert ministrations of Dr. David could not be discounted, of course, but there was no denying the fire the raw liquor had built within his body.

It was an effort to dress but he kept at it doggedly until, gun at his hip, he was ready to go about the plans he had earlier formulated. He started for the door, reeled dangerously, and caught himself by bracing his right hand against the wall. He grinned wolfishly. He wasn't as strong as he'd thought.

Resting briefly, he made his way into the adjoining room, and found it empty. He heard noises out in the back yard and fumbled his way to the open doorway. David was watering a small garden planted against a weathered fence. The physician glanced up as Luke halted in the opening. He smiled.

"You've got more guts than an Army mule. A wound like that would keep an ordinary man in bed for a week."

"Not if he had things to tend to," Wade replied. "Like to settle up with you, be on my way."

David put the watering can aside and moved toward Luke. "First I'll have a look at things," he said. "Didn't expect you up quite so early. . . . Sit over there."

"Already lost too damn' much time," Wade grumbled, backing into the room and sinking onto a hard-backed chair.

"You rush things too fast and you'll find yourself in that bed again," the physician warned.

"I aim to take it easy."

David made no answer. Using a pair of scissors, he snipped the bandage encircling Luke's head. With gentle fingers he examined the angry groove left by the bullet.

"That'll do fine," he said. "Just don't scratch it. Now, pull off your shirt so I can see the other little souvenirs your friends gave you."

Wade complied. David removed the bandage. Lips pursed in his habitual manner, the doctor probed the two lesions thoughtfully.

"Good, good," he murmured. "They'll be all right if you don't pull some fool stunt and break them open."

He left the room momentarily, and returned with a tray of bottles and fresh bandages. Quickly and efficiently, he dressed the wound, applying more antiseptic and a cooling salve.

"I'll leave the bandage a bit looser this time," he said. "Closure is not important now. Just a matter of healing." Finished, he stepped back. "What do you plan on doing?"

"Soon as I run down that cattle buyer we were supposed to meet here, I'm heading west. Got to locate the herd if I can. Lot of people depending on the money from the sale."

David shook his head. "Riding's not going to do you any good. Apt to break that wound open again."

"Can't be helped," Luke said, reaching into his pocket. "How much do I owe you?"

"How about two-fifty? Suit you?"

Wade produced his supply of change and counted out the specified amount. "Fine with me, but it hardly seems enough.

Fact is, I'd double it if I had the cash, but you're looking at my pile."

"Two-fifty's the going rate, and I don't believe in sticking the cash customers just because everybody else is on credit." He thrust the money into his pocket. "Wait here. I'll bring up your horse."

Luke followed the physician out into the yard. "I owe you for his keep, too, don't I?"

David grinned. "It's on the house. Everybody mostly pays me in hay and grain. If I had ten horses, they couldn't live long enough to eat up what I've got stored in my barn. What about the boy's buckskin?"

"Be obliged if you'll let him stay. I'll have somebody pick him up."

David nodded and disappeared into a small, sagging structure at the rear of his lot. Within a few minutes he returned leading the sorrel. He passed the reins to Luke.

"Be smart now. Go easy."

Wade grinned, and pulled himself carefully onto the saddle. His left arm and shoulder were still somewhat stiff, but on the whole he didn't feel too badly. There was just the weakness.

David said: "The cattle buyer you're looking for will be at the hotel . . . there's only one in town. You'll likely find him at the restaurant right next door, this time of the morning."

Wade nodded, and headed on to the dusty street. He paused there, vaguely dizzy, and scanned the double line of high and low false-fronted buildings that strung off to his left. The Westerner Hotel was about halfway down. A café sign hung above the plank walk just beyond. He swung the sorrel toward it.

Pulling in to the hitch rack, he dismounted awkwardly, wrapped the leathers around the crossbar, and entered the restaurant. It was a small place, no more than half a dozen tables and a short counter. A waitress in a starched apron looked up at him expectantly.

"I'm hunting that cattle buyer," Wade said, coming straight to the point. "Has he been here yet?"

The woman smiled. "No, but he's about due."

"I'll wait for him at that back table," Luke said, motioning at a back corner. "And while I'm waiting, bring me something to eat. Double order of eggs and bacon. And a pot of coffee."

"Yes, sir," the waitress said, then frowned as Wade staggered slightly. "You all right, mister?"

"All right," he muttered, and moved for the corner table.

Wade had just begun to eat when a nattily dressed individual, wearing a derby hat cocked to one side, entered. Smiling brightly, the waitress hurried to him. She spoke a few words, pointing to Luke. Apparently this was the man he wanted to see.

The buyer made his way through the tables, halted before Wade, and extended his hand. "Name's Bishop. Hear you're looking for me."

"If you buy cattle, I am," Wade said, shaking hands. He introduced himself and Bishop sat down. Luke explained what had happened to the Mangus Valley herd.

Bishop toyed with his gold watch chain. "Too bad. I was expecting it in today. Guess there's no point in hanging around any longer."

"That's what I wanted to talk to you about," Luke said, leaning forward. "I'm asking you to give me a few more days. That herd's out there somewhere, and I'm heading out to find it and bring it in."

"Maybe," the buyer said doubtfully. "Rustlers have a way of disappearing quick with the steers they've grabbed."

"Maybe so . . . but, hell, two hundred steers don't just fade into nothing."

"You any idea where they might be?"

"A little. I remember crossing a shallow river west of here. . . ."

"That'll be the Penasco. About twenty, twenty-five miles out."

"Laying in that bed at Doc David's I had a chance to do some thinking. I've got a hunch I'll find a trail somewhere along that river."

Bishop wagged his head. "That'll take you three or four days, maybe a week. And for two hundred head it's hardly worth my while to wait."

"It's mighty important to those people back in the valley that this sale goes through," Luke said earnestly. "And it could mean plenty to you later on. It's a small herd, sure, and you're dealing with small ranchers. But little ranches grow into big ones . . . and you'd be putting yourself in strong with every one of them. They wouldn't forget the favor and I expect you'd have first crack at every head they raised in the future."

Bishop stroked his mustache, and cast a sidelong glance at the smiling waitress. "Well . . . if you're putting it that way, I might just hang around until Saturday. . . ."

"I'll appreciate it," Wade said, relaxing slightly. "You won't regret it."

"Always happy to help new ranchers get on their feet," Bishop said expansively. "Pays off eventually. Now, if you'll excuse me, I'll have my breakfast."

Luke opened his mouth, intending to invite the cattle buyer to sit with him, but Bishop was looking at the waitress, who stood expectantly beside a table on the opposite side of the room.

"All set, then," he said as the man rose. "I'll see you by Saturday, if not before."

Bishop bobbed his head. "Good luck. I don't know how you can manage it, but I'll wait around to see if you do."

"I'll manage it," Luke replied quietly. "I've got to."

XII

The heat was brutal. Piercing rays, like sharp, white-hot lances, speared from a cloudless sky, stabbed into him, and steadily drained the juices from his already weakened body. His shoulder pained considerably and he learned that, when it became unbearable, relief was to be had by dismounting and walking ahead of the sorrel for a time. It slowed his progress, but conversely it served also to rebuild his lagging strength.

As a result it was noon when he reached the Penasco River. Luke had intentionally swung to the south, determined to search along the banks of the stream for prints of the stolen cattle. He didn't believe the rustlers had cut to that direction—it was logical to assume they had veered northward—but he was bucking a time deadline and he could not afford to whip back and forth endlessly searching for the trail.

He halted at the broad, shallow stream and spent a quarter hour soaking his head, washing his face and neck in the cool water, while the sorrel took his fill. He felt much better after the refreshing pause, and soon moved on.

Crossing to the Penasco's west bank, he headed upstream, his eyes now on the soft mud under the sorrel's hoofs. Although events subsequent to the ambush were hazy in his mind, he was fairly certain the herd had been driven across the river, and not turned north along the west slopes of the low lying hills. Unless they had been driven up the Penasco.

His thoughts came to an abrupt halt at that possibility. . . . Up the river, between the walls of the cañon through which it flowed. The stream was shallow, scarcely hoof deep, and soft earth, covered with grass and the flat-leafed cone-centered plant they called cowslips back home, extended back on either side for several yards. It would have been simple to drive a herd up the cañon.

Eager now, he urged the sorrel to a slow lope, ignoring the pain in his shoulder. Somewhere ahead he would intersect the hundreds of hoof prints left by the cattle; if he were right, they would march up to the edge of the river and there disappear.

Minutes later his probing eyes picked up the tracks left by his sorrel and Joe Dee Kline's horse where they had crossed two nights previously. The imprints had crusted over—but they were there. Encouraged, he hurried on.

The flat began to lift and meet the slopes of the low string of hills, bringing to Luke Wade a faint doubt. He was drawing nearer to the first bluffs marking the mouth of the cañon. Unless he encountered the trail left by the herd soon, he would have to conclude that he was wrong, and that the rustlers had followed some other course.

But the tracks were there—hundreds of deep-cut imprints in a narrow band. The herd had entered the river and the cañon at the very foot of the opening.

Relief flowing through him, Luke Wade halted and swung from the saddle. He ground-reined the sorrel at the base of the bluffs and walked slowly upstream, eyes scanning the spongy green earth. For the first 100 feet he saw nothing, but now there was no doubt in his mind and so he pressed on.

A short distance later, hoof prints began to appear on the Penasco's banks. It was clear then what had happened. The cattle had waded the stream for a time, then begun to string out on solid ground. Here and there he spotted droppings, and with that final assurance Luke turned about and retraced his steps to the sorrel. He had only to follow the river through the cañon, and eventually he would come to the missing herd.

It was pleasant within the confines of the walls. Squat cedars, piñons, and scrub oak brush dotted the rocky slopes, and now and then bright splashes of vivid reds, yellows, and whites marked beds of wildflowers. The floor of the cañon, fifty feet wide on the average and nearly level, was covered with grass and other lush growth that softened the heat and made the passage easy for both Wade and the sorrel.

Gray squirrels darted in and out of the rocks, and white-breasted bluebirds and sharp-tongued jays with their arrogant crests uplifted flitted ahead of him. Several times the sorrel's progress disturbed drab gray dipper birds, teetering on stones in midstream, and sent them skimming off, barely clearing the water.

The cañon twisted continually, never becoming deeper or shallower. The sun dropped below the rim to the west and long shadows began to stretch across the stream. It was still hours until sunset, Luke knew, but darkness would come early along the bottom of the cañon.

He grew hungry and ate again from the sack of grub old Caleb had prepared. Coffee would have helped considerably, but he was reluctant to stop and build a fire. Smoke might reveal his presence. He had no idea, of course, how far ahead the herd might be. He had lost a day and two nights at Anson's Fork in addition to the time spent riding back and forth. Unless the rustlers had halted somewhere along the way, he could have a long ride before him.

It ended much sooner than he had hoped.

The cañon angled sharply to the left a half mile farther on. He made the turn, the sorrel trotting slowly along at the edge of the water, and pulled up short when he beheld a wide, sunlit mesa stretching out beyond the end of the hills. Immediately he swung the horse away from the river, gained higher ground, and spurred him into a lope, anxious to see what lay beyond the cañon's northern mouth. When he reached the wide opening, he again halted. A low whistle escaped his lips.

A deep swale, at least a mile across, lay to his left, a lush, circular oasis on the surface of the prairie. Tall, thick-trunked cottonwood trees spread their branches over the entire area and at the lower end an ample watering pond shimmered in the afternoon light. Near the center stood a squat ranch house. Four horses waited, hip-shot and heads low, at the hitch rack fronting it. Farther back Luke could see a barn and a scatter of outbuildings. And in the corral, shifting restlessly, were the missing cattle.

XIII

Luke Wade assumed it was the stolen herd. There appeared to be about 200 head, and the trail out of the cañon led toward the ranch. But it was too far to be positive—and closer inspection would be impossible until darkness fell.

He rode the sorrel off to one side and drew up behind a tangled clump of junipers. There he would be visible neither from the house nor to a rider who might chance to come out of the cañon. He swung stiffly from the saddle, suddenly excessively tired and wishing for a drink of whiskey, or at least some strong coffee to bolster his sagging strength, but both were out of the question.

He ate again, sparingly, from his supply of food, washing down the hard bread and now paper-dry beef with water from his canteen. The sorrel contented himself with browsing on the thin grass growing in the open spaces between the rocks.

Just what he would or could do was not clear in Luke Wade's mind. He had tracked down the stolen cattle, the proof of which he would obtain as soon as night came, but from there on his course was uncertain. One thing was clear. He had to get the beef to Anson's Fork as soon as possible. Bishop would not wait much longer—certainly not beyond the Saturday deadline he had stated. And while the herd below was, at that point, likely little more than a long day's drive from the settlement, there was not time enough to return to Red Hill, gather the ranchers concerned, and bring them in to help. The same held true with the railhead. And he could not do it alone. No one man, however expert and experienced, could manage 200 obstinate steers by himself. He shook his head, disturbed by the problem—and then dismissed it from his mind. He would find some way to meet the issue when the moment came.

Finished with his sparse meal, he hung the sack back on the saddle and, favoring his wounded shoulder, climbed to a somewhat higher ledge on the side of the hill where he could look out over the mesa and see the ranch.

The sun was falling slowly into a blaze of golds and yellows beyond the Sacramentos, and long streaks of clouds hovering about the peaks and ridges were assuming varying shades of purple. As he watched the fiery glow spread, until it extended the full, sprawling length of the great hills, which grew steadily darker beneath the changing purples.

Back in the cañon a dove *cooed* mournfully and a squirrel *chattered*. Up on the slope something moved—a rabbit, most likely—and a small cascade of gravel spilled over a ledge, disturbing the hush. A door slammed, the slap of it hollow and distant.

Instantly Wade turned his attention to the ranch house. A man, carrying a water bucket, came off the rear porch, slammed a second, screened door, and entered the yard. He walked lazily to the well a dozen paces to the back of the structure. Placing the bucket on the sill, he began to crank the windlass, setting up a dry squeal that echoed through the quiet. The sorrel paused in his foraging, looked up inquiringly, and then resumed his chore.

The outlaw slopped his bucket full from the keg he had lifted from the depths of the well, turned, and started for the house.

He gained the porch. The screen slammed once more—but there was no second slap. He had left the inside door, probably leading into the kitchen, open. In deference to the heat, Luke supposed.

Smoke began to trickle from the chimney at that end of the house. It was mealtime and the men were preparing to eat. Minutes later yellow lamplight blossomed in a corner window of the same room.

Luke glanced toward the Sacramentos. The sun was entirely gone and the golden glow had turned to a leaden gray—but it was still too light to move in closer.

An hour later, with his shoulder paining in a persistent, aching manner, he watched the lamp go out in the kitchen and come alive again in an adjoining room. The outlaws had completed their meal and had moved into other quarters where they would pass the evening playing cards, drinking, and swapping stories. It should be safe enough now to move out, he judged. He was anxious to have a look at the cattle.

Returning to the sorrel, he crawled onto the saddle and cut back. Circling wide across the mesa, he waited until the bulky shape of the barn stood between him and the ranch house, and then rode directly forward.

He reached the weathered structure, halted, and again dismounted. A tautness gripped him as he secured the sorrel to a tough, squat cedar. He paused, an odd thought crossing his mind: *I've gone through six kinds of hell, and now I'm risking my neck for a man I'm going to kill. Makes no sense. . . .*

He stood there in the dim light, half crouched, considering that truth, wondering at his own inconsistency. And then he eased his outraged sensibilities by telling himself there were other men involved, good men, honest men who deserved his help. It was wrong to penalize the whole of Mangus Valley because of one evil member.

He moved on then, working his way along the splintery boards toward the corrals. He could hear no sounds issuing from the house and concluded the outlaws were unusually quiet or else had turned in for the night. Perhaps they were all in a drunken stupor. He grinned wryly at that bit of wishful thinking; a man just didn't run in that kind of good luck.

He gained the corral, where the cattle heaved and shoved restlessly. Drawing in close, he hurriedly examined the nearest flank for its brand. It was a bold A-D, freshly burned. There was no doubt in his mind now. The steer belonged to Albert Dunn. It was the stolen herd.

He pulled back into the deep shadow of a cottonwood and studied the house. Light still showed in the dusty square of the window and there was yet fire in the kitchen range, judging from the trail of smoke winding lazily into the night sky. It was probably a hangover from coals still alive in the stove, Luke guessed. Such men would spend little time cooking; they would boil coffee and fry meat, but other than that they would have no use for a stove.

Still undecided as to his next move, he slipped in closer to the house, dodging from shadow to shadow, always careful to avoid the open areas. There was no way of telling if any of the men were looking out, and he took no chances. Reaching the structure, he eased up close to the lighted window and peered in.

There were four men, as he had concluded earlier from the number of horses at the rack. They were grouped about a table, engaged in a desultory game of poker. Small piles of matches served as chips.

Surprise rippled through Luke when he recognized one as the red-headed friend of Del's. Red was the man who had hurriedly departed when invited to take up the fight where Del and the Mexican had left off. The others were strangers to Wade; all were hard-faced, whiskered men with the stamp of outlaw upon them.

"Reckon we better be gettin' at them steers, come mornin'," one of the men said, laying down his dog-eared cards and reaching for a sack of cigarette makings. "Be a helluva job, workin' over them brands."

"What's the rush?" the rider sitting at his left demanded. "We got plenty of time. Besides, Jim'll be here tomorrow or next day. He can help. Five of us'll do it quicker'n four."

"Suits me," the man with the tobacco said. "I ain't honin' to get at it any more'n you. I recollect up. . . ."

"All right, Todd, you playin' or ain't you?" Red cut in impatiently. "Either bet or back off."

"I'm playin'," Todd said calmly. "Openin' for two bucks." He tossed the necessary matches into the center of the table, then settled his small, dark eyes on the redhead. "You're mighty jumpy. Somethin' eatin' you?"

Red glared at his cards, swore in disgust, and slammed them onto the table. "All that's eatin' me is my stinkin' luck . . . and this waitin' around."

"That and thinkin' about how his pal, Del, got his guts blowed out by that drifter. That sort o' thing sure can get to a man. . . ."

"Well, you're square with him now," the fourth rider said. "He's cold turkey, layin' back there in the hills. By now the buzzards'll have picked him clean."

Red picked up his cards, grunted, and settled back. He seemed relieved. "Expect you're right, Chino. He's been paid off and I got to quit thinkin' about it." He shifted his attention to the fourth man. "Willie, there any more rotgut in that there bottle?"

Willie reached down and held aloft an empty quart bottle. "Nary a drop," he said. "Been sucked bone dry."

Red swore softly. "Nothin' to do but wait . . . and nothin' to drink while we're doin' that. Damn if I ain't ridin' in to the Fork tomorrow and gettin' a jug."

"Jim'll be bringin' some," Todd assured him. "You'd be makin' the trip for nothin'." He leaned back, yawned. "Gettin' powerful sleepy. How about you birds . . . want to quit?"

"Couple more hands and I'm ready," Chino said. "Whose bet?"

Luke Wade stepped back from the window. A plan was taking shape in his mind—a wild, desperate plan in which the odds would be stacked high against him, but it was one that could work if he were careful.

He faded into the shadows and made his way to the barn. On impulse, he entered the wide, open doorway, halting just inside. A pile of hay was at the far end of the runway, offering itself as a comfortable bed for the night. He could use some rest.

He crossed over and examined the window behind it. The sash was loose in the frame, held in place only by two rusting nails. Pushing them aside, he lifted the window out and leaned it against the wall. It was an instinctive precaution. He now had an escape exit other than the door if anything went wrong.

The sorrel was almost directly below the window; taking up a quantity of hay, he dropped it where the big red could reach it. That done, he made himself comfortable in the corner, prepared to rest and work out the details of the plan he had in mind.

Immediately his pulse quickened as his ears picked up the slow beat of approaching horses. He had overlooked the fact that the four animals out front would likely be stabled for the night.

He thought of the window, but decided it was too late for that—his injured shoulder would hinder him too much if he endeavored to make a hasty escape. He lay back, drew his gun, and pulled hay across his prone body, leaving only his eyes exposed. Nerves taut, he watched the doorway.

It was Chino. Lantern in hand, leading the horses, he stepped into the runway. He paused briefly to hang the light on a peg, then continued on. No danger, Wade thought, then felt fresh alarm when he saw that the outlaw was not putting the horses in stalls but was bringing them on to the pile of hay.

Scarcely breathing, Luke watched as Chino came in close—no more than half a dozen paces away—and stopped. He dropped the reins to the floor and moved in behind the animals. Shouldering his way between them, the outlaw slapped them sharply on the rump, forcing them in to where they could help themselves to the hay. He did not trouble to remove the bridles or loosen the girths.

Chino paused beside one of the horses, evidently his own, and began to fiddle with the saddle, making some repair or adjustment. The moments dragged. As he lay, tense and rigid, Luke's shoulder began to throb more acutely. He needed to shift his position slightly to relieve the pain but he dared not move. To do so would startle the horses and reveal his presence to Chino.

The rustler worked with aggravating slowness. The weak light of the lantern was behind him and Wade could see his jaws moving methodically as he chewed on a cud of tobacco. One of the horses lifted his head. Luke froze, not even breathing. The animal had picked up his scent, and now stared suspiciously at the mound of hay that Wade had drawn over his body.

At that moment Chino completed his chore and stepped back. The horse lowered his long head, gathered in another mouthful of dry fodder, and began to grind it between his teeth. Luke felt the tension ease. The outlaw turned and retraced his steps down the runway, his boot heels rapping a lazy cadence on the hard-packed soil. He retrieved the lantern and stepped out into the yard. There was a loud *squeak* as he closed the doors, a faint *jingle* of metal when he fastened the hasp.

Luke changed his position, easing the pain. All four horses jumped at the unexpected movement, but he gave it no thought. He could still hear Chino walking toward the house.

He pulled himself about until he lay facing the window. He needed to keep close tab on the hours. When the first hint of light broke in the east, it would be time to start. His plan could prove a deathtrap if he waited too long.

XIV

Luke Wade got little sleep. The vital importance of timing to his scheme, and the dull, infuriating pain in his shoulder, combined to keep him restless and wakeful. He dozed for only short periods, awaking each time with a start to stare anxiously at the window.

Finally, in disgust, he gave it up and, rising, brushed the hay from his clothing and moved to the opening in the wall. The outlaws' horses, frightened, shied away at his abrupt appearance, but after a few moments they quieted. Since Chino had closed and locked the doors he was forced now to use the window. Slowly and painfully he hoisted himself through the empty framework and dropped to the ground.

It was an hour or more yet until first light, but he was going ahead with his plan, regardless—better to be early than late. Releasing the sorrel, he led him around the barn to the corral where the cattle were gathered. He tethered the horse to a small tree a few paces back from the enclosure, and then returned to the barn. Using utmost care, he opened one of the doors, doing it slowly to minimize the *squeak* of hinges. The rusting metal set up a dry *screech*, nevertheless, but the sound was suppressed and he doubted if anyone had heard it.

There were rifles slung from the saddles of two of the rustlers' horses. Pulling both free, he levered one and assured himself that it was fully loaded. The other he tossed into the pile of hay. He examined the saddlebags next, but found no hidden weapons in any of them. Gathering up the trailing reins of the four animals, he led them to the corral. Side-by-side, he tied them to the top bar of the pole enclosure, placing them at a point where they stood near but in front of his own sorrel. He hung the rifle upon his saddle, then turned to study the house.

It lay in complete darkness. Smoke no longer drifted from the kitchen chimney and he guessed the fire was finally out. He waited out a long minute, then, taking a deep breath and pulling his pistol, he moved toward the rear door, hopeful that it had not been closed and barred by the outlaws.

He reached the screen and stepped cautiously onto the porch. A sigh slipped from his tight lips. The door to the kitchen stood open. Holding to the screen to prevent its slamming, he allowed it to swing shut, then crossed the dust-covered board floor and entered the house.

Trapped heat still hung heavily in the small room, along with the odor of well-boiled coffee. Luke, eyes straining into the darkness, glanced hungrily at the stove, wishing he dared pause for a cup, but he decided against it; the most dangerous part of his plan was before him, and, until he had that mastered, all else would have to wait.

Holstering his gun, he leaned down and removed his boots. Again taking out the weapon, he crossed the kitchen, weakly lit by the moon and starlight, and passed through the opening that led into the room where he had earlier watched the outlaws at their card game.

It was deserted. He had half expected to find some of the men asleep in chairs or on the sagging couch placed against the wall; snoring sounds deeper in the house, however, bespoke bedrooms. On silent feet he made his way along a narrow hall toward the noise.

The outlaws had quartered themselves in two rooms. Halting in the doorway of the first, he recognized Red and the one called Todd. They were sprawled on a ragged bed, sleeping soundly despite the stuffy, sweat-permeated air. Chino and Willie would be farther down the corridor. Luke grinned tightly into the darkness. It made things easier.

Quietly, careful not to stumble against a chair or some other item of furniture, Wade crept into the room. Halting in the center, he looked about, peering through the faint light. Red and his companion lay motionless, only partly unclad. A moment later he saw what he was searching for—the outlaws' gun belts. They hung from the bedpost.

He stepped in silently, lifted them without sound, and backed to the doorway. Both belts were heavy with cartridges, and supporting them with his left hand brought quick pain to his shoulder. He returned to the kitchen and looked for a place in which to hide the weapons. His glance picked up the flour barrel. Lifting the lid, he dumped the equipment into the half-full container.

He went then to the room where Chino and Willie slept, followed a similar procedure, and dropped back to the kitchen. Removing one of the revolvers, he thrust it into his own belt, thus providing himself with an extra weapon, and then added the remainder to the barrel.

Breathless from tension and effort, he sank onto one of the hard-backed chairs. That much was over with. Now, if he could pull off the rest. . . .

He drew on his boots and lit the lamp. Taking up the chair and light, he moved to the corner of the room nearest the inside door. There he placed the lamp on a shelf behind and somewhat above. He considered that for a few moments, and decided he was in the best possible position for the outlaws when they came into the room, since he would be to their backs, more or less. This would afford him a favorable advantage. Satisfied, he sat down to wait out another hour.

The smell of coffee beckoned to him. Rising, Luke moved to the stove and laid his hand against the side of the smoke-streaked pot. It was lukewarm. Picking up a cup, he poured it full and lifted it to his lips.

It was strong and the bitterness of it jolted him like a blow to the belly, but it scattered the cobwebs gathering about his brain and brought him to a full alert. He glanced out the window. It was still too dark to begin; he had to have enough light to see by.

Taking the pot and cup with him, he returned to his chair and sat down. Refilling the tin container with the last of the pot's contents, he nursed it until the darkness beyond the doorway began to fade. He got to his feet then, and turned down the lamp. Drawing back into the corner as far as the walls would permit, he lifted the metal coffee pot and hurled it through the window.

At the sudden *crash,* yells erupted in the bedrooms. A gun in each hand, Luke Wade stood poised, waiting, listening to the utter confusion the shattering glass had evoked. Todd was cursing in a wild, steady way. He could hear Chino shouting questions, Red answering. Moments later there was the hammer of hurried boots in the hall, and in the adjoining room. All four of the outlaws crowded into the kitchen.

Todd was a step ahead. He was fumbling with the buttons of his shirt, mouthing curses. "Where'n the hell did I leave my iron . . . ?" he began, then pulled up short as his sweeping glance fell upon Luke.

The others hauled up abruptly, and turned to follow his stricken gaze. Their jaws sagged, sleep-heavy, red-rimmed eyes opening wide.

"For the love of God," Red muttered in an awed tone.

"Where'd he come from?"

Luke motioned with his right-hand gun. "Line up over there . . . in front of the stove. Keep your arms up . . . high."

Chino and Willie crossed over slowly and took up positions near the range. Red and Todd shuffled into place beside them.

Todd said: "You get our hardware?"

Wade nodded. "You won't be needing it. I've got the rifles, too, in case you're thinking about them."

The outlaw shrugged, spat. "So you've got the drop on us. What comes next?"

"We're making a cattle drive," Wade said blandly. "We're getting that herd you rustled into the railhead by dark."

The four men stared, mouths hanging open. Then Todd laughed. "You've cut yourself one hell of a chore, bucko, if you think you can make us do that. Four to one . . . ? You can't watch us all and drive cattle."

"You'll do the driving," Luke said coolly. "I'll be watching . . . right down the barrel of a rifle all the way. First one of you to make a wrong move gets blasted out of the saddle."

"Maybe you could try. . . ."

"No maybe about it. I can do it . . . ask Red."

Todd said no more, lapsing into a sullen silence. Chino glanced toward the stove. "How about somethin' to eat?" he said, a slyness in his voice. "Long ride. . . ."

"You'll eat when we get there . . . in Spilman's jail," Luke said. "Now, head out that door, single file. Your horses are at the corral."

He stepped to one side, intending to move nearer the exit. His foot caught against the leg of the chair in which he had been sitting. He went momentarily off balance, came up hard against the wall with his injured shoulder. A paroxysm of pain flashed across his face.

"He's hurt bad!" Chino yelled. "Knew damn' well we'd got

him back there in the rocks!"

The rustlers halted, wheeled slowly. Wade, lips tight, rode out the hushed moments while the breathless pain gradually subsided. He wagged the pistol in his good hand menacingly.

"Keep going," he ordered. "Nothing wrong with. . . ."

"Jump him!" Chino shouted, and lunged. A knife glittered in his fingers.

Luke took a half step back and fired from the hip. At such close quarters it was impossible to miss. The impact of the heavy bullet smashing into Chino drove the outlaw back. He *thudded* against the wall, eyes wide, mouth agape, and sank slowly to the floor.

Wade, watching the others through coils of acrid smoke, again moved his weapon. "Anybody else?"

There was no reply from the remaining outlaws.

Luke said: "Get this straight. I've got nothing to lose . . . and I'd as soon kill you as take a breath after what you did to my friends back there on the flats. Now, take my advice and do what you're told. Understand?"

Red nodded sullenly. "Reckon so."

"I'm interested in one thing . . . getting that stock to the rail-head. Help me do that and you'll get there alive. Buck me and you'll end up being buzzard bait. That's the choice you've got." He hesitated, allowing his words to sink in. Then: "We ready to pull out?"

For answer the three men wheeled and walked silently out into the yard.

XV

"Hold it!"

Luke Wade barked the command as the outlaws drew up behind their horses. It was ticklish business keeping them under close watch; at any moment they might decide to turn on him.

It would be worse once the drive was under way.

"Stand pat . . . and look straight ahead!"

He wanted to be in the saddle before they mounted. Holding to both guns, and favoring his throbbing shoulder, he hauled himself onto the sorrel. Thrusting one of the pistols into his belt and holstering the other, he unslung the rifle, cocked the hammer, and laid it across his lap.

"All right," he said. "Climb aboard. Red . . . you drop the corral bars and let the stock out . . . then head them up. We're taking the shortest trail to the railhead . . . around the end of the mountain."

The last was a shot in the dark. He wasn't certain such route even existed, but logically it would seem so. He watched the outlaws' expressions for a reaction that would telegraph to him that he had erred. There was none. He breathed easier. He had guessed right.

In the gray light the rustlers swung to their saddles. Red cast a side glance at Luke, his face grim with hate, and walked his horse toward the sliding bars that closed the corral.

"You . . . Willie!" Wade snapped. "Ride left swing. That puts you on the right, Todd."

Todd's eyes squeezed down to slots. "Where'll you be? Trottin' along behind?"

The outlaw was thinking of the dust that ordinarily swept along in the wake of a moving herd—thick dust that could choke a man, blind him, and hide all else from him.

"I aim to be 'most everywhere," Luke said coolly. "Back of you . . . back of Willie . . . and looking at the back of Red's neck. Won't be one second when this rifle's not lined up on your shoulder blades." He paused, watching the redhead push aside the poles that made up the corral's gate. "I got one more bit of good advice for you . . . all of you. It won't be healthy to turn around, trying to see me. You've driven cattle before, so you know what your job is. Do it . . . and you'll stay alive."

The herd was beginning to stream out into the open. Red swung back onto his horse and rode forward slowly, angling toward the upper end of the hills. The lead cattle began to mill uncertainly. Wade motioned impatiently at Willie and Todd with the muzzle of his rifle.

"Get in there, damn it, and start them moving!" he snarled.

The two men wheeled in to take their assigned positions. Shouting, flaying with their ropes, they got the herd under way.

As before, there was not too much dust. The earth was covered with grass and the small number of cattle made for a minimum of disturbance. Falling in behind the swaying, bawling, heaving mass, Luke studied the thin yellow drift. It was shifting right to left. The slight breeze was out of the south. Accordingly he angled the sorrel for that side.

Willie flung a blank look at him as he swung in close. Wade scowled and shifted the carbine. The outlaw's lips moved as he apparently swore deeply. He faced about and fell to his task.

Up ahead Luke could see Red a few yards in front of the lead steer. He was glancing neither to right nor left. Red was the one he could have the most trouble with, Wade knew. Heading up the herd, he was in the best position to make a run for freedom, since he would be at all times the farthest away.

But Luke was gambling on the redhead's reluctance to tempt death. He had backed down in Red Hill—and again at the ranch house. It wasn't likely he would take any chances on stopping a bullet now.

He turned his head and gazed to his left across the humping backs of the steers. Todd, slumped on his saddle, rode near the tail of the herd. He, too, was holding his eyes straight on, doing nothing more than to keep pace with the cattle.

Luke slowed the sorrel, faded back into the trailing dust, and spurred quickly to the opposite side. He veered in behind Todd unnoticed, and pulled up until the sorrel's bobbing head was alongside the rump of the outlaw's buckskin.

"Get the lead out of your tail end!" Luke shouted harshly. "I aim to reach the Forks by dark!"

Taken unexpectedly, Todd jumped visibly. His head swiveled about and his jaws worked furiously, but whatever he said was lost to the racket of the herd. He lifted his rope and began to fly about angrily. Several steers broke into a shambling run, and shortly the entire bunch was moving at a faster pace.

Wade re-crossed the trail, and loped in behind Willie. He saw Red twist about, glance back, spot him—and quickly resume his position. Luke sighed softly. So far, so good. He had the outlaws thoroughly buffaloed—but for how long was problematical. Later, as the day wore on, they would begin to realize they were losers regardless of what they did. As rustlers, and once in the hands of the law, they stood no chance. Under the threat of his rifle, they also could not win if they attempted an escape. It would be a hard choice.

The sun broke over the eastern horizon in a vast yellow spray of long fingers, and the coolness began to fade. By mid-morning the heat was upon them full blast, and the continual riding, the lacing back and forth, and the tension all combined to heighten the ragged pain in Luke Wade's shoulder.

He kept it hidden from the rustlers, who continued to do their jobs under his hard, relentless stare and the deadly promise of the always cocked and ready rifle. By noon they had dropped off the broad, grassy mesa and were on a second, seemingly limitless flat, but one almost barren of growth. The dust increased and maintaining a watch over the outlaws became more difficult.

Near the middle of the afternoon, sweat-soaked and dust-caked, his eyes smarting fiercely, his shoulder paining with a dull, maddening intensity, Luke Wade began to sense the possibility of failure. He doubted if he could maintain the constant vigilance over the outlaws for much longer. He was approaching both physical and mental exhaustion—yet he knew he could not quit, that he must get the cattle to Anson's Fork.

The reason for that had somehow become clouded in his flagging mind, and he was too worn to puzzle it out. And oddly the primary purpose for his being in that part of the country had also gotten mislaid somewhere during the past few violent and tension-filled days. The man with the saber-scarred chest had retreated into some remote corner of his memory and had become of minor importance.

Everything centered now on the herd and its critical value to the ranchers of Mangus Valley. Of equal consideration was the need to avenge the ruthless murders of young Joe Dee Kline, of big, smiling Helm Stokes, and the quiet-faced cowpuncher, Leggett. Avenge their deaths by process of law—he had no desire to assume the chore of dispensing justice personally unless forced, that was up to Spilman and other authorities. He would bring the rustlers in, even aid in hunting down the remainder of the gang, but no more than that.

And here again Luke Wade was at variance with the life he had led since Ben Wade had been murdered. Vengeance had been his only goal, and the search for it had been his daily bread. The killings of Joe Dee and the other men were different, however; it was a matter for the law. Had his mind been clear enough to reason, Luke might have wondered at that fine line of differentiation he had drawn, and perhaps questioned himself.

It was late in the day when, barely able to stay upright in the saddle, he saw smoke on the horizon ahead. His hopes immediately soared, and with them also rose his strength. Only a little farther and he would have it made. Three, four miles—possibly less. Then the hard, murderous trip would be over, the cattle would be safe in the pens at the railhead—and the rustlers would be locked in Amos Spilman's jail.

He shifted his attention to Todd, a dozen paces to his right. He must be doubly watchful now. If the outlaws intended to make a break, it would come soon. They had little time left.

Todd felt Wade's eyes upon him, and half turned. His dust-grayed face was drawn into a hard sneer. "There's your town, bucko. I'll give odds you'll never make it."

Luke's expression did not change. "I'll make it. Could be you won't."

The outlaw's lips parted in a toothy grin and he looked away. Luke held his position for several more minutes, then dropped back, circled through the trailing yellow pall, and rode in behind Willie. The rustler was hunched forward over his saddle, chin pointed straight ahead. He appeared to be watching Red, now slightly out in front of the herd—a little more than usual, Luke thought. Suspicion lifted swiftly within him. He spurred up to Willie's side. The outlaw swiveled about to face him.

"Whatever you're thinking . . . forget it!" Luke warned. "I'm close enough to that town now to get along without you . . . all of you!"

"Who's thinkin'?" Willie demanded with a transparent show of innocence.

"You are!" Luke shot back angrily. "Try something and I'll put a slug through you!"

Wade came about sharply as sudden confusion on the opposite side of the herd caught the tail of his eye. He spun, and pulled away from the cattle for a better look. Through the thin edge of the pall he saw Todd, low over the saddle, cutting away, starting to make a try for the distant hills to the rear.

Luke snapped the carbine to his shoulder. He took hurried aim and pressed off a shot. The bullet dug sand immediately in front of the outlaw's horse. The buckskin shied, and reared. Luke fired again, this time purposely placing his shot as near to the outlaw's head as possible.

At the first *crack* of the rifle the herd began to run. Wade glanced at Willie, saw he had no problem there, and swung his eyes to Red. The rustler was standing in his stirrups, his gaze on Todd as his horse broke into a lope to keep ahead of the cattle.

Luke drew close aim on the redhead. He sent a bullet *whirring* over his shoulder. It was so close the outlaw flinched. Instantly he dropped back onto his saddle and resumed the chore of leading the onrushing steers.

Waiting to see no more from that position, Luke raced through the dust to where he could watch Todd. The rustler had managed to bring his frightened horse under control finally. His face was working with rage and a steady flow of curses poured from his crusted, cracked lips.

"God damn you!" he yelled as Wade rushed in. "You ain't takin' me to no lynchin'! Not me . . . you'll sure as hell have to shoot me first!"

"That's just what I figure to do!" Luke snarled, and brought up the rifle again. He took dead center aim at the outlaw.

Todd's face froze. His eyes spread, filled with fear. Abruptly he lifted his arms. "Now . . . hold on a bit," he stammered. "Wait . . . you can't. . . ."

The carbine in Luke's hands did not waver. "You're the one asking for it," he said coldly. "I'll tell you same as I told Willie . . . I don't need any of you now. I can take this herd the rest of the way by myself. And nobody'd fault me if I brought in a dead rustler."

Todd settled deeper onto his saddle. He shook his head slowly. "All right, Wade. I reckon you're holdin' all the aces."

Tension began to sweep from Luke Wade's taut frame as he lowered the rifle. He had expected them to make a break for freedom and had been alert for it. It had come—and now it was over with. He had weathered the emergency.

He raised his eyes wearily to the east—toward Anson's Fork. It couldn't be far now, and the cattle, frightened by the gunshots, were moving at a good trot. It wouldn't take long. . . .

Luke's thoughts halted. A frown crossed his face. Three riders were approaching, slanting in from the southeast.

Tension again rose within him. These could be the rest of the rustling gang, the ones Todd and the others had spoken of. He thumbed back the hammer of the carbine, and waited.

And then, as the riders drew nearer, fading sunlight glinted upon a bit of metal worn on the vest of one. Luke squinted through the dry haze, and relief hit him with sudden, joyous force. It was Amos Spilman. With him were Bishop, the cattle buyer, and another man he did not know.

XVI

As the gate to the maze of cattle pens at Anson's Fork swung shut, Luke Wade leaned forward and wearily laid his forearm across the horn of his saddle. That was it; the herd had been delivered. He watched as Bishop and the two men he had hastily hired on to handle the cattle made a final check of the hasps.

Satisfied that all was secure, the cattle buyer passed some silver to his assistants, and then walked briskly to where Luke waited. Town Marshal Spilman and his deputy had already gone, taking their prisoners off to jail where they would remain until the arrival of the circuit judge.

When Bishop drew near, Luke straightened. There had been no opportunity to talk earlier; now he voiced the question that had been in his mind.

"How did it happen you and the marshal and his deputy came out to meet me?"

"We didn't," Bishop replied, leaning against the graying, unpainted cross boards of a loading chute. "I mean intentionally. Gilligan . . . the deputy . . . had a matched team he wanted to sell. I was interested, went out to see it. Spilman was along for the ride. Coming back, we heard gunshots. Headed over that way to see what it was all about. Saw it was you. . . ."

"Lucky for me," Wade murmured. "I was about done in. . . . How many you tally?"

"Two hundred and eighteen. Glad now I waited for that herd. All prime stuff. I'll go top . . . eighteen dollars a head. Think that'll make your rancher friends happy?"

Luke nodded. "I know it will. Can we settle up now?"

Bishop smiled. "Sure, if you say so. But you're not figuring on riding back tonight, are you?"

Wade said: "Why not? No reason to hang around here. I thought I'd eat, lay around until midnight, then head out."

Bishop frowned. "Man, you're ready to fall off that horse now! And from the look on your face I'd say that shoulder of yours is giving you holy hell. Spend the night here . . . as my guest. Get some sleep. A few more hours aren't going to make any difference to those ranchers."

"It's not them I'm thinking about," Luke said quietly. "I want to get this chore done with. Got some business of my own to look after."

Now that the cattle were safe, the need to find the man, the killer with the saber scar on his body, had again pushed to the fore.

Bishop stared at Luke's set face for several moments. "I see," he said. "Well, it's up to you. I'll meet you in the hotel lobby in an hour."

"Good enough," Luke replied, and turned away.

He left the sorrel at the livery barn and gave instructions to rub him down good, then feed and water him, paying for the job in advance. He told the hostler he'd return around midnight.

He went then to the water trough in the yard behind the barn, stripped to the waist, and washed himself thoroughly, being careful not to soak the bandage around his chest. He felt better after the cold dousing and wished it had been darker; he could then have disrobed completely and taken a bath all over. But it could wait until he reached Red Hill.

He walked the short distance to the café after that and spent almost the last of his available cash for a good meal.

When that was over, he returned to the street, and leaned back against a porch roof support to kill time until he would meet with Bishop.

Evening's coolness was setting in, and lamps in stores and nearby homes were beginning to glow. A few persons were out, strolling along the plank walks enjoying the break in the day's slashing heat. Music was issuing from several of the town's saloons, and down at the end of the street a church bell tolled the faithful to prayer services.

"Glad to see you're still kicking!"

At the sound of a familiar voice Luke wheeled. It was Dr. David. He grinned. "Thanks . . . but there's been times when I felt better."

"I expect so. Medically, you've got no business even being alive. Man with a hole like you've got through you ought to be in a pine box. It giving you trouble?"

"I know it's there, for damn' sure," Luke said ruefully. "But I made out."

"You would. Let's step over to my office so's I can get a look at it. Bandage probably needs changing."

Wade shook his head. "Hell, Doc, I'm broke. Just spent my last. . . ."

"No charge," David said. "Just ordinary professional interest. Goes with the original fee."

Luke grinned. "If that's the way it is, all right." It wouldn't hurt to have the wound cared for. A long ride lay ahead of him and treatment could make it less painful.

He moved off the porch that fronted the café and fell in beside the physician. In silence they walked down the street, heading for the doctor's combination office and residence at the far end. They reached the gate and started to turn in.

Wade halted suddenly. A rider materialized from the shadows beyond the corner of the house. Metal glinted in his hand.

"Look out!" Luke yelled, and, shouldering the physician roughly into the shrubbery, he threw himself to the ground.

A gun *crashed* twice in quick succession, its explosion flaming bright orange in the darkness. Wood splintered just beyond Wade. He rolled fast, ignoring the pain that seared through his shoulder, drew his gun, and bounded to his feet—too late. The rider was already hammering off into the night, offering no target.

Luke stood in angry silence, looking into the darkness into which the ambusher had disappeared. Back in the direction of town he could hear men running, coming on the double to see what all the shooting was about.

David's voice came to him from the blackness of the yard. "You hit?"

"No," Luke said, turning to the physician. "How about you?"

"Got myself a couple of scratches, that's all. Obliged to you for shoving me out of the way. Never was much hand at doctoring myself. See who it was?"

Wade shrugged, and winced at the movement. "Didn't get a good look. Happened too fast . . . and it was too dark."

"Well, he was no friend of yours, that's for certain. Likely one of the rustlers you didn't get."

"Must've been. I know they were waiting for one man . . . called him Jim, I think. There could be more."

Marshal Spilman, accompanied by a dozen or more townsmen, pounded up, panting for breath. The lawman's face was red.

"What's going on up here?"

"Somebody took a couple of shots at Wade," David said. "Got away before we could see who he was." The physician paused. "You right sure those three outlaws are still locked up?"

"It wasn't one of them, if that's what you're hintin' at," the lawman said, his voice rising. "I was sitting there talking to them when I heard the gunshots. He do any damage?"

"Only to my fence," David said. He glanced at Luke. "Let's go."

Wade, deep in thought, turned to follow the physician into his office. The man on the horse had to have some connection with the rustlers; it was only logical to believe he was the missing member, the one they had been waiting for. But somehow it didn't make sense. Outlaws ordinarily weren't that faithful to their comrades in crime. They might attempt a rescue, particularly if it could be done before the jailing was complete, but to risk gunning down a man who had been no more than an instrument in their capture hardly seemed plausible. It just didn't jibe.

One thing was now certain: he'd have to leave that night as he'd originally planned. The would-be assassin could return and hang around for a second try. The sooner he got out of Anson's Fork, the better.

David found the wound to his satisfaction. He applied more ointment and a fresh bandage, and stepped back.

"Now, all you need is some rest. Take the same room you had before. Bed's ready."

Luke pulled on his shirt, smiling faintly. "Sorry, Doc, but I've got to pull out tonight."

David smacked his hands together. "Damn it, Luke! I'd like to go around bragging about how I saved you from dying, but if you keep pushing your luck. . . ."

"If I hang around here, I'm a sitting duck for whoever that is that's pot-shooting at me. I don't feel like making it easy for him."

"Of course," the doctor said soberly. "Better keep your eyes peeled when you leave here. Probably be smart to go out the back."

"I'll do that," Wade said. "So long . . . and much obliged to you."

"So long," the physician said, following him onto the porch. "Take care of that shoulder."

Luke made his way down the dark alley behind the buildings until he was opposite the hotel. Then, turning into a trash-littered passageway between a saloon and a harness shop, he crossed the street and entered the hotel. From a deep leather chair in a far corner, Bishop rose to meet him. He came forward, arm outstretched.

"Glad to see you're all right!" he boomed. "Heard about the close call you had."

"Little dark out there for good shooting," Wade commented dryly. "You set to do business?"

Bishop reached into his pocket for a leather fold. He opened it and extended a draft. "All made out. Three thousand nine hundred and twenty-four dollars. You can turn it over to your friends and they can cash it anywhere. All I need now are the papers on the herd . . . the bills of sale."

Bills of sale!

Wade felt his spirits sink. He hadn't given the necessary papers a moment's thought. Stokes had been carrying them— likely they were still on his body. The rustlers wouldn't have troubled to take them; they would have planned to blot brands and make papers of their own.

"You've got bills of sale, haven't you?" Bishop asked, frowning.

Luke said: "Matter of fact, no. One of my partners was carrying them when he got killed. I'll have to get new ones made up."

The cattle buyer's face fell. He folded the draft and put it back in the leather fold. "Guess we'll have to put off settling up until you can get them," he said. "Matter of good business, you understand. I trust you . . . but my company. . . ."

"I understand," Wade broke in, angry and impatient. More delay now faced him. It meant riding all the way to Mangus Valley, collecting new papers from the ranchers who had furnished stock for the drive—then returning to the railhead. And after that would come the long trip again to the valley.

"Any chance you riding back with me?" he suggested hopefully. "Save us both a lot of time."

Bishop laughed. "Not much. I'm no saddle man. Couple of hours on a horse and I've had enough to keep me walking for a week. . . . Besides, I'm overdue in El Paso now."

"That mean you can't wait for me to get new papers?"

Bishop scratched at his ear. "Like I said, I'm way behind now . . . but I guess a few more days won't make much difference. Tell you what I'll do. I'll give you a receipt for the herd, and put the draft in the bank, then I'll stall around a few more days. Anything comes up and I have to leave, just present the papers to the banker and he'll hand over the draft. That agreeable?"

"Agreeable," Luke said. "Now, if you'll just write out that receipt, I'll get on my way."

Bishop produced the leather fold once more, removed a blank sheet of paper, and began to write.

"Too bad you can't take all that money back in hard cash to your rancher friends," he said. "Expect it would sure look good to them."

No thanks, Luke thought. The unknown rider in the dark could be planning a second ambush. This time it might not fail—and he wasn't about to make a rich man of him, whoever he was.

XVII

The receipt for the cattle tucked into his pocket, Wade departed Anson's Fork a short time later. He had slipped out the rear entrance of The Westerner Hotel, hurried along a shadow-filled alley, and gained the livery barn unnoticed. Leaving the stable by the back, he led the sorrel through the back to the edge of the settlement and only then mounted. When he was finally on the main road west, he felt certain he had not been seen.

The weight of the long, sleepless hours bore heavily upon him now, and, as the big red horse loped easily on through the silvered night, he dozed intermittently. His shoulder pained little, thanks to Dr. David, and during the periods of wakefulness he planned ahead.

Soon the responsibility of the cattle would no longer be his. He had only to hand the receipt over to Travis McMahon and he was finished with it; McMahon or one of the other ranchers could make the trip to Anson's Fork and claim the money. When that was done, he could resume his grim quest.

It wasn't precisely clear in his mind as to just how he would go about finding his father's killer. That it was one of the Mangus Valley ranchers he was still certain, but still he just couldn't walk up to a man, rip open his shirt, and look for a scar. Find work on the various ranches, that was the answer. Volunteer to help out for a few days, at no wages if need be. Ranchers too poor to hire hands were always happy to furnish meals and a bed in exchange for labor. And being acquainted with most of them should make it simple.

The opportunity of looking for the saber slash would present itself; perhaps it would come while working in the open and a man peeled off his shirt to escape the heat. Or it could be at wash-up time—or possibly during a suggested swim in the creek. He'd get his chance; it would turn up. The important thing was to get started at it. He'd lost considerable time already.

The miles rocked by steadily. The sorrel, refreshed by rest and care, enjoyed the coolness and easy run. Several times he tried to increase his pace to a gallop, but Luke held him down; a long hot day faced them once the sun broke over the horizon.

He halted at dawn to ease his own stiff muscles and breathe the sorrel. While waiting, he ate the last of his food, now dried to hard tack and leather, and wet it down with water.

Thirty minutes later, as he stepped back into the saddle, he threw his glance to his back trail. He was considerably south of the trail he had crossed previously with the herd, and the land was somewhat rougher and broken with low buttes and brushy arroyos.

He sat motionlessly on the sorrel, squinting into the rising sun while a frown pulled at his brow. Far back he could see a dark shape just below the horizon—and the thought crossed his mind that he was being followed, that he had not escaped Anson's Fork unnoticed after all. But the blurred object did not move, and Luke, finally deciding that it was a scrub cedar or piñon, rode on.

He was drawing near to the Penasco River. On the yonder side he would start watching for the bodies of Leggett and Helm Stokes. Buzzards would likely tip him off to where they lay, he realized grimly. The word of their deaths, and that of young Joe Dee Kline, would take the edge off the good news he brought concerning the sale of the herd. Three men dead—the drive had been costly, even though successful.

He paused long enough at the Penasco to water the sorrel and refill his canteen, and then pushed on, his glance now alternately sweeping the broad land before him and the bright sky above. Even though the vultures and coyotes had probably gotten to them, there would be remains.

Three riders broke suddenly into view.

They appeared abruptly on the crest of a low rise far ahead, and striking east. Wary, Luke continued, his eyes fixed on the horsemen. They could be the rest of the rustlers. He grinned. He guessed he was getting overly suspicious. He had thought the same when Spilman, Bishop, and the deputy had met him with the herd. Likely they were ranchers going to the Fork on business.

The trail at that point had curved farther south, and now followed along the edge of a sandy wash well studded with mesquite, rabbit brush, creosote bush, and other rank growth. He considered dropping down into the arroyo and keeping himself concealed until he had passed or was at least certain of the men. But he didn't like the idea. It made him feel as though he were hiding, running, and that rubbed against the grain. It was bad enough that he had had to sneak out of the settlement. So he rode on, the three men coming into sharper focus as they drew nearer. Luke's gaze settled on the rider to his left. He frowned. There was something familiar to him, something about the way he sat his saddle. He narrowed his eyes to cut down the glare. The man in the center—he appeared familiar, too.

McMahon!

Surprise swept through Wade. It was McMahon on the left. Something had happened—they had gotten word of trouble and were riding to the railhead. Relief gripped Luke. It was a bit of luck he had not counted on. And then he straightened in the saddle.

"Stokes!"

The name exploded from his lips as he recognized the rider in the center of the group. The big rancher had somehow escaped the rustlers. Pleased and further relieved, he lifted his hand in salutation, and signaled them, now eyeing the third man more closely. He wasn't sure but he thought he was Joe Dee's father, Otis.

He touched the sorrel with his spurs and broke him into a gallop. Immediately McMahon and the others halted. He wondered if Kline knew that his son was dead, and decided he probably did not. Stokes, making an escape, likely had been too occupied to see the boy go down. Or he could have; that would account for Otis's being in the party. He could have come along to search for his son's body.

Luke waved again, lifting his hand to indicate his recognition. McMahon replied with a half-hearted gesture. Luke shrugged. His welcome was anything but cordial—and then it came to him that the men were on a sad journey. The deaths of Joe Dee and Leggett had affected them deeply.

He reached the bottom of the rise upon which the ranchers waited, and sent the sorrel trotting up the gentle grade. Gaining the top, he slanted toward them. Smiling, he bobbed his head in greeting.

"Mighty happy to see you . . . ," he began, and stopped short. Helm Stokes, his face a curious mixture of shock and surprise, was looking at him over the barrel of a cocked revolver.

"What . . . ?"

"Climb down off that horse, you thieving bastard!" the big rancher snarled. "We've got you dead to rights!"

XVIII

Startled, Luke Wade stared at Stokes. His eyes shifted to McMahon and Otis Kline. Their faces were set, impassive. Anger lifted suddenly within him.

"What the hell's this all about?" he demanded in a rough voice.

Kline swore deeply. "He's got the guts to set there and say that! I ain't a man given to violence nowadays, but right now I could blast him off that saddle . . . and never take a deep breath doing it."

"Let Stokes handle it, Otis," McMahon murmured. "He knows what he's doing."

Luke's anger continued to rise. "I'll say it again . . . what's the trouble? You've got no call jumping me this way, not after I've worked my guts out trying to. . . ."

"You getting off that horse, or do I shoot you off?" Helm Stokes cut in coldly. "Makes no difference to me."

Wade raised himself in his stirrups and swung from the sorrel with great deliberation. His mind was churning, seething, struggling to understand what had happened, just what it was that had brought about the change of attitude on the part of the ranchers. A few days ago he had been a friend; now he was a mortal enemy fit only for death.

"Keep your hands up!" Stokes warned. "And walk over here where we can watch you."

Luke crossed in front of his sorrel, arms uplifted. McMahon dismounted. Kline followed suit. Last of all Stokes came to ground. Ignoring him, Wade placed his attention on McMahon; he might be his chief suspect insofar as the murder of Ben Wade was concerned, but he was also the man he knew best.

"I still want to know what this means. I've done nothing to make you throw a gun on me. . . ."

"He's done nothing." Stokes echoed mockingly. "He had his bunch all lined up to rustle our herd. He shot down Joe Dee, left him laying out there on the flats for the buzzards, and now he's got the nerve to say he's done nothing!"

Struck dumb momentarily by the outrageous accusations, Wade simply glared at the rancher. And then his fury boiled over.

"That's a lie . . . and any man who believes it is a plain fool! Sure, rustlers jumped us. They left me for dead in the Sacramentos, and drove off the stock. I got to my horse later and managed to reach the railhead. Found Joe Dee's body on the way. Figured they'd got you and Leggett, too, so I kept watching. . . ." Luke paused, his eyes bright with anger. "How'd you get away?"

"They drove him off," McMahon said. "Sort of like last year. Ain't heard from Leggett. You say you've been to Anson's Fork?"

Wade nodded, again centering his attention on McMahon. The big rancher seemed interested in getting the straight of the matter.

"I was in pretty tough shape when I hit town. Somebody hauled me off to the doc's and he fixed me up and kept me in bed for a couple of nights and a day. But quick as I was able, I headed back this way. Figured the herd had to be around here somewhere."

As he spoke Wade's temper began to cool. McMahon and the others had things all wrong somehow. It was up to him to clear it up.

"Finally located the stock at a ranch on the upper end of the Penasco. Four men were looking after them. Had a bit of trouble with one, but I made the others drive the herd on in to Anson's Fork. Buyer by the name of Bishop was waiting. He took the lot."

McMahon's jaw sagged. "You got the cattle to the railhead . . . and sold them?"

"Just the way we figured. . . ."

"You're a fool to listen to that!" Stokes said harshly. "Nothing but hogwash. He's stringing you . . . trying to save his own neck." The rancher paused and looked up, his eyes reaching to the flat beyond Luke. The faint, rhythmic beat of an oncoming horse hung in the calm, heat-charged air.

"You mentioned my boy," Kline said gently. "His body . . . where's it now?"

"Waiting for you at Anson's Fork," Luke replied. "Marshal took charge. I'm sorry, Mister Kline. Wasn't anything I could do for him. He was already dead."

Kline bowed his head. "However this turns out, I'm obliged to you for not leaving him lying out there."

"I didn't shoot him. It was one of the rustlers. Could have been the one I had trouble with at that ranch. Or it could have been one of the others. There's three of them in jail now at the railhead."

The approaching hoof beats grew louder. McMahon, shading his eyes with his hand and squinting, said: "Say, that looks like your man Leggett, Stokes."

Surprise again rushed through Luke. Both Stokes and Leggett alive! Only he and Joe Dee had dropped under the rustler's guns.

Stokes said: "It sure is him! Now, maybe we can get the straight of this. Expect what he'll tell us will prove Wade's a damned liar."

"It's no lie," Luke said softly. A calmness had settled over him as a vague suspicion began to grow. "I can back up everything I've told you."

"Oh, sure," Stokes said in an offhand, crooked-grin way. "Your kind always has ways of proving things. People that'll swear they saw you. . . ."

"I've got the receipt for the herd," Wade cut in unhurriedly in a quiet voice.

Stokes's face hardened. His words died in his throat as his brow pulled into deep corrugations.

A smile began to spread across Travis McMahon's lips. "A receipt, you say!"

"Right. There's a draft waiting for you at the bank. I couldn't get it because I didn't have the papers on the herd."

There was a long moment of silence, and then McMahon

boomed: "By God, can't be no better proof than that! Stokes, you're all wrong somewhere. Let me see that receipt, Luke."

Shifting his glance to Stokes, still covering him with his pistol, Wade dug into his right-hand pocket and procured the fold of paper given him by Bishop. He extended it toward McMahon.

"That cattle buyer's in a hurry to move on. You ought to. . . ."

"I'll take that!" Stokes snapped, and grabbed the receipt from Luke's fingers. He whirled about, and abruptly stood facing all three men. "You won't be needing it."

McMahon's beefy face flushed. "Now, what the hell does this . . . ?"

"Just stand tight," Stokes said. "And keep your hands in front of you. Leggett'll be here in a couple more minutes and we'll wind up this little shindig."

Understanding came then to Luke Wade. Stokes and Leggett were both in on the rustling. Jim Leggett—Jim—that was the name Todd and the other outlaws had mentioned, the man they were waiting for. Stokes was probably the leader of the bunch. He swore, angered by his own blindness. Why hadn't he been able to see it?

Otis Kline found his voice. "You mean you're the one who's been stealing our stock?" he asked in an unbelieving tone. "It . . . it was you last year?"

Stokes smiled. "You guessed it, Otey. It was me. Had myself a pretty good thing going. . . . Still would have," he added, flicking a glance at Luke, "if my boys had done the job on him they were supposed to."

"But Joe Dee . . . a boy. Why did you . . . ?"

"Real sorry about that. Tried to scare the kid off, but he wouldn't run. I couldn't have him carrying tales, so one of the boys had to take care of him."

A deep sob broke from Kline's throat. McMahon, his words cold and squarely spaced, said: "You're the worst kind of a son-of-a-bitch, Stokes! Making out like you were a friend, letting us trust you while all the time you were robbing and killing. . . ."

"Forget it, Travis!" the rustler snarled. "No need to get all riled up. You won't have to stew over it much longer."

"Meaning what?"

"One thing, of course," Stokes said. Behind him Leggett had pulled out of the arroyo and halted. "Come on up here, Jim!" he called, not turning his head.

Leggett, leading his horse, moved in.

McMahon asked again: "Meaning what?"

"Now, I can't just leave you three running loose, can I? I'd be a damned fool to do that."

Kline's voice showed no fear, only surprise. "You aim to kill us?"

"Got to, Otey. Hate it, but I got no choice."

Luke listened in silence. He was calculating the odds, trying to find an opening somehow. But Leggett's arrival had complicated and narrowed the chances.

"How you going to explain this to the people waiting back in the valley?" McMahon said. "Us just dropping out of sight's going to be hard to cover up."

"Don't figure to," Stokes said. "Nothing left around here for me now, not the way it worked out this year. I'll just ride on in to Anson's Fork, hand over this receipt and the papers I'm carrying, and collect the money. Then I'll move on."

"We'll move on," Jim Leggett corrected quietly, coming up behind Stokes and halting by the tall man's shoulder. "Things sure have blowed up."

"They have, thanks to you," Stokes replied angrily. "We could have strung it out for a couple or three more years if you hadn't bungled the job. How's it happen you didn't take care of this saddle bum?"

"We did!" Leggett said protestingly. "Hit him twice while he was up there in the rocks. Then next thing I knew, there he was in the Fork. Tried again when I got the chance, but it was too dark and I missed. I hung around, looking for him, but he snuck out of town. Followed fast as I could. . . ."

"Well, no matter now. I've got what we need to claim the money. Next thing's to get rid of these three. Over there in that arroyo ought to be a good spot. Then we'll pick up the cash and head north."

Travis McMahon shook his head. "You'll never get away with it, Stokes. It's cold-blooded murder you're talking . . . and a lot of people know we rode out together."

"And we're all disappearing together," Stokes said with a broad smile. "You think of that? Something happened to all of us, that's what people'll think. I've got everything figured down to a hair, Travis. That's one reason why I've got by all these years. I figure ahead."

He turned to Luke. "And you, cowboy . . . I don't know where you got that gun, but I want it. It's mine."

XIX

Cold rage soared through Luke Wade. He forced himself to remain calm.

"Your gun? What makes you think so?"

"Spotted it first time I laid eyes on you. Got lost a couple years ago up Wyoming way. Had me some trouble with a crusty old codger who tried slicin' me in two with a saber, and I dropped it somehow. . . ."

"You're . . . him!" Luke yelled, and, heedless of all else, he lunged at the killer who for so long had been but a dim shadow before him.

The outlaw's gun roared in his ears. He felt the hot slash of the bullet as it seared across his rib cage. But he knew no pain—only a surging exultation as his clawing fingers encircled

Stokes's neck. Guns blasted—twice. There was no sickening impact. Vaguely he realized it wasn't Stokes's weapon that had fired.

"I been hunting you . . . years!" Luke heard his own voice shouting. "That was my pa you murdered . . . an old man . . . crippled up . . . couldn't protect himself. I swore on his grave I'd track you down and make you pay!"

His flaming mind became aware that Stokes had collapsed beneath him; that he was kneeling on the outlaw's chest choking him; that his shoulder was screaming with pain.

He became aware, too, of hands dragging at him, pulling him off. Travis McMahon's voice dinned into his consciousness.

"Luke! Luke! Let him go! Save him for the hangman!"

Gasping for breath, Wade staggered back. Pain was writhing through him like a thing alive. He sagged against the sorrel. The yellow haze that filled his eyes began to fade and he looked about. Leggett lay on the sandy earth, glazed eyes staring into the hot sky. A broad, red stain covered his breast.

Those were the gunshots he had heard. McMahon, or Kline, had taken care of Leggett. He shifted his glance to Stokes, now stirring weakly. The outlaw's mouth was gaped, and he made dry, rasping sounds as he struggled for breath. Luke swayed to him, leaned over. He grasped the man's shirt front in his trembling hand and ripped it open. The long, thin mark of Ben Wade's saber ran the full length of his torso.

Hate and anger burst again through Wade. He drew back a stride. The ornate pistol—the killer's own gun at his hip—came swiftly and smoothly into his hand.

"Got to kill him," he murmured in a tight voice. "He's got to die . . . can't trust it to the law. . . ."

McMahon's words were low and soothing. "Easy now, boy. Reckon I understand now what's been bothering you. Don't say as I blame you for how you feel . . . but don't make the mistake of killing him."

"It's no mistake," Luke said woodenly.

"Your doing it would be. This vengeance hunt you've been on for so long wouldn't die with him . . . not really. It'd keep right on living, because you'd keep on thinking how you'd killed him, how you'd finally squared things for your pa . . . and it'd be the wrong kind of satisfaction. It's not the good kind, because down deep you'd know all the time you were a murderer, too . . . no better'n him. . . ."

"Listen to him, son," Otis Kline said quietly. "He's talking gospel, pure gospel. I know . . . I been through it."

"Let the law finish it for you," McMahon said. "Then you'll sleep easy the rest of your time. And the law'll do it . . . you've got my guarantee. I'll see him right up to the gallows. Expect Otey'll give you the same promise."

"You can bet on it," Kline said in a hard voice. "He owes me, too . . . for Joe Dee."

Luke Wade looked down at the weapon in his hand. It no longer was the sleek, efficient bit of beauty it had always seemed—no longer the symbol of what he had to do. Now it was a heavy, ugly machine of death—the very one that had snuffed out his father's life. Suddenly he wheeled, and hurled the weapon off into the loose sand of the arroyo.

"I reckon it's finished," he said wearily. He stepped back and pointed at Stokes. "Let's get him to the Fork and hand him over to the marshal."

McMahon's thick shoulders settled in relief. He smiled. "Figured I wasn't wrong about you. If you've got no place special you're aiming to go, how about coming back to the valley? Expect folks would be right pleased to help you get started . . . and the country can always use a good cattleman."

"You'd be welcome to move in with us," Kline added. "Got an empty room now, and . . . and I could use a son. . . ."

Luke felt a lump rise in his throat. He was silent for a long minute, then: "Obliged to you both. . . . Sure would be fine, tying down to one place again."

Real fine, he added to himself—*with Samantha close by. . . .*

★ ★ ★ ★ ★

PANHANDLE GUNMAN

★ ★ ★ ★ ★

I

He stood in the hush, staring at the shimmering heat waves that lay upon the land below the buttes. A jay scolded nearby, and high overhead lace-edged clouds sped swiftly along on the upper wind currents.

He raised his hand, brushed the sweat from his forehead. A low sigh of despondency slipped from his cracked lips. It was finished . . . done. He could forget Circle S—and all else now. There was nothing left to do but load the body of the dead lawman on his horse, move down to meet Carl Glyde and the posse, and tell his story.

They would not believe him, for he had nothing to substantiate his words. They would arrive quickly at an inevitable conclusion—that the lawman had encountered him, attempted an arrest, and had been killed for his efforts. That he had troubled to bring the body in would count for nothing. To most it would appear a desperate move toward saving his own skin, one calculated to cast a shadow of doubt on his guilt. He could, of course, ride, climb to the crest of the buttes, strike eastward, and lose himself in the endless stretches of Texas, the Indian Nations, and beyond. Someone would find the lawman, if not today—tomorrow, or the next. But he could not bring himself to consider that; it would solve nothing, merely insure the addition of another murder charge to the one now standing against him. And he was of no mind to spend the rest of his life running. Three days ago it had been different. . . .

II

The wind was dry and hot. To Mace Seevert, it was a welcome discomfort for it meant that, at last, he was home. Five years the war had sliced from his life; three he gave to combat, one sacrificed to the tedium behind the high walls of a prison, and the fifth lost to a Union Army hospital as the disastrous result of an attempt to escape. But that was in the past now; the thundering guns, the sickening slaughter, the wild, reckless charges, the shrill cries of the wounded and dying were just echoes fading from his memory. He had returned, ready now to pick up the ruptured threads of his existence, no more or no less better, perhaps, than any of those who had entered the conflict as boys and emerged as men.

Adjustment would be difficult. He was aware of that fact, but it could—it would—be made, although he must do it alone for Tom Seevert was dead. Mace, as the only son and heir, now owned the Circle S. It had been a fine, growing ranch when he rode off to join Nathan Forrest and his cavalrymen; in the idle years since his father's death it likely had changed little.

Shading his eyes, he looked ahead eagerly. It was not far now—the rim stretching before him was the extreme southern lip of Panhandle Valley. The Circle S lay within its broad expanse, although it was much farther north. It was the same fertile land, however, and, noting the dark richness of it, Mace guessed there had been a wet spring. Abruptly anxious, he put the sorrel he was riding to a lope and soon gained the summit of the rise. He halted, and a long sigh slipped through him. Below, in gently billowing waves of crested grass, his homeland unfurled before him. It extended north as far as the eye could see, and then beyond. To the west ran the dark, forbidding banks of lava beds, commonly termed the *malpais;* thirty miles to the east stood the frowning, red-faced buttes known as the Piedras Rojas, and towering behind them were the rugged

Sacramento Peaks.

Here and there clusters of green-capped cottonwood trees marked the location of springs, and twisting, sparkling lines, like arteries of silver, traced the course of numerous creeks and streams. From where he stood, Mace could see only one of the dozen or so ranches that lay in the valley, but the others were there, nevertheless, hidden by the lifts and falls of the undulating land, or lost simply to distance.

Tom Seevert had chosen well when he selected the Panhandle Valley as the place to build his home and raise a family, and he had shown wisdom in the site picked for the Circle S. He had erected its buildings below a line of bluffs that shielded them from the cold north winds of the winter months. Morning sun struck first the front of the main house, and Mace could remember many times during the war, when he was chilled and miserable, how the memory of his warm room had cheered him.

Cottonwood Creek, kept bank-full by a spring, formed a swift-flowing boundary to the west. The stream flattened out into a small lake a half mile below the cluster of buildings and there became a natural swimming hole, or in more practical terms a watering pond for stock.

The greater portion of the ranch, near 30,000 acres of deeded land and free range, lay to the south and east of that point. It was better than average pasture, well able to support several herds of ordinary size, and with the demand for beef strong in the market places—a 1,000-pound steer was bringing as much as $5—Mace felt the opportunity for becoming a successful rancher was his.

Getting the financial backing to start was the first hurdle to be faced, for like most men who had served with either the blue or the gray, he was returning home broke. But he expected little difficulty. Old Henry Tubbs, the banker in nearby Berrendo

Crossing, had always been a friend of the family. He had staked Tom Seevert in the beginning, had aided him during the lean years, and Tubbs had never lost a dollar on the Circle S. Mace was certain the banker would not refuse him—so certain, in fact, that he had already contracted to purchase several small jags of cattle from various ranchers as he made his way across Texas.

Sighing again, wishing it were reality instead of still in the offing, Mace put the sorrel into motion and headed down the long slope. A time later, reaching the bottom, he swung north. He crossed a wide flat, climbed to another crest, and again moved downward into a broad swale.

Anticipation began to build within him. In another two hours or so, he would be home. Already he was entering country he knew well, areas he had, as a boy, roamed with his best friend, Yancey Harper. Familiar landmarks began to catch his eye, specific places that held special meaning for him. To the left lay the narrow band of brush where he had hunted often for rabbits and fleet-footed blue quail. In the small grove west of that he and Yancey, together, had once slain a deer. It had been near Thanksgiving, and the two families, their ranches adjoining, had pooled their food resources on that holiday and feasted on tasty venison.

Recalling that incident brought Tom Seevert again to his mind. His father would not see the fruits of his labor; he would never look upon the ranch he had worked so hard to build, and watch it become what he always claimed it could be. His faith in the country had been boundless and during hard times he had fought on stubbornly, never losing sight of his dream. His faith would now pay off, if all went well.

Mace came to a narrow stream—Comanche Creek—and paused to let the sorrel water. The wind had faded to a whisper and the heat of the young summer morning was beginning to make itself felt. He removed his battered campaign hat, his last vestige of the war, mopped the sweat from his forehead. He grinned. It was good to be hot again, to sweat—not from the heat of battle or the barrels of overworked guns, but from the clean, burning sun reaching down from a cloudless sky unmarred by smoke.

The sorrel's thirst satisfied, Mace pressed on. He could see the hill that marked the extreme southwestern point of the Circle S now, a vague, bluish mound that lifted from the level of the valley and silhouetted, like a monstrous beehive, against the horizon. His pulse quickened. He was making better time than he had anticipated.

Still, he would go home first, as he had planned, clean up and look around a bit, and let old Chopo Rosales, the ranch foreman, and whoever else was there, know he was back. Then he would ride on to Berrendo Crossing and talk with Henry Tubbs. The machinery of banking set in motion, he could then spend a little time around town, renewing old acquaintances and finding out about Yancey and other friends. He had lost track of them all while he was away. It would be good to see them again. They would be happy and pleased to hear that he planned to restock and continue the Circle S. Chopo would be particularly happy. The old *vaquero* had been around the ranch for as long as Mace could recall, serving as Tom Seevert's *segundo*—and filling the rôle as second father to Mace. He had been more a member of the family than an employee. Rosales would continue to be ranch foreman, Mace had already decided, as he was a good hand with cattle—and having him close by would go far in filling the void left by Tom Seevert's death.

Mace rode out another lengthy swale, began to climb the yonder slope. The sorrel trotted easily, a tough little gelding that seemingly was tireless. He had bought him in Tennessee, picked him up for little money and had. . . .

The sudden, rolling report of an explosion brought Mace Seevert up short. For one fragment of time he was again in the war, with the monstrous guns booming out their fearful challenge, and then, quickly, he was back in the hot, peaceful solitude of Panhandle Valley. Shaken, he turned half about, threw his glance into the direction of the blast. A great bulge of smoke was lifting upward beyond the ridge to his left. The Cargill place lay there, he remembered—an elderly couple, friends of his father and mother. He had ridden over to see them many times, taking them some especially prepared bit of food or just carrying a message from his father. What could have caused so powerful an explosion?

Frowning, he swung the sorrel off the trail and spurred toward the rim. He gained the top, halted. The Cargill ranch was a half mile distant. Smoke boiled about the scatter of old buildings and flames were beginning to leap upward from what Mace guessed was the barn. He was too far and there was too much dust and smoke to determine anything else. One thing was certain, however—the Cargills were in trouble. He sent the gelding down the hill at a gallop, crossed the flat, and pounded to the opposite crest. Again he halted. The Cargill place was just below. He took in the confused scene with a swift glance.

The barn and several outlying, smaller buildings were a seething mass of flames. He could hear the terrified *shrilling* of livestock, the excited *clatter* of chickens and geese above the *crackling* of the fire. In the doorway of the main house the figure of a woman lay sprawled, her bright calico dress a splash of color in the swirling haze. In the center of the yard two men wrestled with the lanky figure of Henry Cargill as they sought to drag him toward the doomed barn. A third rider, still in the saddle and holding the reins of the other horses, watched from nearby.

III

Fire—explosion—death. It was the war all over again. Momentarily it gripped Mace Seevert, hurled him into a boiling cauldron of flaming memories, and then once again he swept it aside, reached for the pistol hanging at his hip. This was not Trenton or Dover; this was not war—this was trouble, trouble in Panhandle Valley where he had expected only peace.

He glanced at his weapon, saw that it was fully loaded. Then, leaning forward on the sorrel, he sent the tough little gelding thundering down the slope straight for the Cargill yard. Halfway he snapped a shot at the men. The distance was too great for a handgun but he knew he must do something to attract the raider's attention and prevent their dragging the old rancher to a fiery death. There was no doubt as to their intention.

At the sharp *slap* of the pistol shot, the trio whirled. The pair holding Cargill released their grasp. The rancher sprawled in the loose dirt. The two riders broke for their horses, vaulted into the saddles. The third man, hastily jerking a bandanna mask over the lower half of his face, spun about. He drew his revolver and leveled it.

Mace saw the quick puff of smoke, heard the drone of lead. He ducked instinctively, threw two answering shots at the trio. Cargill had recovered his footing, was now up and running in that faltering gait of the very old toward the house. Either he was going for a weapon, or he was hurrying to the side of his wife.

Seevert reached the foot of the slope, surged out onto a flat stretch of ground that had been recently plowed and planted. The sorrel at once slowed, having difficulty in the soft, broken soil. More gunshots erupted from the yard as the outlaws recognized the disadvantage. Instantly Mace cut away, drove hard for a tamarisk windbreak off to his left.

He gained that, mindful of the *whining* bullets singing all around him, and plunged into its dense cover. He spurted again into the open for a short space, fired two hurried shots at the raiders. He grinned wolfishly as he saw one flinch and reel on his saddle. Abruptly he was behind a second stand of brush.

His weapon was almost empty. Kneeing the sorrel, he began to whip in and out, offering no target while he hurriedly thumbed bullets from his cartridge belt and fed them into the cylinder of his pistol. He came to the end of the windbreak with the loading gate of his six-gun still open. A yell went up as the sorrel burst into view. A half a dozen reports cracked through the dust and smoke and once more Mace Seevert was aware of passing bullets. But he was ready now; his pistol was loaded. He turned his attention to the yard.

Cargill was down again, this time stretched out full length. He was not moving. Mace swerved to his right. One of the raiders had pulled a rifle from its boot, was trying to sight along its barrel. Mace threw a shot at him. The slug grazed the man's shoulder. He pulled back suddenly and his horse reared. Seevert tried again. The bullet struck the outlaw's saddle near the horn. There was a puff of wood splinters and leather fragments, the eerie *screech* of ricocheting lead. Once more the frantic horse began to buck and plunge.

Taking advantage of the confusion, Mace spun, doubled back, heading for the thick brush growing at the lower end of the yard. He laid another shot at the raiders. They were milling about, two of them endeavoring to aid their companion in his attempts to bring his fractious mount under control. Suddenly they wheeled and rushed for the trees a half mile up the valley.

Mace snapped a final shot at them, and then, reloading as he went, he urged the sorrel into the yard. Churning dust, smoke, and layers of heat from the burning structures hung in a dense cloud over the hard pack. A large tree standing adjacent to the barn had exploded into flames, becoming a many-fingered torch. Mace could hear no more sounds from the livestock and guessed that all had perished.

Making his way to Cargill, he dropped from the saddle. Hanging onto the reins of the nervous sorrel, he knelt over the rancher, lying face down in the dust. There was no need to turn him over. He had been shot in the back, likely died instantly.

Anger throbbing within him, Mace Seevert rose and continued to the house. He squatted beside the crumpled shape of the woman in the doorway. It was Mrs. Cargill, as he had suspected, and she, too, was dead. There were no marks on her. She had died of heart failure—of fright.

Seevert pulled himself to his full height while a towering rage hammered at him. What sort of men were these who could ruthlessly attack and murder two such defenseless people? What had happened to Panhandle Valley—always a quiet, settled world where men lived in peace, were never troubled by violence such as this? What was going on?

After a few moments the fury dwindled and a sober realization of what must be done came over him. He tied the sorrel to the hitch rack and returned to the doorway. Slipping his arms under the frail body of Mrs. Cargill, he lifted her and carried her into the skimpily furnished bedroom. When he had placed her on the soft padding, he went back for Cargill, brought him in, and placed him beside his wife. He stood for a time studying their gaunt, toil-scarred features while he again wondered about Panhandle Valley. It seemed it, too, was a battleground, one of a different sort than that to which he was accustomed—but equally deadly, nevertheless. He reached down, took up a handmade patch quilt that was draped across a nearby trunk, and covered the rancher and his wife. Turning, he strode to where the sorrel waited.

He glanced toward the barn. The fires had burned themselves down and there was no danger of their spreading to the main structure. The bodies of the Cargills would be safe. He could not go home now, as he had planned. He must first ride to Berrendo Crossing, report the murders to Town Marshal Kilgore. He could furnish only a meager description of the raiders, but one of the outlaws had been wounded, and that would slow them down considerably. If he moved quickly, Kilgore could run them down with ease.

IV

The years had wrought little change in Berrendo Crossing. This Mace Seevert noted as he turned into the settlement's single, curving street and pulled the loping sorrel down to a fast walk. Hansen still ran the saddle shop. McGillivray's name remained on the sign above the general merchandise store. The restaurants, saloons, the bank, feed store, and livery barn were not altered, appeared only to have grown more weather-beaten. H. Wallace, M.D., one of his father's first friends, still practiced medicine from the corner office of his residence.

He saw few familiar faces, however, among the thin scatter of persons moving along the sagging boardwalk. Some glanced at him curiously. It struck him as odd that he recognized none of his old friends, and that thought gave him cause for wonder.

He hurried on, pointing for the jail at the opposite end of the dusty street. He was anxious to see Kilgore, make his report of the tragic affair at the Cargills', and volunteer for the posse. He would learn, too, if this was an isolated incident, or if there were other similar occurrences. If so, he would offer to do his part in bringing such murderous activities to an end.

He reached the jail, pulled in to the hitch rack, and dismounted. For a moment he stood there, looking back down the familiar yet alien street. Wheeling abruptly, he stepped up onto the narrow landing and moved toward the door.

In the interests of coolness, it had been propped open by a

brass cuspidor. Avoiding this, Mace walked to the center of the small room and looked at the man hunched over the desk. It was not Kilgore. Kilgore's hair had been snow white years ago. This was a younger man.

" 'Morning," he said by way of announcing himself. "I'd like to talk to the marshal."

"That's me," the young man said, and looked up.

Mace Seevert rocked with surprise. "Yancey . . . Yancey Harper!" he yelled, and stepped forward impulsively, hand outstretched. "Never figured you for a lawman!"

Harper came to his feet, grasped Seevert's fingers in his own. Shock held him speechless. He was much the same, Mace noted, a bit heavier, but the same red hair and ruddy face.

Finally he recovered. "Mace . . . how . . . where did you come from? You're dead . . . or supposed to be. . . ."

"Long story," Seevert replied. "Tell you about it later. What happed to Kilgore?"

Harper settled back onto his chair, folded his arms across his chest. "Dead. I've been town marshal for the last couple of years." He hesitated, stared hard at Seevert. "Can't get it straight in my head that you're here . . . and alive. He said. . . ."

Mace lifted his dark brows. "Who said? Who's he?"

Yancey only frowned. "Hard to believe. After all this time."

"Well, it's me, and a long way from being dead. Some friends of ours, however, aren't so lucky. The Cargills."

Harper's features stiffened. "What about the Cargills?"

"Three men raided their place an hour or so ago. I rode up too late to do anything about it. Their barn had been blown up and about everything but the main house was burned down. Missus Cargill was dead from fright, I suspect. Cargill was murdered . . . shot in the back."

"You get a look at the three men?"

"Not a good one. Winged one of them, though. Saw him

flinch when my bullet hit. I figure they haven't got far. You round up a posse and we can go back and pick up their trail. They'll move slow with one of them carrying lead. What's going on around here, anyway? I thought I'd left the war behind me."

Yancey Harper's voice was winter cold and a remoteness settled over him. "Nothing's going on, far as I know."

"Nothing!" Mace exclaimed. "You mean two murders are nothing?"

"Things like this happen," Harper said coolly.

Mace studied the young lawman. This was not the Yancey Harper he had known; this was a different man, one wary and sore-edged.

"Something new in Panhandle Valley then," he said. "You want me to tell Doc Wallace . . . guess he's still the coroner . . . to ride out there while you're getting a posse together? We ought to move pretty fast."

"Best you leave it to me," Harper said in a quick way. "I'll look after it. Wallace's not the coroner any more."

Mace sighed. "Reckon I'm away behind things." The remainder of Yancey's words suddenly registered. "You mean you're not taking a posse after those killers?"

"I mean I can handle it alone. Posse would just get in my way."

"Alone?" Mace echoed. "Yance, those jaspers are cold-blooded killers! You'll need help. . . ."

"I can take care of them," Harper assured. "Obliged to you for dropping by and bringing word. Now," he said, rising, "expect I'd best get busy. See you around," he finished, offering his hand.

"No doubt," Seevert replied, not missing the reserve in Harper's manner. He was being brushed off, told politely to mind his own business. He nodded, turned toward the door. Reaching the opening, he paused, again studied the lawman, wondering what had brought about so great a change in Harper. A thought struck him. Perhaps there had been more such incidents in the valley. Yancey hadn't been able to do anything about them and it was a sore spot with him. He was touchy on the subject. At that rationalization, Mace grinned, bobbed his head.

"Sure you don't want me to help?"

"I'm sure," Harper said in a clipped tone. "My job. No need for anybody else mixing up in it."

He lowered his head, began to thumb through a stack of printed dodgers on the desk. Mace wheeled, stepped through the doorway, halted.

"I'll be here to testify against that bunch when you bring them in. Send word out to the Circle S."

Yancey did not look up. "I'll keep it in mind. Glad to see you back, Mace."

There was no warmth in his words. *Like hell you are,* Seevert thought as he moved into the hot sunshine. A stranger would have been accorded more cordiality than Yancey had shown him.

He stopped beside the sorrel, pondering the strangeness of Harper's actions. It was as though Yancey resented his return, disliked the fact that he was not dead. But that was foolishness. What reason would Harper have for that? And the manner in which he had received the news of the Cargill murders; it had not been the outraged reaction of a lawman being told of a ruthless killing in his domain, followed swiftly by hurried preparations to begin a search for the outlaws involved. Instead, it was a calm, almost disinterested acceptance of a fact and an indefinite indication to do something about it—alone.

None of it made sense. His earlier assumption that something was wrong in Panhandle Valley flourished anew, and to that was now added another suspicion: whatever it was, Yancey Harper was up to his neck in it.

Mace laid one hand on the saddle horn, took up the sorrel's leathers. He glanced down the street; there must be someone to whom he could talk, someone who would tell him what it was all about. His eyes settled on the office of the town's physician.

Doc Wallace. He would have the answers. He swung onto the gelding and struck off for the distant corner.

V

A red-wheeled buggy stood in the Wallace yard, and, as Mace entered the shadowy parlor of the physician's home, which served as a waiting room for patients, he could hear a woman's voice in the adjoining office. Restless and disturbed, he moved to one of the windows and stood there, his gaze on the low hills beyond the town. He could not get Yancey Harper out of his mind.

After a time the woman came from Wallace's inner sanctum. He watched her cross the room, trailed by the squat figure of the doctor who saw her onto the porch. At least Wallace seemed not to have changed, Mace thought. He was the same, solicitous little man he had been.

After a few final words of encouragement to the woman, the physician wheeled and reëntered the room. Cocking his head to one side and smiling with professional gentleness, he peered at Mace.

"What can I do for you, sir?"

Seevert stepped into the shaft of sunlight that slanted through the window. He extended his hand. "You can say welcome home for one thing, Doc."

Wallace started visibly. Mace saw the same astonishment run through him that had claimed Yancey Harper.

"Love of God, boy! Where did you come from?"

Impatience ripped through Mace Seevert. "What's the matter

with everybody around here? Took me a while to get back from the war, but I made it. People act like I've got no business being alive!"

Wallace stepped forward impulsively. He grasped Seevert's hand, squeezed it tightly. "I'm sorry, Mace, but seeing you was a bit of a shock. We were all given to understand that you were dead. He told us. . . ."

The physician's voice trailed off. Mace looked at him sharply. It was the second time he had heard that statement begun and then pointedly dropped. No doubt when he turned up missing after that last fracas at Day's Gap, many had thought him dead—but who was making such a big case out of it, and why? This time he would have an answer.

"Who's so all fired interested in me being dead, Doc?"

Wallace stopped, glanced through the window. Turning on his heel, he crossed the room, closed the door, and slid the bolt. Motioning to Mace, he continued on into his adjoining office. Pointing to a heavy, leather-covered chair, he sat down at a massive roll-top desk. His moon-like face was serious as he picked up a blackened pipe and began to stuff it with tobacco shreds.

"When did you ride in, Mace?"

An angry impatience again whipped at Seevert. "Just now. Don't dodge my question, Doc. What's so surprising about me not being dead? And who told everybody I was? I asked Yancey that and he gave me the run around, same as you're trying to do. What's the deal?"

Wallace said: "Yancey? How come you were talking to him?"

"Went there looking for Kilgore. Found him instead. The Cargills were murdered this morning. I saw it . . . or most of it. Wanted to report what I saw and offer to join a posse. Yancey the same as told me to mind my own business. He didn't seem to appreciate much my coming in."

Wallace was only half listening. "The Cargills," he murmured. "Too bad. Nice folks. . . ."

Seevert came to his feet, eyes snapping. "Damn it, Doc! Quit dodging around the bush! Give me some straight answers!"

The physician laid his pipe aside. He looked up at Mace, his face solemn. "Sit down, boy. You're not going to much like what I've got to tell you."

Wallace waited until Mace had again settled himself in the chair. He leaned forward. "You know a man named Fallon? Con Fallon?"

Surprise flowed throughout Seevert. "Fallon? Sure, he was my commanding officer. What's he got to do with it?"

"Everything. He blew in here about a year before the war ended. Brought a couple of men with him. Maybe you know them, too . . . Charlie Zapf and Ben Childers?"

Mace nodded. "Remember them both. Zapf was a sergeant in my outfit. Childers was our powder jack . . . the man who handled the explosives. We did a lot of that kind of fighting . . . blowing up bridges, supply dumps, roads, and such." He paused, frowned. "Can't figure why they'd come here. Seems to me they were from the East, or somewhere along the coast."

"Wouldn't know about that, but they ended up here. Fallon had been wounded and discharged. Don't know how Zapf and Childers got out. Maybe they'd been wounded, too. Doesn't matter. The thing that does is that Fallon had a letter from you . . . a sort of deed."

Again surprise blanked Mace Seevert's face. "Deed?"

"Yes. Looked all right. Had your signature on it. And it had been witnessed by Zapf and somebody else . . . don't recollect the name. It turned your place over to Fallon, gave him full ownership."

Seevert lunged to his feet. "It did what?" he shouted in a strangled voice.

"Signed over the Circle S to Fallon. He told us you had been in his company, that you two were close friends. He said you were always talking about your ranch and what you planned to do with it when the war was over. Then, right before that last battle you were in, I think he called it Day's Gap . . . somewhere in Alabama . . . anyway, he said you came to him. Claims you had a feeling you might not come out of it alive. You'd made up this deed and wanted him to keep it, in case your hunch was right. You explained you wanted him to have the ranch. Said you couldn't stand the thought of it being taken over by squatters, or having it lost because of back taxes. And since you two were such good friends, you'd like it if he'd accept."

Mace stared at the physician. His jaw had dropped and a fierce light burned in his eyes. "Fallon's a damn' liar," he managed finally. "A stinking, lousy liar . . . along with a few other drawbacks. I never said anything like that, or even thought of it. And I never signed any deed. As for him being a friend . . . only reason I was around him was because I had to be. If I was out picking friends, he's about the last man I'd choose."

"Figured it was a bit odd," Wallace said. "So did a lot of other people, but there wasn't much argument to be put up. He had that deed . . . and you never came back. Where were you all that time?"

Mace shrugged. "Got captured at Day's Gap. It was in the spring of Eighteen Sixty-Four. Yankees sent me to the prison on Johnson Island, up in Ohio, along with a dozen more Confederate soldiers. I was there almost a year when a bunch of us tried to break out."

"The war was about over then," Wallace murmured.

"We didn't know that, of course. If we had, we could have saved ourselves a lot of trouble. Anyway, we made a run for it. We didn't make it and I got shot up . . . three balls, one of them in my head. I spent the next six months or so flat on my back in a Yankee Army hospital, then three more getting back on my feet. They turned me loose finally, and it took a little more time working to get enough cash so's I could buy a horse and head for home." Seevert paused. Anger hardened his mouth, glittered in his eyes. "Now I'm here . . . at last . . . only to hear this jack-leg Fallon had stolen my ranch."

Wallace reached forward, wrapped his fingers about Seevert's wrist. "Easy, son. Nothing's gained by getting all riled up. Maybe. . . ."

"He won't keep it long," Mace said, pulling away. "Just long enough for me to see him . . . call him a liar and order him off. Where'll I find him?"

"The old Harper place."

"Hashmark? What's he doing there? Where's Yancey's folks?"

"They've been dead quite a while. Fallon bought the ranch from Yancey."

Mace found that hard to believe. "How did that happen? Why didn't Yancey just keep running Hashmark?"

Wallace rubbed at his chin folds. "I expect he's the only one who can answer that. It happened right after Kilgore got killed, about the same time Yancey got the job as marshal. Some people figure it was Fallon's backing that pinned the star on him. And now. . . ."

"Now he's Fallon's dog, is that it? Is that what you were about to say?"

Wallace stirred his thick shoulders. "You're saying it, Mace, not me. Yancey makes out that he's no friend of Fallon's, but sometimes you wonder."

Seevert stood, motionless and silent, staring down at the physician. Then: "What's the big trouble around here? I got the feeling something was wrong the minute I rode down the street. And this Cargill thing . . . people like them getting murdered in cold blood. Everybody seems to be running scared . . . even you."

Wallace's face colored and he looked down. "Easy for you to say that," he murmured. "You're an outsider. . . ."

"The hell I am! This is my home . . . I own a ranch here in Panhandle Valley!"

"I mean . . . you've been gone. You don't know. . . ."

"That's why I'm asking. I want to know. Spit it out, Doc!"

Wallace pulled back into his chair, gave Mace a quick glance. "And you've got a right," he said, coming to a decision of some sort with himself. "You named it when you said the town was running scared. It's more than that. It's the whole valley. Con Fallon's got the entire kit and caboodle knuckling under. You saw a sample of it this morning . . . the Cargills. Fallon gets what he wants, one way or another. He started with your Circle S and the Harper place, and kept going. Now, I'd say he owns or controls a half a million acres in the valley. He's been building up ever since he moved in, collecting ranches and farms like old women collect seashells and butterflies. Some he bought out, some he just took over when the owner wouldn't sell or run . . . like the Cargills."

"If everybody knows this, why the hell doesn't somebody do something about it?"

"Knowing and proving it are two different things. And then, if you could prove something, you got yourself another chore getting something done about it."

Seevert spun angrily on his heel, stamped across the room. "Well, I aim to do something . . . about my place, anyway. Con Fallon's not crooking me out of the Circle S, no matter how tall he stands around here!"

"You'll be on your own," Wallace warned. "Keep that in mind. Merchants mostly favor Fallon because he's brought a lot of business into town. They just sort of close their eyes to what's going on . . . leave it up to Yancey. And what ranchers are left are afraid to buck Hashmark."

"So I'm on my own," Mace snapped, coming back around. "I won't ask for help . . . I won't need it."

"Maybe. You're up against a big outfit. It's not the Hashmark you knew. Fallon's got himself a dozen hardcase toughs riding for him, on top of a regular crew."

"Long odds," Mace said grimly. "Seems I've never run up against any other kind. You said Fallon was at Hashmark. What's he done with my place?"

"Started out living there. Then, when he took over the Hashmark, he moved. Uses the Circle S as a line camp and for storing feed."

Mace was quiet for several moments. Then: "Have you been by there lately?"

"Not for quite a spell, but last time I saw it, it was in pretty bad shape. Don't expect much, boy. You'll be disappointed. Place hasn't been worked since right after your pa died."

"Rosales . . . Chopo? Is he still around?"

"Haven't seen him, either. He tried to keep things going at first, but there wasn't much to work with. What beef hadn't been rustled and sold to the Army, disappeared quick after Tom died. Then Fallon showed up and Rosales just dropped out of sight."

"They could've killed him, like they did the Cargills. Circle S was the only home he ever had." Frustration and a wild sort of fury possessed Mace. "And everybody just stands around and lets things like this happen!" he shouted. "Isn't there a man in town with any guts at all?"

The physician got up slowly, making no reply. He placed his glance on Mace and said: "No, I guess not. And you could be making a mistake, too. You're up against a bunch of ruthless men. Fallon's the worst of them all. And he's big, stands high.

He won't take kindly to being made out a liar and a cheat. You sure Circle S is worth it?"

"It's worth it," Seevert snapped, and stalked to the door. He jerked the bolt free, stepped out onto the porch. He paused there, looked back over his shoulder.

"Figured I was through with fighting," he said in a grim voice. "Seems now I'm just starting."

VI

Mace Seevert rode down the center of the street, his glance, bold and defiant, cutting back and forth. He knew the reason for the coolness, the restraint now; he was the prodigal returned—and most unwelcome for they saw in him greater trouble for the already stricken Panhandle Valley. It irked him deeply to realize that men who had been associates of his father, who had known him since he was a youngster, now lacked sufficient courage even to speak; it hurt more to find that those who had been his friends were now strangers, placing their backs to him.

His shifting gaze caught Henry Tubbs, peering through the wavy glass of his window. When their eyes locked, the banker turned away. McGillivray, sweeping the freshly settled dust from the porch fronting his store, lowered his head, continued at his task. There were others. He cowed each with his contemptuous stare. But beneath that flint-hard veneer he had assumed there was a dull ache. He didn't need their friendship, he told himself; he could get along without them—all of them. But it was a hollow assurance. His homecoming had turned out far different from what he had expected.

He reached the edge of the settlement and swung onto the road leading northeast. It followed a meandering course over the flats and through brushy arroyos and choppy hills, eventually touched the lower corner of the Circle S. From there it pointed directly for the sun, skirting Hashmark, the Harper—now the Fallon—spread.

In the first glowing rush of anger he had determined to ride directly to Hashmark, confront Con Fallon with his lie, and order him off the Circle S. Now, as he drew nearer to his land, the urge to look upon the house where he had been born, to see again the things he had thought of a thousand times in the past five years, overpowered his will. Fallon could wait.

He rode on, pulse quickening as he drew nearer. He topped the last grass-covered rise, pulled to a halt. Below, with the frowning buttes standing bleakly in the hot sunlight, lay Circle S—or rather, what remained of it. A lump crowded into his throat. Doc Wallace had warned him there would be little resemblance to the ranch he had known; even so, he was not prepared for the desolate, forlorn scene he looked down upon.

The smaller outbuildings were rotting frames, some wholly collapsed. The corrals were gone, their logs carried away, likely for firewood. The barn was a shell. Only the main house, built by Tom Seevert to withstand the elements, stood firm, but it, too, was a forsaken hulk, its windows shattered, its doors sagging drunkenly from a single hinge, or missing entirely. A gaping hole presented a dark patch in the roof and the stout uprights supporting the porch were tilted and appeared about to fall.

The circular well housing Tom Seevert had so painstakingly constructed lay on its side, several boards ripped off and missing. Bits of frayed rope still clung to the rusting pulley. Nearby a bucket, riddled by bullets, had been turned bottom up on a stake to provide a target for marksmen whiling away their time.

Mace, his spirits sinking lower with each moment, allowed his eyes to travel over the once well-tended yard. Waist-high weeds, sunflowers, clumps of greasewood, dove weed, and other rank growth had closed in, unchecked, upon the house. His mother's lilac bushes, so assiduously cared for in happier days, were stark, unclothed sentinels lining the south wall of the structure. Jenny Seevert had planted them there in order for their sweet perfume to fill the rooms in summer, he recalled. Now their branches, like gaunt arms, reached up in pitiful supplication, begging someone to clear away the relentless, choking weeds and permit them to bloom again.

A heavy sadness descended upon Mace. He should have known; he had expected too much. He should have realized the place would go to ruin during his absence. *Nothing stands still,* he told himself. The marks of war, of prison and pain lay heavier across his features now, placing a stillness, a somber shadow there, and his acquired age, much greater than his actual years, made itself more apparent.

Head bowed, he touched the sorrel with blunted spurs and started down the short slope. He gained the neglected yard and hauled up before the falling hitch rack. For a time he sat, staring at the front of the dilapidated house in moody silence. Finally he dismounted.

He crossed slowly to the doorway, looked inside. The room had a vile stench, and quick anger rushed through him. Once it had been the parlor. It had contained a sofa, a walnut table—butterfly table his mother had called it—a deep, comfortable rocking chair, and one or two ladder-backs. There had been pictures on the walls, stern-faced relatives held in rigid suspension by photographer's head clamps; a braided rug had covered the floor. Now it was being used for other purposes.

He passed on into the adjoining room, his parent's bedchamber. It was filled now with irregular blocks of crudely baled hay. The kitchen, the stove overturned and broken, the shelving ripped from the walls, contained several sacks of grain. An empty whiskey bottle stood on the sill of one window.

He had no heart to look farther. The rear entrance, the door gone, was before him and he stepped out into the sunshine again. Other reminders of the past greeted him: the garden plot his mother had tended, now a weed bed, the small chicken yard where he had gone daily to collect the few eggs begrudged him by the fowls, the crude cage in which he had kept a pet squirrel until it gnawed its way to freedom.

He stood there, unseeing, his eyes on the useless litter. Everything was in shambles—worthless, rotting relics of days far in the past. But the land remained, rich and steadfast—and permanent. At that thought Mace Seevert stirred and from it he took hope. Circle S could be rebuilt. It would mean hard labor, privation, and sacrifice, and he would have to do it alone, for now there was not even the faithful Chopo Rosales to help. But it could be done. First, however, came Con Fallon and the threat he posed to the future. The sooner he faced him, got him out of the picture, the sooner he could begin. His spirits rising, he wheeled, started for the sorrel.

Abruptly he halted, faculties suddenly alert as a warning sang through him. Someone—or something—had moved in the shoulder-high brush across the yard. Mace held completely still, eyes drilling into the tangle of stalks and leaves while his ears strained to catch any uncommon sound. His hand drifted downward, settled on the butt of his pistol. It could be some of Fallon's riders. His jaw tightened. If so, the reckoning could just as well begin here on Circle S property as elsewhere. It was a poor place for a showdown, however; he was in the open, an easy target, while whoever skulked in the brush was invisible to him.

He waited another half minute, then, ducking low, he whirled and threw himself around the corner of the house. He did not stop but hurried on and circled the structure. When he again halted, he was at the opposite end of the building where he had a complete view of the weeds while still protected by the south wall of the house. Gun in hand, he probed the rank growth with his glance.

Off toward the bluffs a meadowlark trilled into the hot sunshine. Insects *clacked* loudly in the weeds, and somewhere a dove mourned. The faint, dry rasp of cloth brushing against dead leaves reached him. Mace felt his nerves tighten. The sound came from the right, only paces away. He rode out the tight moments, scarcely breathing. It was the war all over again, the deadly hush before a battle began.

The muted scrape came again, much nearer. Tops of several stalks shifted gently, swung back into place. Mace, keeping low, darted silently across the narrow strip of open ground and slipped quietly into the weeds. Whoever it was, he decided grimly, was in for a surprise; he would not wait; he would act first. Motionlessly he listened. The dragging noise came once again, now only a step away. Mace tensed and gauged the location of the sound.

"Hold it!" he yelled suddenly, and lunged.

He collided with the intruder and both went down in the *crackling* brush. Seevert rolled to one side, bounded to his feet. Anger pulsing through him, gun ready, he glared at the figure sprawled before him.

"Who are you?"

At the question the man turned over. He looked up, a thin, dark-faced individual with glittering black eyes. A sound escaped his throat, a low cry.

"*¡Madre de Dios! ¡Muchacho mío!*"

Mace fell back a step. Astonishment gripped him at the familiar term; Rosales had always called him *muchacho*. He looked closer. A broad smile parted his lips.

"Chopo!"

"*Sí*, it is I!" the old man cried, scrambling to an upright position. Tears were streaming down his lined cheeks. "It is I . . .

Chopo . . . who welcomes you from the dead!"

VII

Mace staggered as the old *vaquero* threw himself bodily upon him, embraced him fiercely.

"A miracle of the holy saints!" Rosales cried. "A holy miracle! You are back from the dead!"

"I'm back . . . but not from the dead," Mace said as the Mexican disengaged himself. "Just took me a long time to get home." He paused, studied the dark, smiling face before him. "Good to see you, old friend. I was afraid. . . ."

Rosales brushed at his eyes. "Forgive me, *muchacho,* if I act as a child. You feared for my life?"

"I heard you'd disappeared. Some figured that you had been shot . . . ambushed."

"It has been tried," Rosales said dryly. "A man quickly learns the shadows are his best friends. You have come only today?"

"Today," Mace said. "Never expected to find the old place in this condition."

"It is sad," Rosales murmured, looking around. "Come, we shall talk of it," he added.

Mace followed the *vaquero* to the back of the house where the sun shone warmest. There Rosales squatted on his heels, shoulders against the wall. He motioned for Mace to join him.

"You have become a man," he said.

Seevert hunkered beside the Mexican. "Doesn't take you long to grow up in war. Speak slower. It's been five years since I used my Spanish. I'm a bit rusty."

"You will learn again. I shall teach you as I did before. But what is to be done, now that you have returned? That one of evil . . . Fallon . . . has he not a paper that tells the *rancho* is his?"

"His paper means nothing," Mace answered. "Everything he

says is a lie. I didn't give him the ranch."

"Of this I was sure. After the *patrón* died, I stay and do what I can to keep the rancho as he would wish. Someday the *muchacho* will return, I tell myself. Then this Fallon and his *hombres malos* come. They show the paper, tell me the *rancho* is theirs, that I must leave. I do not believe. The *muchacho* would not give away the land of his father, I say, even in death. But they do not listen. I go then to the marshal. . . ."

"Yancey Harper?"

"No, the old one . . . Kilgore. I ask if this thing I am told is true. He says it is so. There is a paper that gives to him the owning of the Circle S. Still I do not believe. I return here. Already this Fallon and those who work for him have come. The things of your father and mother are in the yard. Fire has been made of them. . . ."

"That's where everything went . . . burned?"

"*Sí* . . . later, when no one looks, there are some things I save before they are lost. I take them to the *jacal* I have built in the *malpais*. They wait for you there."

Mace was silent for several moments after Chopo Rosales had finished. He laid his hand on the Mexican's knee, said finally: "Thank you, *amigo*. Nothing we can do about that . . . but we can build ourselves a new ranch. The two of us. . . ."

"How can that be? Has he not the paper?"

"The paper is what is called a forgery . . . a lie. It means nothing. I aim to see Fallon and tell him so and take the paper from him."

The *vaquero*'s face clouded. "It will be a thing of danger, *muchacho*. He has many men who will kill without thought."

"You don't have to tell me that. I saw the Cargills murdered this morning. I think it was Fallon's bunch."

Rosales moaned softly. "*Ai-eeee* . . . the old *señor* and his fine lady . . . good people. May the Virgin take them to her breast."

141

The *vaquero* crossed himself devoutly. Then: "You saw this?"

Mace related the incident. When he had concluded, Rosales nodded slowly. "It is as the others. Always a great noise of exploding, one of mighty force. After comes the fires. Some have died in the flames. There are those, also, dead from bullets."

"And nobody ever does anything about it?"

"No one. The law, like the small animal that lives in the ground, is blind, *muchacho*. It sees nothing. This you did not know?"

"I'm learning fast," Mace replied, a hard edge to his words. "After I saw what happened to the Cargills, I went straight to Yancey and told him about it. Got nowhere. Then I talked to Doc Wallace. He gave me a line on the way things have been going here in the valley. Seems Fallon's got everybody walking his chalk line."

"It is so," Rosales said. "Wallace . . . you did not tell him of your plans?"

"Sure," Mace replied, frowning. "I told him I was going to see Fallon, order him off my land. Why?"

The *vaquero* shrugged in the customary way of his people. "It is unwise to speak loudly of such to any man. In this country there are no longer friends, only men who are strangers, although from the moment of birth they have been at your side."

"You mean Doc's lined up with Fallon, too?"

"That I do not know. It is only that it is wise to trust no one. Even brave men walk softly when there are serpents in the house."

Mace nodded thoughtfully. After a time he said: "Tell me about Pa, Chopo. How did he die?"

"Not of violence, if that is in your mind. He took the fever sickness in the cold months and could not rise. I think he cared little. The *patrón* was lonely for you and for his *señora*. There was nothing to fill his heart. He sleeps beside the *señora*, in the small yard on the hill where I placed him."

"Thank you again," Mace said huskily. He stared off toward the bluffs. He should have written home; it would have meant much to Tom Seevert, never quite himself after his wife's death. But somehow there had never been time or opportunity. Forrest and his cavalry were continually on the move, and, when imprisonment came and it was possible, Tom Seevert was dead.

"The small yard blooms with flowers," the *vaquero* said. "I come often to this place when Fallon's men are not here. I come to look, to remember, and to hope. It is my home, also, *muchacho*. I have no other."

"And it will always be," Mace said in a quiet voice. "Long as I'm alive." He rose to his feet. "I'm on my way to see Fallon now. You hang around here, but keep out of sight. If I'm not back by dark, ride in and tell Doc Wallace. I don't know if he'd do anything about it or not, but he might."

The *vaquero* also came upright. "Is it not best that I, too, go? This thing you cannot do alone."

"I figure it's the smartest way to handle it . . . alone. I don't want it looking like a delegation. The fewer people in on it, the easier it will be for Fallon to back down."

"But how . . . ?"

"He thinks I'm dead, too. Showing up will work in my favor. I know him, from the war. Call his hand to his face and he'll fold. . . ."

There was a sound at the edge of the yard. Mace whirled. Three men, guns in hand, faced him. They had come in, apparently, from the far side of the house, dismounted, and eased their way up silently. The one nearest, a powerfully built individual with a scar on his face, stared at Mace.

"Seevert . . . sure as hell," he muttered. A sly grin crossed his

143

features. "What's the matter? You don't recognize me?" he asked, brushing his hat to the back of his head.

Mace started. It was Zapf, older, darker, heavier, and with the same hard-edged way about him. "I recognize you, Charlie," he said coldly. "Weren't wearing that bullet track last time I saw you."

"Little souvenir I got at Memphis. Figured you for dead."

"Seems about everybody thought the same. Going to be a disappointment to your boss."

Zapf hawked, spat. "Well, don't go bragging too much about it," he drawled. "Expect the major'll be doing something about it." He bobbed his head at the man to his left. "Get their guns, Tuck. We're taking them back to Hashmark."

VIII

Hashmark was in striking contrast to the crumbling Circle S. Seevert took note of this as they rode into the yard. The buildings were clean and in excellent repair. There was an air of prosperity that could not be missed. Horses stood in the corrals; the cook's garden was green with growing vegetables; plump fowls scuffled in their pens and several milk cows grazed on the grassy plot reserved for them. Across the front of the house flowers laid a colorful blaze and the huge cottonwood tree that he and Yancey had climbed so many times in years gone by spread a broad, cooling shadow over all.

Seevert's heart ached as he looked upon it. This was what he had envisioned, in time, for Circle S—a fine ranch, comfortable, complete, and well-paying. He wondered now if it could ever come true; he had only ruins with which to begin—and that claimed by another man.

The full import of the warning given him by Doc Wallace, and further emphasized by Chopo Rosales, was registering more forcefully upon him now. Fallon would not give up easily; he was building an empire and he would resist anyone's efforts to block its progress. Having his look at Hashmark convinced Mace Seevert of that. Perhaps he had been a fool to think he could just walk in, call Fallon a liar to his face, and order him off Circle S property. But there had been no other recourse; it was the only thing he could do.

"Draw up there in front of the house," Zapf ordered harshly. "Major'll be in his office."

Mace brushed aside his dark thoughts, angled into the neatly whitewashed rail. As Chopo and the others pulled in next to him, he saw the curtains of a corner window in the house sweep back. The face of a young woman appeared. She considered the riders briefly, curiously, and then the folds of lace dropped again into position. Fallon's daughter, Seevert guessed, or possibly his wife although she seemed much too young for the one-time officer.

Two men came from the doorway, one with an arm in a sling. A bandage was wrapped about the biceps. The other was Ben Childers. His eyes flared with surprise when he saw Mace, but he made no comment, simply watched in a quiet, suspicious way.

Zapf motioned to the riders with him. "Tuck, you come with me. Rest of you get over to the bunkhouse and wait. Likely we'll be needing you in a few minutes."

Childers and the two others continued on across the yard. Mace watched them go thoughtfully. He glanced at Zapf.

"That bandage wouldn't be covering a bullet hole, would it?"

Zapf's jaw hardened. "Inside, both of you," he snapped, and pushed Rosales toward Seevert.

Mace suppressed his anger and stepped up onto the gallery. He could not be sure, but he thought the wounded man had been one of those encountered at the Cargills'—the one he had managed to hit. He appeared to be about the same build and wore similar clothing. He wished he had gotten a better look.

He reached the house and entered. It was cool and shadowy, all familiar. He turned, from previous knowledge of the arrangement, toward the room where Yancey's father, Sam Harper, had maintained office quarters.

"Watch 'em," Zapf said to Tucker, and crowded ahead.

The sour-faced rider lifted his hand. "Hold up," he said, leaning back against the wall.

Zapf's hunched shape blocked the doorway. "Got a little surprise for you, Major," he said, his voice faintly exultant. "Found him hanging around the old Circle S."

Zapf reached back, grasped Mace by the arm, and pulled him into the room. Con Fallon, a balding, red-faced man with small, black agate eyes, glanced up. Shock traveled across his feature. He leaped to his feet.

"Seevert!"

Mace grinned wolfishly. "And a long way from being dead."

In the space of a quick breath Con Fallon had recovered himself. He nodded. "So I see. Glad of it, Mace."

"I'll bet," Seevert said dryly. "It was a mighty fancy lie you palmed off on folks around here about me handing over my ranch to you. You'd have been smart to put a bullet in my back yourself . . . made sure I wouldn't be showing up someday. It was a mistake to leave it to the Yankees."

"Now, you know I wouldn't do a thing like that," Fallon said smoothly. "I always looked out for my men . . . my friends."

Fallon had not changed, Mace noted; he still had the same sly, confident manner. He said: "Only when you had something to gain. Who did the forgery on that paper, Con? Zapf?"

"Can't see that it matters. It was done in the interests of keeping things straight. A signed paper simply saved a lot of explaining, and avoided legal problems."

"Still a lie," Mace snapped. "I'm serving notice on you here and now to get off my land and stay off."

Fallon, deliberate and cool, reached for a bottle of whiskey on his desk, filled a shot glass to the brim. He tipped it to his lips and downed it in a single gulp. He made no offer to anyone else.

"No point in getting all worked up over this," he said cheerfully. "Never saw a problem yet that couldn't be talked out."

"Nothing to talk about," Mace replied. Fallon's indifferent manner infuriated him, but he hung tightly to his temper. He had learned long ago it was wise to keep your head when you dealt with Fallon. "I'm warning you to clear off Circle S. And while I'm here, I'll take that paper you put my name to."

Fallon sat down, toyed with his empty glass. His eyes lifted, met those of Seevert, and held. "I figured you were dead. Everybody did. I knew you wouldn't want your place falling into the hands of land sharks or homesteaders, so I took steps to prevent it."

"Obliged to you," Mace said sardonically. "Seems you've been taking a lot of steps here in the valley."

"A man looks out for himself," Fallon replied blandly. Glancing at Zapf, he added: "And his partner."

"Maybe, but it always catches up with him. But that's not what I'm here for. You have a crew over to my place in the morning and clean that feed out of there. If you don't, I'm putting fire to it. And if you're running any stock on my land, get them off. Now . . . hand over that paper."

Fallon placed his hands together, formed a bridge with his fingers. "Don't see why this can't be straightened out to our mutual satisfaction. . . ."

"The only way to do it," Mace cut in roughly, "is get off Circle S and stay off."

"Not so simple as that. You've got to bear in mind I've quite an investment there. Quite a bit involved. . . ."

"Your problem, not mine. You had no right taking over in the first place. Everything you did, you did on the strength of a lie. Now make the best of it and back off."

"I might consider paying you for the place . . . say five hundred in gold."

"It's not for sale," Mace barked. "Not for five thousand."

Seevert became aware of Rosales's fingers plucking at his arm. He glanced at the *vaquero*. The Mexican pointed to an ancient musket hanging over the fireplace at the end of the room. Fresh anger rolled through Mace. It was an old weapon that had belonged to his father, a long-barreled muzzle-loader, complete with powder horn and hand-fashioned leather bullet pouch. It dated from Revolutionary War days and had been passed down through generations to the elder Seevert.

Fallon became aware of his attention. "It's yours, of course," he said easily. "Just couldn't let it get lost . . . not a fine old weapon like that."

The man's glib tongue served only to add more fuel to the fire simmering within Mace Seevert. Fallon was putting on the pose of having committed no wrong at all, of actually having done him a favor.

"You're damn' right it's mine!" Mace snarled. "And there was some other stuff your hands burned they had no business touching!"

Fallon shrugged. "Most of it you would have destroyed yourself . . . items of no value to you or anyone else. However, that's beside the point. I was thinking . . . why not throw in with me . . . us? We could use a third partner in Hashmark."

"The hell with that!" Zapf shouted, coming to sudden life. "I ain't splitting . . . !"

"I'll do the talking, Charlie," Fallon broke in sharply. "You keep listening." He swung his flat eyes back to Mace. "Hashmark's a big ranch. Plenty here for all of us. You could live right here, maybe put up a nice house for yourself . . . and the Mex, if you want. . . ."

"Forget it," Mace said flatly.

"Let me finish. That ranch of yours is worthless, run down to where you can never do anything with it. Fact is, it's dead. Take a fortune to get it going again."

Fallon paused for comment. Seevert remained silent, merely stared.

"Come right down to brass tacks, it's not worth much to me, either," the Army man continued. "Makes a fair line shack and feed depot for my west range. And there's water. Outside that, it's nothing. When you consider it, I'm being generous, offering you a part of Hashmark just to let things ride."

"Not interested," Mace said stubbornly. "You heard my terms. That's where I stand. I won't change."

He sensed he was suddenly on thin ice, decided quickly there was nothing to do but bull on through. He turned to Zapf. "I'll take our guns, Charlie."

Zapf frowned, glanced at Fallon. Tucker, pistol still in his hand, raised the weapon slightly.

"Forget it," Fallon said, his manner undergoing a swift change. His voice was sharp and his eyes had taken on a dull glitter. "I'm giving you a choice, Seevert. See it my way, or I'll be forced to protect myself."

"By taking care of us like you did the Cargills and a few others around here?"

"Nobody stands up to Hashmark," Fallon said. "I get what I want."

"Not this time. I'm a couple of jumps ahead of you. Told a friend I was coming here. He'll have spread the word by now. If anything happens to me, everybody'll know who was behind it."

"And do what?" Fallon asked lazily. "One thing you'd better understand, Seevert . . . I own this valley . . . and the people in it, as far as that's concerned. They jump when I holler frog. They don't listen to anybody else."

"You don't own me," Mace shot back, his voice trembling with rage. "You never will. I'll fight you. . . ."

"The hell with it," Fallon said suddenly, his attitude changing. "If you think I'll stand by and let you foul up my deal here, you'd better think again!"

The one-time officer poured himself a drink with casual deliberation. In the quiet of the room the liquor made a small slapping sound. He studied the glass with brooding eyes briefly, then raised his glance to Zapf.

"Get this renegade out of here, Charlie. Take care of him. And the Mex, too. I'm tired of him skulking around in the brush, watching me."

IX

Con Fallon made the pronouncement of death as coolly as he would have ordered a meal in one of Berrendo Crossing's restaurants. The bloody conflict between the North and South had marked some men thus, leaving them callous of heart, scarred in mind. The life of a man meant nothing to them.

Mace stared at the officer. Fallon was a hard one; he had become aware of that during the war, but now that the fighting was done with, it somehow surprised him; it seemed odd, unexpected. It should not have come as a shock, he realized a moment later. Wallace had warned him of the man's ruthlessness, so had Rosales, and even Yancey Harper, in a left-handed sort of way. He should have listened to them—but yet, how can you step on a snake without getting close?

He squared himself before Fallon. "You're making a mistake," he warned. "Maybe the last one of your life."

"I hardly think so. Get them out of here, Charlie."

Mace felt the muzzle of Tucker's pistol dig into his side. "Get movin'," the rider said in a low voice.

All of the anger that had been building steadily within Mace Seevert since he had ridden into Panhandle Valley peaked in that moment and exploded into driving fury. He spun on his heel, his movement only a blur. He caught Tucker with his left elbow, knocking the man's gun away. Maze's right fist went down, Tucker's weapon dropping from his nerveless fingers and skittering across the floor.

In that same instant Chopo Rosales leaped upon Zapf. The husky sergeant, caught by surprise, staggered back and came up hard against the wall. He recovered immediately. As the old *vaquero*, ignoring the difference in both age and size, rushed in, Zapf met him with two hard blows to the head. Rosales halted in his tracks. He staggered, fell across the corner of Fallon's desk.

Mace whirled to aid the *vaquero*. Too late to intercede, he crowded in on Zapf as Chopo slid to the floor. He drove a stiff right to Zapf's belly. The man buckled forward. Mace straightened him with a whistling left to the chin. The husky man failed to go down, braced himself, swung wildly. Seevert ducked, lashed out again.

A warning sang through him. He threw a glance to the side. Tucker was up, had recovered his lost weapon, and was moving in. Mace hammered two more blows into Charlie Zapf, wheeled to meet this new threat. Con Fallon's cool voice checked him.

"Let it be, Seevert."

Mace came about slowly, lungs heaving for breath, his face clothed with sweat. He could hear Zapf, sagged against the wall, retching weakly. Rosales lay on the floor at the end of the desk, and behind it, with a long-barreled cap-and-ball Colt in his hand, stood Fallon. The big hammer of the pistol was pulled to full cock position.

"Try that again and I'll have to handle you right here myself,"

Fallon said quietly. "Try to keep such goings-on away from the house. I've got my step-daughter living here, and things like this are a bit hard to explain to her." He shifted his gaze to Zapf. "Well, how about it? Think you can take care of him now?"

There was scorn in Fallon's tone. Zapf pulled himself erect. His face was flushed, eyes abnormally bright. "I can handle it . . . I'll call the boys. . . ."

"No you won't!" Fallon snapped. "This job I want you and Tucker to do. Nobody else."

Zapf swore. "What the hell difference . . . ?"

"Makes plenty of difference. You heard what he said about telling where he'd gone. The fewer who know what happened to him, the less likely it is to leak out."

A closeness came over Zapf. "I thought you wasn't scared of anybody . . . or anything."

"I'm not, but I'm no fool, either. You're doing the job yourself . . . you and Tucker. That'll keep you from ever talking about it. I know I don't need to worry about Tucker. That right, Tuck?"

"Yes, sir, Major," the squat rider said, and moved in behind Seevert. He jabbed viciously with his pistol. "Goin' to be a pure pleasure, doin' this little chore for you."

Mace flinched as pain shot through him, but he made no sound. Fallon opened the top drawer of his desk, laid the old Colt inside. He sat down slowly, turned his gaze on Zapf.

"Well, Charlie?"

Zapf stirred. "All right, Con. You're calling it." He looked down at Rosales. "Get up, Mex!"

The *vaquero* struggled to a sitting position. He rubbed at his jaw, seemingly dazed. Nodding, he said—"*Sí, señor.*"—and, bracing himself by placing one hand on the corner of the desk, he rose.

"Get over here with your *compadre*," Tucker ordered, jerking his head at Seevert.

Again Rosales nodded. He took a half step forward, and then in a totally unexpected move he spun, leaped behind Fallon. Steel glittered in the light from the window as a knife, hidden somewhere on his person, flashed into his hand. He jabbed the point against Fallon's throat, grinned wickedly at Tucker and Zapf.

"I have changed my mind, *señores*," he said in a voice soft as velvet. "Drop the guns or this *asesino* dies in his own blood."

Fallon's face turned to chalk. Tucker and Charlie Zapf made no move. The Mexican pressed harder with his knife. A drop of blood appeared on Fallon's skin.

"Do not test me, *amigos!*" Rosales warned. "I am of many years. I have seen much and I am prepared to die. For the *muchacho* I will do anything. Drop the *pistolas, por favor.* Quick!"

Fallon's face was a glistening, distorted mask. "For God's sake, do it!" he blurted frantically.

Tucker's pistol *banged* against the floor. The weapons he had had taken from Mace and the *vaquero* followed. A moment later Zapf dropped his.

Seevert wheeled, scooped up the handguns. Taking possession of two and tossing the *vaquero*'s to him, he kicked the other into a far corner of the room. He grinned at Rosales.

"Turn him loose, *viejo.*"

Rosales did not stir. "Is it not wise to slay the wolf when you have him trapped?"

"No doubt, but we'll need him to get out of here."

Reluctantly the Mexican lowered his knife. He leaned forward, jerked open the drawer in Fallon's desk, procured the cap-and-ball pistol.

"I pull the teeth of the wolf, anyway." He grinned and threw the weapon onto a chair.

"Good. Now keep that pig-sticker handy. You may have to

use it yet, if he doesn't do what I tell him."

Fallon, probing his throat with his fingertips gingerly, glared at Zapf. He swiveled his attention to Mace, eyes glowing. "You see the kind of help I've got around here? A pack of fools! It'd be worth a lot to have a man like you in with me, Seevert. The Mex, too, if you say so. How about making it a half interest in Hashmark? Just you and me cutting it right down the middle."

"Not by a damn' sight!" Zapf yelled, surging forward. "You can't . . . !"

Mace stopped him with an outstretched arm, shoved him back.

"You got nothing to say about it, Charlie," Fallon continued, ignoring the interruption. "I let you in, now I'm letting you out. I've got a belly full of your bungling."

"You're wasting your breath, and my time," Seevert said impatiently. "Now, I'll take that paper. Hurry it up!"

Fallon frowned deeply, shook his head. He looked down. "Not sure where it is. . . ."

"Use that knife, Chopo," Mace said. "Maybe it'll prod his memory some."

The *vaquero* grinned broadly, seized Fallon by the hair, and drew back his head. Instantly Fallon pulled open the drawer of his desk. He fumbled through an envelope of papers, selected one, and tossed it onto the countertop.

Thrusting one gun into his belt, Mace unfolded the paper, glanced at it. Satisfied, he drew a match from his pocket, scratched it into flame, and dropped it onto the sheet. It flared up, began to burn. He turned then to Fallon.

"Go to the window. Call in your boys. Tell them you want them in here."

"What for?" Fallon demanded.

"Don't be asking me any questions! Do it, and be damn quick about it unless you want to lose some more blood!"

Rosales's dark face split into a smile, but there was no humor in Mace Seevert's voice. Fallon got up hurriedly and went to the window, raised the sash.

"Childers!"

A door *creaked* in the yard. Childers called back: "Yeah, Major?"

"You and the rest of the crew get over here."

"Right away, Major."

Fallon wheeled. His eyes had narrowed and he took on a sly look. "If you're figuring what I think you are . . . you'll never get away with it."

Mace smiled. "We'll see," he said quietly. "Now sit down . . . and keep your mouth shut."

X

Rosales, his swarthy face a dark study, stepped to the window. He glanced out, shrugged. "There are many, *muchacho mío* . . . seven I count. Is there not a better way?"

"Too late now," Fallon said, a note of triumph in his voice. "You've overplayed your hand this time, friend Seevert."

"Maybe," Mace said.

It was a long chance, he knew, and time was beginning to press. There would be others in the house: the cook, possibly the handyman, even members of the crew. And the girl was there. She could happen by at any moment, glance into the room, and, realizing something was wrong, set up an alarm. Discounting the possibility of that, there were the seven hard-case gunmen now moving across the yard; they would not be easy to manage. It was a desperate gamble but Mace Seevert could see no alternative if he and Rosales were to leave Hash-mark alive.

"Stay put in that chair," he said to Fallon. "Get behind him, Chopo. Hold that knife on him. First wrong move he makes, drive it in to the handle."

"A pleasure," the *vaquero* said maliciously, and slipped in between Fallon and the wall.

"You two," Seevert said then, facing Zapf and Tucker. "Get over there where I can watch you." He pointed to the opposite side of the room. "No need my telling you that if you yell out, you'll be the first to die."

When they had taken their places, Mace stepped behind the door. Holding both pistols at waist level, and standing clear of the door's arc, he waited. Outside on the porch there was the *scuffing* of boots, then the hollow *clack* of heels as men entered the hall. Seevert steeled himself for the moments ahead.

"Yeah, Major?"

It was Ben Childers. Fallon remained silent. He jerked convulsively as Rosales shifted.

"Come in . . . damn it!" the rancher snapped irritably.

There was a brief pause and Childers, followed by the others, filed into the room. When the last had entered, Mace kicked the door shut. All wheeled, their faces going slack. Childers, a little apart, muttered an oath. His hand dropped swiftly to his pistol.

Mace said—"Don't."—in a quick, clipped way. "You'll never make it."

Ben Childers hesitated, his jaw working spasmodically. Mace nodded to him and the other men. "Raise your hands . . . up . . . keep them there. Play it smart and you'll still be alive come sundown."

Childers did not move. "Odds a bit high, ain't they? Seven to one . . . two, counting the Mex."

"Like to see just how high?" Mace asked softly.

Fallon flinched again. "Don't argue with him!" he yelled. "Do what he tells you!"

Ben Childers looked down, slowly lifted his arms. "Sure, Major," he said.

"Now, one at a time . . . walk over there and drop your guns in that chair," Seevert directed. "Use your left hand. Then get over with Zapf. Move!"

It was done quickly and without incident. When all were lined up along the wall, Mace motioned with one of his weapons.

"Turn around . . . put your hands flat on that wall. And don't look back if you want to keep a whole skin!"

Sweat was standing out on his face. The butts of his guns felt clammy in his palms, and tension was setting his muscles to quivering. It was taking far too much time—time he could not afford to lose.

"Hurry it up!" he snapped.

Finally it was accomplished. He motioned to Rosales, pointed to a table standing in the corner of the room. "Get that cloth, dump their guns into it. We'll take them with us . . . at least until we get outside."

The *vaquero* hastened to comply. Seevert, his eyes on Fallon, said: "Get up. You're coming along."

The Army man did not hesitate, something in Seevert's manner chilling any opposition he may have harbored. He pulled on his hat and walked stiffly to the center of the room. Rosales slung the square of cloth, bulging with weapons, over his shoulder. Abruptly he wheeled, crossed to the fireplace, and took down the old musket and its side equipment.

"We do not leave this for these *cucarachas*," he said, holding it in the crook of his arm.

Mace smiled, turned as a thought came to him. His glance swept the men lining the wall. Singling out the rider with the bandaged arm, he spun him about.

"You're the jasper I winged at the Cargill place this morning," he said, shooting in the dark. "Same one that plugged the old man in the back . . . murdered him. Figured you'd like to know the law will be coming for you. . . ."

The man's eyes flared. "No . . . it wasn't me! Maybe I was there, but it sure. . . ."

"Shut up, Gabe!" Childers yelled. "He don't know nothing! He's only guessing."

"You were there, too, Ben," Mace said. "That explosion was your work. Always were a good hand with blasting powder."

Childers made no reply. The man called Gabe swung his face back to the wall. Seevert felt a glow of satisfaction. He had been right about the killers. Gabe and Ben Childers were two of the three he had seen. Gabe, if crowded hard, would talk. It wouldn't be difficult to get the whole story out of him—all of which would lead back to Con Fallon and Charlie Zapf.

"What good do you think that'll do you?" Fallon asked, again calm and easy-going. "Nobody around here will pay you any mind."

"Maybe not around here," Mace said quietly. He jerked his head toward the door. "Walk in front of us. Keep thinking about this gun I've got pointed at you. If anybody tries to stop us, I'll kill you. Goes for this bunch in here and any of your crew outside. Understand?"

"I understand," Fallon said glumly. "Charlie, you keep everybody right here until I'm back."

"If you come back," Zapf muttered.

"He will," Mace said, "as long as he does what he's told. I don't go in for murder."

Zapf lapsed into silence. Fallon, preceding Seevert and Rosales, marched out into the hallway, across the porch, and into the yard. They mounted up, the rancher taking, one of the horses at the rail. Mace, feeling the hard crash of urgency more strongly now, gave the outbuildings, the bunkhouse, and the corrals a swift scrutiny. No one was in sight.

"Move on," he ordered.

They swung about, headed for the high, pole-arch gate. Rosales curved off, paused by the horse trough, and dropped the sack of weapons into the water, then hastened to catch up. He rejoined them as they left the yard.

"This isn't the end," Fallon warned when they reached the road. "My turn to sing is coming next."

"I knew you'd figure it that way," Mace replied. "The trouble with your kind is you never know when it's time to quit. If you were smart, you'd forget the whole thing right now."

"I'm smart," Fallon said. "You'll be finding that out."

They rode for another half hour with the lowering sun in their faces. When they reached a sharp bend in the trail at the edge of the short hills, Mace drew to a halt.

"Far enough," he said. "It looks like your hired hands mind real well."

Fallon, hands folded and resting on the horn of his saddle, spat. "Have your joke now, Seevert. You won't be laughing for long."

Mace shook his head. "It's no joke to me, but if you aim to push this further, you know where to find me. I'll be at my ranch, working. I'll mention that feed you've got stacked in my house again. Unless it's gone by noon tomorrow, you won't need to send for it."

"You won't be alive come noon," Fallon snapped, and, jerking his horse about savagely, he headed up the road.

Rosales watched him go. Finally he turned to Mace. "It is not the end of trouble, *muchacho.* It is the beginning. Now they will come."

Mace said: "I hope they do."

The *vaquero's* brows lifted. "Not to fight. There are too many. There is something you have not spoken of to me. A plan, perhaps?"

"There is, *viejo.* We're going to let Fallon hang himself. I got the idea back there at his place. Let's go to your *jacal* and I'll explain it to. . . ."

"Wait!" Rosales broke in, lifting his hand. He cocked his head toward the south. "Someone comes."

Mace listened into the fading afternoon. The rapid drumming of a galloping horse was a steady sound in the hush.

"Better see who it is," he said, and, spurring the sorrel off the trail, rode in behind a clump of brush.

XI

Hunched over his saddle, Mace Seevert kept his eyes on a curve in the road little more than fifty yards distant. Beside him Chopo Rosales also waited.

"He rides fast, this *extraño*," the *vaquero* commented.

Mace agreed. But stranger or not, whoever it was, seemed to know exactly where he was going. It could be one of Con Fallon's men on his way to Hashmark from Berrendo Crossing. He doubted that; few hired hands were ever in so great a hurry to report for work.

The rider hove into view. Coming around the bend, he was, for the space of a dozen seconds, moving directly toward the two men hiding in the brush. And then he swept on by. Mace glanced at Rosales and shrugged.

"Yancey Harper," he said. "Paying his duty call."

The Mexican frowned, not understanding the military phrase. He rubbed at his grizzled chin. "He rides hard for one not going to visit a friend. Perhaps he is, how you say . . . *hombre de dos caras.*"

"Man with two faces . . . two-faced," Seevert translated. "You could be right," he added, listening to the receding hoof beats. "Nobody seems to know for certain where Yancey stands. He might be going to see Fallon on business . . . about the Cargills. I understand he makes out like he's against the Hashmark crowd to everybody."

"It is possible," Rosales said, but there was no conviction in his words.

They swung about and struck off across the open country. Mace puzzled the matter of Yancey Harper in his mind, endeavored to put together some sort of pattern, some reasonable answer, but he could settle nothing. He could be misjudging Yancey, believing him to be hand in glove with Fallon. Yancey could be trying to do a job but was simply in over his head. He never had been one to choose the hard road, always looked for the easy way out of a tough situation.

They reached the lava beds, and Chopo moved forward to lead the way. For a time they followed a narrow trail, one almost hidden by greasewood, red sage, and other desert growth, and came finally to a deep gash in the face of the black, forbidding buttes. Rosales turned into this, and after a short climb they broke out into a small clearing where a shack, constructed of piecemeal lumber and other odds and ends, had been erected.

"It is humble, but here it is safe," Chopo said, pulling to a halt.

"Looks good to me," Mace declared, dismounting from the sorrel. He glanced at the *vaquero*. "I've got to be moving on . . . soon as I get a bite to eat. Anything I can do to help stir up some grub?"

Rosales studied the younger man with quiet eyes. That he was surprised to hear that Mace intended to ride on was apparent, but the inherent politeness of his kind held him silent, forbade questioning. A man's deep thoughts were his own. Besides, Mace had told him earlier he would speak of a plan. This the *muchacho* would do when he was ready.

"There is no need," he said, handing Seevert the old muzzle-loader and its parts. He took up the reins of the sorrel and his pinto, started toward the rear of the clearing where a pile of hay and a trough of water awaited them. "I have but to put fire under the *caldera* and boil coffee. In the *jacal* are the things of the *patrón* that I have saved. Examine them while there is delay, if you wish."

The fading rays of the sun were filling the shelter with a pale gold light as Mace stooped and entered. The items Rosales had spoken of were wrapped in an old blanket and were placed on a small platform of sticks built off the ground to discourage pack rats and similar nuisance animals.

He squatted down before the bundle and unrolled it. Familiar objects met his eyes: several scratched and fading tintypes of his parents, the family Bible, odds and ends of clothing, some silverware—the last, pitiful representations of two lives. It was a sad reminder and for a time he simply sat and stared, unseeing, at the small assemblage, while he thought of the past. The *vaquero*'s call brought him from his reverie.

"All is ready, *muchacho.*"

He returned the articles to the blanket, placed the bundle on the platform, and, after standing the musket in the corner behind it, he moved to where Chopo hunched by a small fire. He laid his hand on the *vaquero*'s thin shoulder.

"It's good to have a few things I can call my own. I'm obliged to you again."

Rosales was spooning a quantity of savory stew into a pan for him. A tin cup filled with strong black coffee was cooling on the ground.

"*Por nada,*" he said. "It is to my disgrace that all was not rescued from those *bribóns.* Had I been wise and with foresight, much more would I have kept for you."

"You did all you could . . . and I'm grateful," Mace said, and, sitting down, began to eat.

It was a tasty meal, one prepared of jack rabbit flesh pounded to tender shreds between stones, seasoned with a mixture of chili, herbs, roots, and crushed beans. It had a bite to it and tears sprang to Mace Seevert's eyes at his first mouthful, but he kept his face tipped down, refusing to let the old *vaquero* notice that he had become a greenhorn where the hotly spiced Mexican food was concerned.

Finished, he sat back. Producing a sack of tobacco and brown papers, he tossed them to Rosales, watched the *vaquero* expertly roll himself a quirly. Then, spinning one for himself, he reached into the fire for a brand. Night had settled over the *malpais* country, and stars high in their soft black bed were laying a silver sheen upon the ragged, ugly rocks, changing them into a different world, one that appeared gentle and inviting.

"I'm pulling out for Crocketville," Mace said, puffing the slim cylinder into life. "Figure to be back by morning."

"It is a long ride," Rosales said simply. "Is this the plan you spoke of?"

Mace said: "Yes. Fallon has to be stopped. I'm taking your advice and Doc Wallace's this time. The two of us can't fight Hashmark. We might hold out for a spell, spill some blood and such, but that's not the way I want it. I've had enough of that. And now that I know who murdered the Cargills, I think I've got my hands on the whip."

"You know this?"

"In a way. That rider, Gabe, was there. So was Ben Childers. Don't know who the third man was, but it can be found out."

Rosales was silent for a time. A young rabbit, attracted by the fire's glow, hopped into the circle of light, paused briefly, and then scampered back into the brush.

"There are those in Crocketville who will help? Good friends, perhaps?"

"It's the sheriff I intend to see. I don't know who he is, but that doesn't matter. He's got authority over the peace officers in the entire county . . . over town marshals like Yancey. I'm going to tell him what's going on here in the valley and that our local lawman can't . . . or won't do anything about it. I think when he hears the story and I tell him I'll testify against Gabe and Childers, he'll be willing to step in. He can't ignore a murder complaint."

Rosales bobbed his head. "It is so. If he is a man of honor, he will come."

"And just to throw a tight loop around things, I aim to bring him in to the ranch . . . to the Circle S. Fallon's going to raid us, either tonight or in the morning. Same as said he would. Having the sheriff standing there when they hit us ought to convince him quick."

Rosales sucked slowly on his cigarette, now a brief stub. Regretfully he flipped it into the fire.

"But if the raid comes tonight, there will be no one there."

"Sure . . . but they'll come back. They'll figure we've hid out . . . so they'll try again. Fallon's got to get rid of us, once and for all."

"It is so," the *vaquero* said.

"Means you're to keep away from the ranch tonight," Mace said, rising. "Don't go anywhere near it. Best you stay right here where you won't run into any of the Hashmark bunch. I'll swing by here with the sheriff in the morning. Then we can all go on to the ranch."

"I shall be waiting, *muchacho.*"

"Good," Mace said. "I expect I'd better be on the move." He reached into his pocket for the sack of tobacco and the packet of papers, and handed them to the old man. "You might as well have these. I sort of got out of the habit during the war."

Chopo's eyes brightened. "*Gracias, hijo mio,*" he murmured happily. "To an old one the *cigarillo* is the good medicine."

"Enjoy it," Seevert said, walking to the sorrel. He looked the horse over critically in the faint light. The gelding wasn't in too bad a condition despite the long, hard day. A meal of freshly cut hay and the brief rest had done him considerable good. But it would be a long trip over the country that lay between the *malpais* and Crocketville.

Jerking the sorrel's reins free, he wheeled the horse around and led him across the clearing. Rosales, a fresh cigarette dripping from the corner of his mouth, studied the gelding.

"Were my animal of better quality than yours," he said, "I would offer him to you. But, alas, he is of small value. Like his master, there is a peak of strength quickly reached."

Mace stepped to the saddle. "The sorrel will make it. He's tough. But thanks anyway, old one. I'll see you in the morning. *Adiós.*"

"*¡Adiós!*" Rosales called into the soft night. "*Vaya con Dios.*"

XII

Go with God. Mace grinned tightly as he guided the sorrel down the steep trail. He would need all the help he could get. Crocketville was a hard ride—and to make the round trip in time, he must cross Hashmark range.

He could go around, of course, follow the usual roads that skirted Fallon property, but that would consume too many hours. And the success of his plan depended upon the sheriff's being there when the rancher's gunmen made their attack. He must risk encountering Hashmark's men, and, while they likely would not be any of the hardcase bunch but only ordinary cowhands, they would still challenge his presence. Any stranger riding across private range, particularly at night, took his chances.

He reached the floor of the cañon, immediately cut to the left. There was a trail a short distance on, he recalled, that led to the opposite rim. By using it he could save a full half hour's traveling.

When he gained that crest, he allowed the sorrel to rest a few minutes, and then, facing east, he struck out. The gelding fell into an easy lope across the grassy flats and Mace wished the entire journey might be so comfortable and pleasant. A cool breeze played against his face and the light from the myriad of stars overhead brightened the land and transformed it into a thing of beauty. Far back in the higher hills a coyote chorus was in progress. He listened idly, always intrigued by the discordant chain of eerie sounds as they echoed from ridge to ridge. Elsewhere other wild dwellers of the buttes and arroyos rested, waited for the coming day and what it might bring to them—continued life or sudden, violent death in the cycle Nature prescribed for its creatures.

What would the day hold for him? He pondered that question as the sorrel moved on through the night. His plan could go wrong; Con Fallon might be more powerful than he thought—his influence reaching well beyond Panhandle Valley. He could be building a snare for himself by bringing in an outside lawman. But his own respect for law and order dictated such a course. Perhaps it was the teachings of old Tom Seevert imbedded deeply in his conscience, or possibly it was the after-effects of the war—a war fought to prove the sanctity of authority. At any rate Mace Seevert looked first to the law to solve the problems that faced him and the valley.

But if that same law, which he held in such lofty esteem, failed to do its duty, one he knew to be just, then he was ready to resort to the old methods—the power and speed of a gun. He might be branded outlaw in so doing, but that would trouble him little. Con Fallon was wrong, and he was in the right; that, as wise old Chopo Rosales had once observed, was all the reason a man required to draw his next breath—to know he is right.

He realized with a start that he was on Hashmark land. Gaining a summit, he halted and dropped from the saddle. Leaving the sorrel to rest, he moved a few paces ahead and threw his glance in a long search across the silvered world. There should be campfires—several of them. And at each there would be Hashmark riders. Abruptly his gaze checked.

To the north a faint, red eye winked fitfully in the star shine. Two miles away, he calculated. He must keep to the south to avoid the camp. He could expect others, however, and for them he needed to be alert. He returned to the gelding, mounted, and pressed on.

A mile deeper in Fallon country he struck a second herd. It had bedded down in a small valley, and Mace cut back to the north, skirted the oblong mass of dark bodies, and the three night hawks hunkered about the campfire, drinking coffee.

He was making good time, and the sorrel was bearing up well. In two more hours, barring accidents and unforeseen delays, he should be in Crocketville. His one worry then would be to locate the sheriff and convince him of the need to step in and take a hand in the affairs of Panhandle Valley. The lawman's return with him to Circle S was an absolute necessity. But if he refused—Mace brushed the possibility aside; it could happen but he would not worry over it until it came to pass. He. . . .

The sorrel reared suddenly, shied to the right. Seevert grabbed frantically at the saddle horn to keep from being thrown, struggled to get the horse under control. They were in a wide, sandy arroyo densely overgrown with brush. He glanced about and tried to determine what had spooked the gelding. A moment later a lone steer, curved horns shining in the starlight, burst into the open.

The old mossyhorn had been hiding in the underbrush and Seevert's approach had startled him. He had bolted down the wash, setting up a loud *clatter* in his passage. A yell went up.

"Who's that?" a raspy voice demanded.

Mace had succeeded in quieting the trembling sorrel. He swore softly under his breath. He had blundered into a third herd, apparently halted nearby. The racket the steer had set up had aroused at least one of the riders. Tension settled over Seevert as he waited, eyes on the rim of the arroyo ahead. Moments later the Hashmark man appeared. He probed the wash with his eyes.

The steer had come to a stand and now there was only the hush of the night. The rider raised himself in his stirrups, looked to his left, then the right. Mace could feel the sweat beads breaking out on his forehead. If the sorrel made the smallest move, their presence would be detected—and he could afford no problems with Hashmark at this point. Motionless as a stone image, he rode out the breathless moments.

A stick popped loudly. The sound came from the direction into which the maverick had fled. In the stillness it seemed sharp as a gunshot. Mace felt relief course through him. The steer had decided to move again. Instantly the Hashmark rider wheeled and trotted his horse along the ravine to investigate the noise further. Seevert relaxed and brushed at the moisture accumulated on his face.

He waited until he could no longer see the silhouetted shape of the cowhand, and then put the gelding into motion. He swung hard right into the arroyo, figuring the herd lay directly ahead. He was right, he saw, when, a half mile later, he caught sight of the camp. Stumbling upon the old steer had actually been a piece of good fortune; had he not, he would have ridden blindly into the camp.

There were no more delays after that and he reached Crocketville and pulled up before the sheriff's office shortly before midnight. The town was closed down except for saloons and the lawman's quarters. Dismounting, he entered. A graying man with a skull-like face sporting a long handle-bar mustache glanced up.

"Something I can do for you?"

Mace nodded. He could see no star on the man's vest. He said: "I'm looking for the sheriff."

"That's me. Name's Glyde . . . Carl Glyde. What's the trouble?"

Mace extended his hand. "I'm Mace Seevert. From over Panhandle Valley way. We need your help." He paused, added: "Ever hear of a man called Con Fallon?"

Glyde drew his brows together, drummed on his desk with his fingertips. Seevert waited. The answer would be all important, if the lawman knew Fallon, was a friend. . . .

"Nope," Glyde said finally. "Can't say as I ever heard of him."

Again a sigh slipped from Mace Seevert's lips. He leaned against the desk. "I'd like to tell you about my problems and ask you to ride back with me tonight."

"Tonight?" the sheriff echoed.

"Yes, sir. It's important that we be there in the morning."

Glyde stirred, settled back in his chair. "All right, Seevert. Let's hear it."

An hour later they were in the saddle, heading back. Mace had laid the situation before the lawman, sparing none of the details. He had finished up by setting forth his plan for trapping Fallon's gunmen when they appeared at Circle S. Glyde had listened attentively and agreed that it was high time something was done.

Now, as they rode on through the night, brightened additionally by a late moon, the lawman said: "I heard talk once or twice about trouble over your way. Howsomever, I figured the marshal would send word to me if things was getting out of hand. Seems I should have done it on my own."

"You'd wait forever if you stood back until Harper sent for you," Mace said. And then, because of friendship and the fact that he was unsure in his own mind of Yancey's exact position, he added: "He's a proud man."

Glyde wagged his head. "A failing that's not good."

Shortly before daylight they reached the *malpais* and joined Chopo Rosales. After introductions, they rode on. The *vaquero*, reserved as always in the presence of strangers, dropped back and maintained a position a dozen paces behind the two other men.

Reaching the crumbling remains of the ranch, they pulled in from the rear after first making a quick survey to be certain none of Hashmark's riders were there before them. Mace wished there were time to look about and determine if Fallon's men had been there during the night, but he dared not risk it. Dismounting in the yard behind the house, Mace turned to Rosales.

"Keep the sheriff's horse out of sight. Leave ours here at the rail."

As the *vaquero* hurried to place the animals, Mace and Glyde entered the structure, took up positions in the one-time parlor where they could observe anyone approaching from the east. Rosales soon rejoined them.

"Unless I'm figuring wrong," Seevert said, "they'll be riding in about now. Fallon's the impatient kind when it comes to something like this. He'll want to get it over with. He can't afford to let me live."

Glyde tugged at his mustache. "Since you're willing to testify against that pair of his in this here Cargill killing, I can't see that it makes much difference."

"Except Fallon will deny he had any part in it. This . . . you personally hearing and seeing what's going to be said and done ought to make a strong case against him . . . so strong he won't be able to squirm out."

Glyde said: "Reckon you're right. If he's big as you claim, it'll take a right smart of evidence to pin something on him. Who'd you say . . . ?"

"They come!" Chopo Rosales warned from his place at the window.

Mace and Glyde moved to the *vaquero*'s side immediately. Four riders broke into the open, and halted. They remained at the edge of the clearing for a time, and then came on slowly. Mace studied them closely, not a little surprised. He had not thought Yancey Harper would be so brazen, so bold about it— but there he was, in company with Zapf, Tucker, and Ben Childers.

"Guess that proves where the marshal stands," he said quietly.

Glyde shifted on his feet. In the pale morning light, his skin, drawn tightly over the bones of his face, looked like parchment.

"What . . . ?" he said, and quickly fell silent as Yancey Harper's voiced reached across the clearing.

"Mace! Mace Seevert, you hear me?"

"I hear you," Seevert replied after a moment.

"Throw down your guns and come out. I'm arresting you for the murder of Con Fallon."

XIII

Con Fallon—murdered! The impact of that statement was like a solid blow to Seevert. The word that the rancher had been killed was shock enough in itself—but to be accused of the crime was incredible. He turned slowly, his senses stunned by the charge, faced Carl Glyde. The lawman's cold eyes were drilling into him suspiciously, questioningly.

"Something's wrong, Sheriff," he said. "They're loco . . . plumb loco. Last time I saw Fallon he was plenty alive."

"Mace . . . you hear me? Come out with your hands reaching. You don't, I'll have to start shooting."

Glyde whirled, stepped through the doorway into the neglected yard. He squared himself before the men. A startled oath ripped from Yancey Harper's lips.

"Sheriff! What the devil you doing here?"

Ignoring that question, Glyde said: "You making a murder charge against Seevert?"

"I am," Zapf broke in. "Doubt if you know me, Sheriff, but I'm Charles Zapf, owner of the Hashmark spread." He paused, apparently to let the proud words sink in. Glyde was unimpressed.

"Seevert ambushed Fallon," Zapf continued. "Was late yesterday."

"You make it sound like you saw him do it."

"He was the only one who could have. Maybe I didn't actually see him pull the trigger . . . but it has to be him."

Anger overcame the surprise that gripped Mace. Zapf was lying unless . . . he spun swiftly and stared at Rosales. The old *vaquero*, hoping to be of help, could have paid Fallon a visit during the evening after Mace had ridden off to Crocketville. He could have slain the rancher and returned to the *malpais* well before daylight.

Rosales, hand resting on the butt of his worn pistol, was watching Zapf and the others through narrowed eyelids. Mace took a step toward him, halted when Glyde's flat, emotionless voice caught him.

"What about all this, Seevert?"

Mace walked into the yard. Meeting Zapf's gaze, he said: "You're a liar, Charlie. And you know it."

Zapf flushed. "Don't know nothing of the kind! You rode off yesterday . . . you and the Mex . . . taking Fallon with you at gunpoint. You threatened to kill him if he didn't do what you told him. When he didn't come back, three, four hours later, me and the boys went looking for him. We found him, all right . . . dead. Bullet in his back."

The sheriff's eyes were still upon Mace. "Seems I recollect

your telling me about seeing this Fallon, but I don't remember your threatening to kill him."

Seevert shrugged helplessly. "I could have said it. Probably did. I was plenty riled at the time, and anxious to get out of there. I knew if I couldn't force Fallon to ride with us, we'd never make it."

The lawman's features were expressionless. "Figuring the hour you walked into my office, you would have had time to circle by Fallon's place. And you were on his range most of the way. Did you see him?"

"Hell, no, I didn't!" Mace exploded suddenly at the end of his patience. "I rode across Hashmark, sure, but all I saw were a couple of cowhands!" Seevert caught himself. Losing his head would only make it worse. He faced Glyde, locked his gaze with that of the lawman. "I never killed Fallon, Sheriff. I swear it. And I haven't seen him since we turned him back on the road."

Zapf shifted on his saddle. "What did you expect him to say? You think he'd admit it? The way he was feeling when he left the ranch house, holding a gun on Con, I'm surprised he didn't do it right there in the yard. He was plenty stirred up, Sheriff. I had a hunch something like this was going to happen."

"Hunches don't count much as evidence," Glyde said dryly. He swung his attention to Harper. "What's your thinking on this, Marshal? You're not saying much."

Yancey smiled. "No need, not with you taking over. I'm still trying to figure out why you're here."

"Seevert came after me last night. Told me about this Fallon and the high-handed way he was doing things in the valley. Said Fallon was trying to take his ranch away from him and asked me to step in before blood was shed."

"He could have come to me," Yancey said slowly.

"Claims he did . . . leastwise about some folks name of Cargill he says were murdered. Told me he couldn't get you to do anything about it, so he figured there was no use going to you on this."

Harper drew himself up stiffly. "I'm working on that Cargill killing, doing my best to find out who did it. But I've got no proof to go on . . . nothing. He seems to think Fallon was behind it, but that doesn't mean anything. You know how things go. Every time something goes wrong, folks blame the big rancher for it."

Mace could scarcely control his voice. "Did you ask that rider of Fallon's named Gabe how he got that bullet hole in his arm? Did you question Ben Childers about being an expert with blasting powder?"

"No proof there, either. Can you recognize the hole a bullet from your gun puts in a man when it hits him?"

Seevert swore in deep disgust. Glyde lifted his hand. "I figure it's a fair question he asked you, Marshal. Did you?"

"He'd be wasting his time," Zapf said with a laugh. "Seevert says this happened at the Cargill place yesterday morning. The two boys he's trying to accuse were on my north range, helping move some stock. I've got a half dozen hired hands up there who'll swear to it. Anyway, that's not what we're talking about. We're talking about who killed Con Fallon."

Glyde looked down. "I expect you're right. It's another matter . . . one I'll be thinking on."

That helpless feeling swept through Mace Seevert again. He was trapped, neatly caught in a web of lies made plausible by his own actions.

"You're lying, Charlie!" he yelled. "I'll say it again! Maybe I was stirred up enough to kill Fallon, but I didn't. The big reason I went for Sheriff Glyde is I didn't want it to come to shooting."

"Or maybe you bushwhacked Con, then went after the sheriff, so's you'd have a good alibi. Makes a fine story, only it won't carry water, mister."

"The hell. . . ."

"All right, all right!" Glyde shouted to make himself heard above Seevert's raging voice. "Just all of you simmer down. Getting all riled won't help nothing. This arguing back and forth won't, either." He paused and looked squarely at Mace. "It boils down to this. You had yourself a big row with Fallon. There was bad blood between you over this property you claim's yours. . . ."

"It is mine!"

"Over your property. You went to see Fallon. . . ."

"I was going on my own, until Zapf, there, showed up with a couple of hardcases and forced my hand."

"Anyway, you say Fallon warned you to get off your property and stay off. Then you left, taking him along at gunpoint as a hostage. Later Fallon was found dead with a bullet in his back. It's circumstantial, but it points to you as the killer, no matter how you slice it. I. . . ."

"That's exactly how I see it, Sheriff," Zapf chimed in, nodding his head in satisfaction. "You won't have no trouble proving it, either."

Glyde, patient to the extreme, remained silent until Zapf had finished. Then: "I don't see how I can do anything but hold you, Seevert. If you didn't do it, you'll get your chance to prove it in front of the judge."

"Chance," Mace echoed bitterly. "How can I do anything locked in a cell? This bunch will rig things to look anyway they like."

The sheriff scowled. "I doubt that. The law does a little better job of looking out for a man than you may think." He reached forward, lifted Seevert's pistol from its holster, and glanced at Harper.

"You want to take over now, Marshal? I expect the circuit

judge'll be through here in a week or so."

Yancey moved his head doubtfully. "Sheriff, I'd consider it a favor if you'd handle it . . . take him back to Crocketville for trial. Con Fallon was a big man in these parts. Well liked and respected. Folks are going to be mighty upset when they hear about him getting murdered, and I sure wouldn't have much luck stopping a lynch party, was it to get started."

"He's right," Zapf said. "Seevert would never live to go to trial around here."

Glyde tugged at his mustache. "All right, I'll take charge. You keep it quiet for the rest of the day, give me time to reach Crocketville. Meanwhile, be getting together all the evidence you can . . . some witnesses if you can find any. I'll drop back in a couple of days and see how you're coming along."

Mace, fighting desperately to remain calm in the face of the inevitable, grasped Glyde's arm. "Sheriff, can't you see this is nothing but a frame up? Somebody else killed Fallon and they're trying to unload the blame on me. It could be Zapf. He had reasons."

"What kind of reasons?" the lawman asked, pulling away.

"He was partners with Fallon. Hearing them talk yesterday, I'd say they weren't getting on so good."

Zapf came up straight on his saddle. "What kind of talk's that?"

"The way you and Fallon were snapping at each other, like a couple of strange dogs. Maybe you got a belly full of doing his dirty work for him. It could be you decided to end the partnership."

"And maybe I could've rode a mule to the moon," Zapf shot back. "Only I didn't. Sure, Con and me had words now and then. Show me a partnership where it doesn't happen. No two men ever agree exactly on everything. I expect that's natural, ain't it, Sheriff?"

Glyde said: "I reckon so, but you can figure on explaining all that at the trial." He faced Seevert. "Let's get started, son. There's a long ride ahead of us."

A protest welled up in Mace Seevert's throat, and then, realizing the futility of it, he let it die. It was best he go along with Glyde who was only doing what he considered right and his duty. Once they were alone, he might, possibly, convince the lawman of certain facts, make him see that it was all a put-up job, that Charlie Zapf was in reality, the best murder suspect.

He said—"I'm ready, Sheriff."—and wheeled, intending to speak with Chopo Rosales. He wanted to tell the *vaquero* to ride to Berrendo Crossing, advise Wallace of the unexpected twist of events. He would need character witnesses, all he could scrape up; the physician was his one hope of accomplishing it.

He pulled up short, masking his surprise. Chopo Rosales had disappeared.

XIV

The possibility that the *vaquero*, out of a misplaced sense of devotion, had killed Con Fallon flashed through Seevert's mind again; his abrupt disappearance now lent further credence to the thought. Striving to make no issue of the matter and thus draw attention to it, Mace moved on toward the horses. If Rosales chose flight, either because of his own guilt, or because he did not relish sharing blame with him, let him go, Mace decided—and good luck.

But such flight was not in character insofar as the Chopo Rosales he knew was concerned. Many changes had come to pass in Panhandle Valley, however, so it was conceivable that the *vaquero* had changed, too. *Not Chopo . . . not Chopo Rosales,* Mace assured himself, stubbornly amending his own thoughts. The old *vaquero* would never forsake him, regardless of the consequences.

But if Rosales's absence escaped Glyde's attention, it was not missed by Charlie Zapf: "Say . . . where's the Mex? You want him, too, Sheriff."

Glyde said—"Hold up a second, Seevert."—and pivoted on his heel. He made a quick search of the room through the doorway. "He was here a bit ago," he said, frowning.

"Him and Seevert's working together," Zapf said. "I figure one's as guilty as the other. You got to hold him, too."

"I know that," the lawman said testily. He came about to Mace. "What happened to him?"

Seevert lifted his hands, then let them fall to his sides. "How do you expect me to know? Last time I saw him he was standing at the window."

The sheriff's eyes narrowed. "You right sure you didn't give him the high sign and send him off somewheres?"

"How could I? I was out here in the yard with you all the time."

Glyde considered that at length. "Well," he said, "there's nothing I can do about it. I expect he just took a notion he'd better run for it. It won't matter. I'll come back for him once you're locked up."

"Leave it to me and the boys," Zapf said. "Won't take us long to lay him by the heels."

"Forget it!" Glyde snapped. "You and your crew stay clean out of it. It's a job for the law, not a gang of trigger-happy vigilantes. Marshal," he said, looking at Harper, "that's a chore for you. Find the Mexican, lock him up in your jail until I come for him. He can't have gone far."

Yancey said: "Sure thing, Sheriff. But I'm thinking something. That Mex has known Mace there since the day he was born. Sort of raised him, in fact. Was I you, I'd keep my eyes peeled for an ambush."

"Good advice," Zapf said hurriedly. "Be glad to have my boys ride escort for you."

"Don't bother," Glyde answered, bristling slightly. "I think I can do my job without any help."

"Whatever you say. Childers and Tuck ain't got nothing else to do, rest of the day."

The lawman, thoroughly aroused, paused beside his horse. He touched Zapf with a withering glance. "If the time comes when I need help taking in one prisoner, I'll shuck my badge," he said.

Unbuckling the straps of his left saddlebag, he thrust Seevert's pistol into it, and then produced a short length of rawhide. Facing Mace, he said: "Hold out your hands."

Seevert did as directed, and the lawman lashed his wrists together. "Now mount up," Glyde directed. "You'll be leading out. Just remember I'll have a gun on you all the time."

"There's not much I can do with my hands tied," Seevert said, and crossed to where the sorrel waited.

The lawman followed him to the rail, waited while Mace climbed onto the gelding. "Just don't get any ideas," he said.

Seevert nodded, and they moved on out of the yard. As they passed Zapf and the others, Glyde ducked his head at Yancey. "I'm depending on you to keep these people in line. I don't want any more trouble over here . . . and get busy hunting that Mexican fellow."

Harper touched the brim of his hat with two fingers. "Yes, sir, Sheriff," he said. There was a tinge of mockery in his voice, but if Carl Glyde noticed it, he gave no sign.

They rode on in silence. Mace was thinking of the warning given to the lawman by Harper. It was possible Chopo Rosales did intend to set him free somewhere along the route to Crocketville. Such would explain his sudden disappearance—and it made more sense than believing the *vaquero* had deserted to save his own skin. If true, he was glad the sheriff had refused

Zapf's offer of escort; against Glyde, Chopo would have an even chance, but opposing the sheriff and two of Hashmark's ablest gunmen, the odds would be too great.

The miles crawled by as the day's heat began to set in. Hunger, too, was making itself felt. Seevert turned, glanced over his shoulder.

"Got anything in your saddlebags a man could eat?"

Glyde said: "No, only some coffee beans and a can to make it in."

"Little coffee'd go pretty good right now."

"Later," the lawman said. "Soon as we reach the hills. I'd like to get away from your place before we pull up."

Mace laughed. "Who're you scared of most, Sheriff? The *vaquero* or Zapf and his crowd?"

Glyde angered instantly. "None of them, mister . . . and don't you forget it! And while we're riding, you'd better be doing some thinking about yourself. You're in a plenty bad way. Was I you, I don't believe I'd do much laughing."

"Meaning you think I'm telling the truth . . . and Zapf's not, and all I. . . ."

"Meaning no such thing. I go by the evidence and so far it appears to bear out what he claims. You got any hole cards, boy, you better be looking at them."

Glyde was right, Mace realized, settling down on his saddle. He was in a tight spot with nothing to back his story. He hadn't shot Con Fallon, of course, but proving it was going to be a big job. He couldn't voice his suspicions of Chopo Rosales, either, as a means for throwing the blame off himself. His feeling for the old *vaquero* was such that he could never save himself at the expense of the Mexican. And if Rosales were not guilty, he'd stay with his belief that Charlie Zapf had pulled the trigger. There was more than just an ordinary, everyday difference of opinion existing between the partners; it was not difficult to see

180

that matters had reached the point of hostility and bad blood. But how could he prove it? Tucker and Childers, and all the other Hashmark men, would swear to anything Zapf asked; he could expect to gain nothing where they were concerned. The same applied to Yancey Harper. He was jigging to Zapf's tune, just as he had been to Fallon's. There was no doubt of it now. Mace swore softly; where does a man turn when he's up against a stone wall?

The morning lengthened, hot and dusty, laying its mark on both Seevert and his weary sorrel. Both needed rest—and food. To take his mind off that, Mace again thought of Rosales. If the *vaquero* did plan a rescue, he should do it soon. There had been better places for ambush farther back on the trail, areas thick with brush; they were heading into open country at this point and opportunities for concealment would be few. But there was no assurance that Chopo Rosales contemplated such a move; it had been no more than a thought, an idea advanced by Yancey Harper. The *vaquero* could be miles away at that moment, riding in the opposite direction for the Mexican border.

Near mid-morning they reached the long, rolling bench of hills that Glyde had designated as their first stopping point. There were no trees to offer shade from the glaring sun, so they halted in a deep arroyo where a scatter of brush provided a smattering of shelter.

"Have some coffee ready in a bit," Glyde said, dismounting and beginning to scrape together a pile of dry sticks and leaves. "Just set yourself down there under that greasewood where I can keep an eye on you while I'm about it."

The lawman was showing the effects of the ride, too, Mace noted as he came off the sorrel. The skin on his face seemed to have stretched even tighter and had taken on a grayish color. But the proud old lawman had voiced no complaints—and he was not likely to.

Mace took time to loosen the sorrel's saddle girth to allow the horse as much relief as possible, then squatted in the thin shade of the bush. Glyde got his fire going and placed a small lard tin, half filled with water from his canteen, over the flames.

"Found a couple of pieces of jerky," the lawman said, reaching into his pocket. "Little old, but it ought to help a bit."

He handed a strip of the tough, dried beef to Mace. "How about a swallow of water?"

"Could use it," Seevert replied.

He took a drink from the canteen, then ripped a piece off the chunk of jerky with his teeth. It was dry as paper, offered little in the way of flavor, but it was something for his stomach. He studied Glyde, at that moment adding crushed coffee beans to the simmering water.

"Sheriff, forgetting for the moment that you're the law, how do you really figure this deal? You think I bushwhacked Fallon . . . that it's the way Zapf claims?"

Glyde dumped the last of the beans into the tin, prepared to lift it off the fire when it boiled up.

"I go by the book, by the evidence," he said. "It sure don't point anywhere but at you. But judging men, and I've been doing that for thirty years or better, I'd be mighty skittish about that man Zapf. The same goes for that marshal you got, too."

"Meaning you'd maybe trust me when you wouldn't either one of them?"

"That's about the size of it."

"Then why not put some of that trust to work, Sheriff? Once I'm locked in a cell, I haven't got a ghost of a chance to prove I'm innocent. Turn me loose for one week . . . seven days, so's I can move around, dig up some facts that I'll need to clear myself. I don't know where I'll find them, or what they'll be, but there's bound to be something, somewhere. If I can't turn them up, I'll ride into Crocketville and turn myself in to you for trial."

"Can't do a thing like that, son, even was I a mind to."

"Why? The way things stack up, I've got nobody left to give me a hand. I have to do it all myself." Mace spat out the tasteless meat, regarded Glyde anxiously.

"I'll be doing all I can," the lawman said. "If you ain't guilty, I sure wouldn't want your hanging on my conscience."

"If a week's too long, make it three days. You've got my word I'll be back."

"Better save your breath," Glyde said wearily, all the friendliness gone from his tone.

The coffee boiled up in a savory bulge. The lawman sat the lard tin on the ground, picked up a twig, and stirred its foamy contents. He rose, walked to his horse, dug around in the saddlebags until he located a cup.

"You can use this," he said, tossing it to Mace. "I'll do my drinking from the bucket. . . ."

His words trailed off into silence. Mace looked up questioningly. Glyde was staring at something beyond him, something at the edge of the arroyo. The lawman's jaw had clamped shut and his eyes were glittering. Mace Seevert's hopes lifted as the familiar voice of Rosales reached him.

"You will please not to move, *jefe*. Even a poor shooter such as I could not miss with the *pistola* at so close a distance."

XV

Mace sprang to his feet. Guilty or not—Chopo had not forsaken him! He grinned at the *vaquero*.

"Been worrying some about you," he said, and moved to his side.

"It was not possible to come sooner," Rosales replied. With his free hand he drew his knife. "Those two *bribóns* . . . Tucker and Childers . . . they have been like coyotes on your trail. I had to keep in the shadows until they turn back." He leaned forward, slashed the cord that bound Seevert's wrists.

Rubbing his hands together briskly to restore circulation, Mace slanted a glance at Glyde. "Seems Zapf gave you an escort anyway."

The lawman made no answer. Mace crossed to Glyde's horse and recovered his pistol. He returned, pulled the sheriff's weapon from its holster, ejected the shells, and shoved it back into its leather case. With a second strip of rawhide found in the saddlebags he bound the lawman's wrists.

"Hate to do this, Sheriff," he said.

Glyde's face was grim. "Then don't. It's only going to make things worse for you."

"Maybe, but I sure couldn't help myself any locked in your jail. I'll stand by my offer. I'll turn myself in to you at Crocketville in seven days, whether I've cleared myself or not. Don't figure it'll take that long. If Zapf's the man who murdered Fallon, I'll dig up proof and bring him in."

"Or kill him."

Mace paused, his features suddenly stilled. After a long moment, he said: "No, Sheriff. I've had all that I want. The reason I went for you in the first place was to keep that from happening. I'll take him alive . . . unless he forces my hand."

"You're a fool if you think he'll just give in. Anyway, I don't figure you'll get the chance to do much. I'll be right on your trail."

"There's the little matter of getting loose and then finding us," Mace said. He held up the lard tin of coffee. "Do you want some of this before you move out?"

Glyde shook his head and turned to his horse. Spurning Seevert's offer of help, he grasped the saddle horn with his locked hands and stepped aboard. Face hard, he looked down at Mace. "What's next?"

"You're going back to Crocketville," Seevert said, and slapped the lawman's horse on the rump smartly.

Glyde struck off up the trail to the east, glancing neither right nor left, his shoulders stiff and set.

Rosales said: "Would it not be better to make of him a prisoner? He has the blood of a badger. He will not quit easy."

"Better, maybe. But we don't want to get crossways with the law any more than we have to. And we better get out of here fast. He's bound to run into somebody before he gets very far that'll turn him loose."

"We go to where?" the *vaquero* asked, dropping back to get his pinto. "There is no safety any place."

"I realize that, but I've got to do some nosing around." Seevert tightened the slack girth on the sorrel and mounted. He waited for Rosales to move in beside him, the question that plagued him now pushing to the fore in his mind. He was still convinced that Zapf was the killer, but there was that one, thin thread of doubt. He caught Chopo's eyes, held them.

"*Viejo,* I need the truth from you."

Rosales frowned. "What is this, *muchacho?*"

"Did you shoot Fallon when I went for the sheriff?"

The Mexican shook his head. "Perhaps this is a thing I would have like to do . . . but I did not."

"You never left the *jacal* during the night?"

"I did not. I give you my word of honor."

"That's plenty for me," Mace said, relieved. He gazed out over the sunlit hills. "Has to be Zapf. He's the only logical one."

"With this I am also sure," Rosales said, having some difficulty with words. "This nosing around, as you call it . . . you have a plan?"

"Nothing for certain. We've got the advantage now. Zapf and the rest of Hashmark thinks I'm with Glyde, on my way to jail.

That'll let us move around easier . . . except they'll be looking for you."

"It will be for them good exercise," Rosales said with an offhand wave.

The horses were walking slowly down the trail. Seevert smiled, still considering their best move. "If I could get into Fallon's office, do some looking around, I might come up with something. Or if we could nab Zapf, take him back in the hills, and make him talk. . . ."

"A frightened man often speaks the truth," the *vaquero* said, "but it would be difficult. He has many to stay by his side. The risk would be great."

"Looks like I'll have to take a few chances if I'm to prove I didn't bushwhack Fallon. Have you got any ideas?"

The *vaquero*'s dark face was solemn. "I am sorry I am of no help. I think of nothing," he said. "But there is a saying among my people that when you would learn of the eagle, go first to the nest. Thus I believe you do the right thing. It is the doing that disturbs me greatly."

"Might not be so hard," Seevert said. "Remember the hill that's right behind the Harper house . . . the one that looks like an old volcano?"

"I remember it well."

"We could hole up there and watch. You can see about everything that goes on around the place. Could just about tell when the house is empty . . . or when Zapf was alone."

"It is never wise to enter the den of a wolf. Better to watch and wait and capture this *bribón* when he has no friend nearby. Also there will be need of food and water."

"I thought of that. You head for your *jacal*, pick us up some grub and a canteen of water. I'll go on to the hill. There's a cave about two-thirds of the way to the top . . . on the side facing the ranch. I'll be there."

"As you say," Rosales murmured. "I will go now. By crossing the mesa here I can save much time. You will have care in reaching this cave, *muchacho?*"

"Careful as I can be," Mace replied. "You do the same. Don't forget they're looking for you."

Chopo smiled, said—"I don't forget. *Adiós.*"—and pulled away.

Mace immediately cut to the opposite direction, also abandoning the trail and striking out across the open country. It was an area of many ravines, shallow washes, and brush, and he had little fear of being noticed unless he blundered accidentally into some of Hashmark's riders. Such was not likely, however; it was a nonproductive section of the ranch, actually wasteland, and there would be no reason for hired hands to be working it.

Late in the morning he reached the plateau that surrounded the bowl-like depression in which Sam Harper had erected his buildings. There was a minimum of cover to be had and Seevert proceeded with greater caution. Because of the land's rolling contour, he was still not visible to the ranch itself, but now there was danger of meeting riders coming up from the hollow on their way to the distant range, and, conversely, returning from it. The cone-shaped hill where he planned to set his vigil stood behind the ranch house and its companion structures, so the most dangerous portion of the journey yet lay before him.

He had just gained the extreme eastern edge of the swale in which the ranch lay, and was congratulating himself on his good fortune, when the *thud* of approaching horses brought him to a halt. He looked about hurriedly, seeking a place in which to hide. There were no rock formations or stands of brush of sufficient size to conceal a man and horse, only shallow washes and arroyos barely below the level of the plain.

Choosing the deepest of these, he rode down into it, and dismounted quickly. He could not tell if the riders were headed directly toward him or not, only that they were drawing near. He listened carefully, deciding finally that there were two in the party. Evidently there was a trail ahead of him but he could not recall it from his knowledge of the country.

The hoof beats grew louder, nearer. Mace caught the drift of voices, wished that he might hear what was being said. But the *pound* of the horse's hoofs only hid their words.

The moments dragged on. The riders need only glance to their right and his presence would be noted—and there would be instant trouble. Such an encounter would have more than mere physical repercussions, however; Charlie Zapf would be made aware of his presence and realize that he had somehow gotten away from Sheriff Glyde. Hashmark would go into action and every rider in the area would be combing the country for him with shoot-to-kill instructions. His life would be worth less than a copper cent.

Abruptly the two men broke into view. They were to Seevert's left and slightly below the mesa. He checked an instinctive desire to duck low, knowing the slightest motion can be caught from the corner of a man's eye and draw attention. He watched the pair pass on by, two he vaguely recognized as having been among the seven he had encountered in Fallon's office. They were engaged in earnest conversation, totally unaware of all else around them.

Mace hung back until they topped a lower rise and started down the long swale that ended in the yard of the ranch, a good half mile to the south. When they were lost behind the hump of land, he mounted the sorrel and resumed the wide, swinging course he had been following. Only then did he realize he had been sweating profusely, that the tense moments had pulled tight his muscles and left him slightly stiff.

But that had worn off when he reached the foot of the hill and turned onto the trail that led to its crest. Dense clumps of brush and piles of rock covered the formation and it was no longer necessary to move with care. About midway he dismounted, picketed the sorrel on a small patch of grass, and continued on foot.

He found the cave filled with weeds blown into its mouth by the winds. He spent several minutes clearing away the powder-dry stalks and leaves, piling them below the opening to form an even better screen than Nature afforded. That done, he sat down to await Rosales, and observe the activities of Hashmark, sprawled below.

XVI

The first hours passed slowly. Mace watched men ride into Hashmark, others depart. Early in the afternoon one of the hired hands brought a buggy to the front of the house. He saw Fallon's stepdaughter and Zapf climb into it and drive off down the road to Berrendo Crossing. Two riders, Ben Childers and a man he did not know, followed. Likely the trip had something to do with Con Fallon's funeral.

By 3:00 p.m., the cave became uncomfortable and the slanting rays of the sun drilled into its shallow depth. Mace, seeking relief, crawled to its outer edge. He wished the *vaquero* would arrive; thirst was becoming a problem and his hunger was more pronounced. Considering the distance involved, Rosales should have made an appearance before that time. Of course, he could have been delayed; he could have encountered Hashmark riders and there may have been trouble. That thought stirred into life a vague worry.

He was becoming drowsy. On his feet without sleep for almost thirty-six hours, sprawled now in the hot sunshine, he found it difficult to keep his eyes open. He fought against it for a while, finally dozed off. He came awake with a start, in time to see the buggy wheel into the yard below. Only Charlie Zapf dismounted from it and Seevert guessed the girl had elected to spend the night in town.

Rosales had not arrived. Something had happened to the old *vaquero;* there was no doubt of it now. He turned his attention again to the yard as he sought to determine his next move. Smoke had begun to trickle skyward from the kitchen chimney as the cook set about preparing the evening meal. Mace swore angrily. He must have slept for the better part of three hours. He looked up. The sun was beginning to slip behind the ragged line of the *malpais* to the west. Night was not far off. As soon as it was full dark, he would leave the hill, start to search. . . .

Riders swept into the yard below, four men. Only a breath behind them came Yancey Harper. All stood for a few minutes before the hitch rack, and then, in a group, they started for the house.

As they mounted the steps, three more horsemen rushed onto the hard pack, coming in from the opposite direction. They halted, dismounted. Mace Seevert sat up abruptly. Something crowded into his throat and threatened to cut off his breath. One of the three, hunched forward and limping, was Chopo Rosales.

Anger ripped through Seevert as he watched the newcomers push the *vaquero* roughly toward the others who had paused on the gallery. The Mexican went to his knees. They jerked him upright, shoved him again. The distance was too great and the shadows too long for Mace to tell if Chopo had been seriously injured in any way by his captors, but it was apparent he had been in for some hard treatment.

Zapf appeared. There was a short period of conversation, and then all came off the porch and pointed for the peak-roofed, hulking barn that stood to the rear of the house. Two of Hash-mark's crew supported the Mexican between them. He seemed to be having trouble staying on his feet.

They passed from Seevert's view when they reached the front of the barn. Mace thought back, recalled the wide, double doors; evidently they were all going inside. Fear brightened in Seevert's mind. What was Zapf up to? If he were having Rosales locked in the barn for safekeeping, the entire party would not have trailed along. No—Charlie Zapf planned something else.

Mace delayed no further. He touched the butt of the pistol at his hip to assure himself of its presence, and then, keeping low, he crawled over the lip of the cave's mouth and began making his way downslope. In the hot flush of anger at Zapf, and his deep concern for Chopo Rosales, his own personal danger was forgotten; he knew only that he could not permit them to take out their hatred for him on the old *vaquero*.

Descending the hill was not difficult. Brush and rocks, coupled with the swiftly closing darkness, allowed him to reach the level behind the barn with no trouble. He crossed the narrow flat that separated the hill from the structure at a trot. When he gained the rough, plank wall of the barn, he halted, placed his ear to the wood, and listened.

He could hear nothing. Zapf and the others were at the far side. Drawing his pistol, Mace circled the building, reached the front. The house lay directly before him now—less than fifty yards distant. Anyone glancing out a rear window would see him.

He ignored that possibility, knowing he must risk it, and moved for the doors. One stood ajar. A lantern had been lit and a rectangle of yellow light marked the opening. He could hear voices, Zapf's and Yancey Harper's he thought, but he could not be certain. He reached the entrance.

". . . spit it out, Mex! You'd better do some talking unless you want your neck stretched! Where's he holed up?"

It was Ben Childers speaking. There was no mistaking his harsh tones. And there was no doubt, either, as to what was taking place inside the barn; they knew of his escape from Glyde, had caught Rosales, and were trying to force him to tell where Mace was hiding.

"I say nothing," the *vaquero* declared, his voice defiant.

"Hoist him up a mite, Tuck!"

Seevert threw caution to the wind. He stepped quickly through the doorway, gun ready in his hand.

"Forget it!" he barked, the fury boiling through him putting a razor edge to his words.

That anger mounted even higher as his eyes took in the scene. Zapf and Harper, with a half a dozen other Hashmark men, formed a circle around Rosales. A rope had been thrown over a rafter and the loop placed about the *vaquero*'s neck. Hands tied behind him, he had been pulled upward to the point where only the tips of his toes touched the dirt floor. He was gagging, struggling frantically.

"Turn loose that rope!" Seevert yelled at Tucker. "Turn loose . . . or, by God, I'll blow your head off!"

Tucker instantly released his grasp. Rosales collapsed in a heap. Eyes flaming, Mace turned on the men, now drawn back into a curved line.

"All of you . . . put your hands up . . . high! Keep them there! Do it quick or I'll shoot. I'd as soon kill you as step on a scorpion."

Harper and the Hashmark men complied immediately. There was no questioning the promise they saw in the raging Seevert. Only Zapf took his time. The corners of his mouth came down into a crooked grin.

"Seems I underestimated you, Mace. Never figured you'd get away from Glyde."

"You've made a lot of wrong guesses," Seevert snapped. "Get those arms up!"

He risked a glance at Rosales, hopeful the old *vaquero* had not been seriously injured. He could not expect to hold eight men at bay for long. And there was the possibility of others coming from the house. Relief flowed through him as Rosales stirred and sat up.

Childers shifted, doing it slowly and carefully. Mace caught the furtive movement and came to sharp attention.

"Don't try anything, Ben!"

Childers froze.

Zapf said: "Better do what he says. Probably figures another killing won't hang him any higher."

The *vaquero* stared at Seevert. His eyes were watery and he continually swallowed. He was still dazed but his senses were steadily returning.

Mace said: "No blood on my hands, Charlie . . . and you damn' well know it. But that doesn't mean I won't shoot if I have to."

"You're a fugitive from the law," Yancey Harper said, coming into the conversation. "I'm ordering you to throw down that gun and turn yourself over to me."

"So your friends can string me up, too?" Mace said with withering scorn. "I'm not that loco. I'll turn myself in after I've nailed the man who murdered Fallon, and not before. When I do . . . it'll be to Carl Glyde, not you."

Some of the tautness was leaving him. Rosales was getting slowly to his feet, a wry smile on his dark face. In the murky depths of the barn his teeth showed whitely as he moved toward Mace, the noose still about his neck.

"The gates of heaven were open for me, *muchacho*," he said. "You came not too soon."

"Lucky I was close," Seevert replied. "Hurry, *viejo*. We're pressing our luck here. Let me cut that rope around your wrists."

Ben Childers moved again. Instantly Mace challenged him. "Keep pushing me, Ben," he said softly, "and you'll get what you're asking for. You had the notion yesterday. You want to try me today?"

Childers shrugged. "You got maybe six slugs in that gun. Can't get us all."

"That's right . . . but there'll be three or four of you go down with me. You want to be the first?"

Zapf said: "Drop it, Ben. Our time's coming up. He can't get far."

Rosales, keeping well away from the Hashmark men, backed up to Mace who, drawing his knife, slashed the pigging string that linked the Mexican's wrists.

"Don't aim to run," Mace said. "Got a little job to finish right here."

The *vaquero* hurriedly pulled the rope from his neck, tossed it aside. Moving swiftly, he stepped behind the men, relieved them of their weapons, and threw them far back into the barn. With his own in his hand, he took up a stand next to Mace.

"There was no water trough nearby, *muchacho*," he said dryly.

Seevert could not suppress a grin. "No need. That will hold them long enough for us to get out of here. Bring your horse."

Rosales pivoted, darted through the doorway. Seevert began to back slowly for the exit. Reaching there, he halted, keeping clear of the opening. It was not going to be easy. The instant he and the *vaquero* were outside, Zapf and his men would race for their weapons, recover them, and open fire. True, there were no doors at the rear of the structure, but there were windows. Their best chance lay toward the hill. With luck they could reach it and be out of range before Hashmark began shooting.

There was a sound behind him. Rosales said: "I am here."

Mace nodded. "Move fast," he said. "We've got to jump clear, slam the door, and drop the bar. Then we make a run for the hill. Your horse will have to carry double."

"The sorrel, he is close?"

"Left him on the slope, near the trail. He's not far."

"It is good," Rosales said. "This *jaca* is of many years and tires soon. He cannot run far with a great burden."

"Just to the hill," Mace said. "All set?"

From his place outside the door, hands on the wooden crosspiece that would lock the heavy panels, the *vaquero* said: "*Sí, muchacho.*"

Seevert gave the sullen men eyeing him from the shadows of the barn a close look. "No mistakes now," he warned quietly. "Zapf's right. . . ."

Instantly he leaped backward through the opening. Rosales slammed the door, hurled the bar into place. A yell went up from the inside as they wheeled to Rosales's pinto. The *vaquero* was slow to the saddle and alarm mounted in Seevert as he vaulted up behind him. The horse came around, struck off across the yard, legging it for the slope.

They reached the narrow flat. Immediately, it seemed to Mace, guns began to *crackle* from the windows of the barn. He twisted half about, flung a shot at the nearest blossom of orange fire. A white hot, searing shock rocked him. An oath ripped from his lips as he almost fell from the laboring pinto. He had been hit.

XVII

Seevert fought to hold his place on the lunging horse. His left shoulder was numb and he had no strength in his arm. With the right, he clung to Rosales as they raced for the shelter of the brush. Behind them he could hear yelling in the yard—shouts to bring horses, curses as men stumbled over one another in their haste. Somehow they had gotten the door open.

The *vaquero*'s ancient horse tired fast under his double load and the steeply rising grade of the slope. Rosales turned his head to the side.

"Where, *muchacho?*"

"Near the trail . . . straight ahead . . . about halfway to the top."

Rosales veered his mount to the left and sliced diagonally across the hill. Seevert's shoulder was coming alive now as the anesthetic of shock began to wear off. Pain stabbed viciously through him with each jolting leap of the pinto. He peered into the half darkness and tried to focus his eyes.

"There's the trail!" he yelled into the Mexican's ear. "I'll drop off! You keep going!"

"To where?"

"Anywhere. Keep riding . . . we got to shake them. Meet you at the *jacal* . . . later."

"Not the *jacal, muchacho.* They know of it."

"Couple of miles north, then . . . where the salt cedars grow," Mace said, and pushed off the rump of the faltering horse.

He struck the ground, went sprawling onto the rocky, uneven surface. Pain wrenched a yell from his lips but he struggled to his feet, turned up the trail to find the sorrel. A dozen yards away Rosales, checked by Seevert's outcry, slowed, started to turn.

"Go on . . . go on!" Mace shouted, motioning to the *vaquero.* "I'm all right!"

Rosales bobbed his head, recovered, and rushed away. Seevert, stumbling over the rocky ground, scrambled on up the trail. His shoulder burned with a living fire and his arm hung limply at his side, but the need to reach the sorrel overrode all else. He could hear hoof beats off in the direction of the barn now and knew that Zapf and his Hashmark crew were getting under way. Yancey Harper would also be with them.

The gelding loomed up suddenly. Seevert gasped his relief. He couldn't have gone much farther. He was sucking deeply for wind and there was a lightness in his head, a vagueness that filled him with a detached, far-off feeling. But the deep-rooted instincts of self-preservation drove him on and forced him to mount the sorrel. He cut off the trail, choosing no particular route except away from the oncoming riders. Given his head, the weary gelding chose the line of least resistance, trotted off downgrade for the foot of the hill.

Mace was conscious of the hammering hoofs behind him as Zapf and the others swept by, moving north. Either someone in the party had spotted Chopo's line of flight, or they had simply assumed it would be the direction taken by the escaping men. He didn't know, or really care.

Some degree of awareness began to take control of his senses and he pulled to a stop. His burning left side felt warm, moist, and he knew he must do something to check the bleeding of the wound. Staying on the saddle, he searched out his bandanna, shaped it into a pad, tucked it beneath his shirt, and pressed it against the hole left by the bullet's passage. Lifting his shoulder slightly, he drew the cloth tighter against the pad and formed a crude pressure bandage.

He didn't know how much good it would do. He had already lost too much blood, and he was having difficulty holding himself upright on the sorrel. But he hung on, both hands locked about the saddle horn as the gelding once again plodded on into the night.

A breeze sprang up, sweeping in from the flats. It was cool and it played against Mace Seevert's feverish face, began subtly to wash some of the fog from his brain. He stirred, winced as pain slugged him mercilessly. He halted the sorrel and fumbled at the pad covering his wound.

The bleeding had ceased, and in the half light he sought to examine the injury. It was a clean wound. The bullet had passed entirely through his shoulder, luckily missing the bone. He wished he had some whiskey with him; washing the bullet hole with raw liquor would effectively cleanse it and stave off the infection that was certain to set in quickly, unless treated. Such treatment would suffice until he could make his way to Doc Wallace for proper medical attention.

But whiskey and the physician were both far beyond his reach—and then his dully functioning brain clutched at a straw; there was a bottle of whiskey on Con Fallon's desk. He had watched the rancher take one, no, two drinks from it the day he was there.

The house would be deserted. Zapf was with his posse somewhere to the north, hunting for Rosales, and, so he thought, Seevert. Fallon's stepdaughter was in Berrendo Crossing. What few hired hands there might be would have retired to the bunkhouse. The risk in entering the house would be small. . . .

It seemed a logical solution to his problem and he lifted his eyes, studied the area about him. He was on the back side of the hill, he saw, recognizing several landmarks. He needed only to cut back around the cone-shaped formation and he would be in the vicinity of the cave. From there it would be downslope to the house.

He swung the sorrel around, his mind clearer now, although that odd lethargy still gripped his body and made it difficult for him to remain straight in the saddle. He left the trail, angled across the hillside mid-distance between the flat and the peak, and gained the far slope. He found himself recalling the earlier descent when he had gone to the aid of Rosales.

The gelding, stumbling occasionally in his weariness, reached the foot of the grade, moved out across the flat, and came to the barn. He would waste no time searching inside that structure for liquor, Mace decided. Likely there would be a bottle or two, stashed by Hashmark riders, but hunting one down would consume time. Besides, there was a bottle waiting for him on

Con Fallon's desk. It would be easy to find.

The yard was quiet, the house dark as he drew up in the shadows at the end of the porch. It was an effort to leave the saddle, and, when his feet hit the ground, he went to his knees. Wondering at that, he pulled himself up, grinned tightly, and walked onto the porch.

He entered the familiar hallway, moved softly as possible to the door that led into Fallon's—now Charlie Zapf's—office. He could not see well, and twice he came up against the wall. Finally he arrived at the doorway to Zapf's quarters and halted. Starlight filtering through the curtains only partly illuminated the room. He hung there, braced against the frame for several moments, eyes straining toward the desk. The bottle was still there.

He started across the room and felt his knee strike against a chair. Ignoring that fresh burst of pain, he lurched on. Breathing hard, he reached the desk. Snatching up the bottle, he pulled the cork with his teeth, spat it aside. Holding the container to his lips, he took a long pull at the fiery liquor.

It hit him with solid, driving force. Recoiling, he sank onto the edge of the desk. After a bit, he helped himself to a second swallow, again paused. New strength was stirring through him, pulsing, setting his blood to racing.

Swaying, he put the bottle on the desk, reached up, and with unsteady fingers pulled his blood-encrusted shirt away from the wound. The pad clung, stuck tightly to the raw, ragged edges of the bullet hole. Angered, he jerked it free, flung it against the wall. The soaring pain shocked him, but he uttered no sound.

The wound began to bleed. Giving it no thought, he again took up the bottle. Placing the mouth against the raw opening, he sloshed a quantity of the liquor into the wound. The white-hot, searing fire that stabbed through him wrenched a gasp from his throat, brought him to his feet. He staggered, lost balance, reeled across the room. His trembling legs caught upon some obstacle. He tripped, went to his knees. Stubbornly clinging to the whiskey, he fought himself to his feet. He started to turn. Danger signals rushed through him as a figure loomed vaguely in the doorway. He dropped the bottle, clawed for his gun. Slowly his hand fell away.

It was the girl—Fallon's stepdaughter.

XVIII

For a time there was only the sound of his hoarse breathing, and then he said: "You! Thought you'd gone to town. . . ."

She stood just inside the room, a lamp in her hand. Through the filmy haze that lay before his eyes, he saw that she was young and pretty. She wore a loose-fitting robe of some dully glowing material that reached to the floor. Her face appeared soft-edged and creamy against its background of dark, shoulder-length hair.

"I came back," she said flatly and directly. "Who are you? What do you want?"

Aided by the liquor and prodded by the urgent need to leave the house before others of Hashmark were aroused, Seevert moved toward the door.

"Don't be afraid," he said thickly. "Just wanted some whiskey . . . borrow it. . . ."

"I'm not afraid," the girl replied calmly. "Who are you?"

"Not important. Sorry I woke you up . . . was trying to keep quiet."

"Quiet!" she echoed. "It sounded like the roof was falling in! If you wanted . . . you're hurt!"

Mace halted. "Yes'm. A little."

She placed the lamp on a table, turned up the wick, and hurried to his side. She examined the wound, her nose wrinkling. "So that's what you wanted the whiskey for."

Seevert said—"Yes'm."—again and continued to edge toward the doorway. He felt her eyes searching his face.

"Now I know you!" she exclaimed, drawing back. "You're Mace Seevert . . . the man they say killed my stepfather."

He nodded. "I didn't do it, though. I'm being framed. That's what I'm trying to do, prove it. . . ."

She studied him for several moments. "You're not going to do anything much until you get that gunshot wound . . . that's what it is, isn't it? . . . taken care of."

"It'll be all right now, ma'am. . . ."

"Stop calling me ma'am! My name is Amanda"

"Amanda. Now, if you don't mind, I'll be leaving. . . ."

"First I'm going to fix that shoulder," she said crisply. "Who shot you?"

He met her frank stare head on. "Your friend Zapf . . . or one of his crowd. They had Chopo, he's a friend of mine, strung up by a rope . . . were trying to make him talk. We managed to get away from them, but I stopped a bullet."

"Zapf's no friend of mine," she said coolly. "The cook told me about some sort of a fight in the barn. He said there was shooting, and then everybody rode off. They were chasing you, I guess."

"And they'll be coming back. I've got to get out of here."

"After I take care of that wound," she said firmly. "Come with me."

Mace did not stir. "But if you think I murdered your father. . . ."

His brain was still a little foggy and he was having trouble understanding her attitude.

"Stepfather," she corrected. "The truth is, I don't know what I think. I talked with Doctor Wallace in town this afternoon and asked him about you. He said he would bet you weren't the guilty man, although he believed you could have done it if you were pushed hard enough. Anyway, I don't think you would come back here if you had."

"I was after the whiskey . . . remembered seeing it," Mace said, utterly honest.

She gave him a quick smile. "I understand the doctor better now," she said. "Just follow me."

He trailed her out into the hall and to a bedroom at its extreme end. Motioning for him to sit down, she poured a quantity of water from a pitcher into a white china bowl. Moving with cool efficiency, she removed his stained shirt and spent several moments probing the wound.

"Not bad," she said, laying a wet pad on it. "Whiskey did a fair job. I'll get some medicine and bandages. Now, don't stir from here."

"Ought to be leaving," Mace said, protesting mildly.

She paused in the doorway. "Don't worry. I doubt if Zapf and the rest will be back for a while yet. Have you eaten today?"

He shook his head. A heavy drowsiness was claiming him, brought about by the loss of blood, the strong liquor, and sheer fatigue. Amanda said something to him that he did not catch and, turning, disappeared into the dark void of the hallway.

He had no idea how long she was gone. When she returned, she brought a plate upon which were several slices of beef, some warm biscuits, and a large cup of black, steaming coffee. Placing them on the table beside him, she said—"Eat."—and again left the room. When she once more stood next to him, she had with her a clean shirt, a bottle of strong-smelling antiseptic, some salve, and bandages.

He ate steadily, wolfing down the food and coffee while she worked at his wound. He began to feel better almost at once, and by the time she had finished, his head had cleared and he was much himself although weaker.

She placed the remainder of the bandages on the table along

with the medicine, and turned to him. Her face was serious.

"If you didn't kill my stepfather, do you know who did?"

"I'm pretty sure, but I've got no proof."

"The cook said you had been arrested and the sheriff was taking you to Crocketville. How did you get away from him?"

"Rosales . . . Chopo, that friend I told you about, gave me a hand." Mace paused, rubbed at his arm to relieve the stiffness. "Not much a man can do, once he's locked in a cell. Had to stay free."

He cast a sideward glance at a window, worried as to the time. But the girl seemed hungry for conversation; he guessed her life was one of loneliness.

"I can understand that," she said. Then: "Everyone is so positive that you did it."

"Especially Charlie Zapf. But Fallon was alive when we left him on the trail yesterday . . . or whenever it was. I've sort of lost track of time."

"It was the last time I saw him alive, too, when you and your friend rode out of the yard with him. He never came back."

Mace, his strength building swiftly now, leaned forward on his chair. "Could be you can give me some help. Did Zapf, or any of the others . . . the ones we left there in the office . . . follow us?"

Amanda shook her head. "No. I came in right after that. They stayed here. It must have been an hour or more before they went into the yard. Then they just stood around, waiting. I guessed from what Zapf said that father had told them not to leave. He was an Army man . . . of course you know that . . . and, when he gave an order, he insisted on it being carried out."

"When did they start looking for him?"

"Quite a while after dark."

Thoroughly perplexed, Mace lifted the coffee cup, drained it of its last, cold dregs. He had assumed Zapf, or some of his closer followers, had set out on the trail shortly after he and Ro-sales, with Fallon as hostage, had ridden off. It now appeared that such was not the case. He rose to his feet, again glanced toward the window. Night still held but it would not last much longer. Zapf and the posse were certain to return by dawn. He faced the girl.

"Do you know when they found Fallon . . . your stepfather?"

"You don't need to be so polite to me about him. We were never close. I was sort of a millstone about his neck and we were less than friendly. They found him about an hour after they left." She stopped, looked squarely at him. "You think it was one of our own men who did it, don't you? Possibly Charlie Zapf?"

The directness of her question jolted him. "I didn't think it showed that plain, but Zapf's my choice. They were partners and they didn't seem to be hitting it off so good."

"I know. Since it happened, I've thought of the same thing. But I don't believe there was anything really serious . . . that serious, between them. There might have been something I didn't know of, of course."

"Zapf had plenty to gain, being his partner."

"Yes, but my stepfather, being the sort of man he was, had enemies. Quite a few. One of them could have happened along and shot him."

Mace nodded. "Could be." He cast a final glance at the window. "Best be leaving here. I'm obliged to you for fixing up my shoulder and for the meal. Hope it won't get you in trouble with Zapf."

"Don't worry about that. This house is mine, not his. And I still own the larger share of the ranch." She hesitated and smiled. "I can't wait to tell him that all the time he was hunting you, you were right here."

Alarm lifted within Mace. "Don't do that! I know Zapf better than you . . . and I wouldn't want you meeting up with an accident."

"I can look after myself," she said lightly. "Where will you go?"

"I don't know. I've got to keep looking. I'm still not sure it wasn't Zapf, or that he's mixed up in it. He might have had somebody else pulling the trigger. I've got a week to find the killer, then I turn myself in to Sheriff Glyde."

She looked at him blankly. "Turn yourself in?"

"Made a deal with Glyde. Told him I'd surrender in a week if I hadn't dug up the murderer. He wasn't exactly in favor of the idea, but I managed it anyway."

She smiled and light danced in her eyes. "Your horse is in the shed . . . the one next to the barn. I gave him feed and water but it probably didn't help much. He's about to cave in. Better take mine."

"Thanks again," Mace said, moving into the hall. "But I reckon not. I don't want them stringing me up for horse stealing, if they get their hands on me again. The sorrel will do all right."

"I hope so," she said. "Use the back door," she added, pointing down the corridor. "It's the second. . . ."

"I know. I the same as grew up here . . . along with Yancey Harper."

He started down the dark hallway, feeling better but vaguely irritated at the weakness that still clung to him. The food and the liquor had done wonders but there was no side-stepping the effects of lost blood. His steps slowed as a giddiness set his eyes to swimming. He would have to take it easier for a bit longer. He reached for the doorknob and heard Amanda call softly.

"Mace . . . are you all right?"

He was surprised at her use of his given name and it pleased him. He half turned, waved. "I'm fine, just fine. *Adiós.*"

"Good bye," she answered as he stepped out into the silent yard.

XIX

A dull, gray haze rested upon the irregular formation of buttes to the east. It extended from the craggy hills in the south, to the long flats of the Calaveras Plains in the north. Mace Seevert gave it a swift survey; dawn was not far off.

Favoring his wounded shoulder, he hurriedly crossed the yard to the shed Amanda had mentioned. He remembered the small structure, the one attached to the barn. The Harpers had used it for storing the family carriage. Fallon had apparently converted it to a sort of private stable for the girl's horse and gear.

He entered, found the sorrel munching grain in a far stall. In the space next to him a tall bay, sleek and showing the signs of excellent care, dozed quietly. He wished he dared accept Amanda's offer to take her horse, but it would have only added to his problems. No one would believe him when he explained that he had her permission—and would give him no time to prove it. Horse thieves in Panhandle Valley, as elsewhere, were accorded short shrift when apprehended.

The sorrel looked better and he moved in beside the red horse, quickly making him ready to move. Amanda must have stabled him when she had left the room. She was a remarkable person and he doubted if Charlie Zapf was fooling her much. He wondered what Fallon had told her about him; had she believed he had given Circle S to her stepfather? That she could have been in the dark about the whole matter hardly seemed possible. She would recognize the brewing trouble and wonder as to its cause. And she had the sort of determination and independence of mind that would get to the bottom of a situation. One thing was sure, Mace realized, and he backed the gelding out of his stall—Amanda was little grieved by the death of Con Fallon. She was, to recall her own words, less than friendly toward him.

The eastern sky had brightened noticeably when he again halted in the yard. The gray had turned to pale yellow and already long fingers of color were spraying upward into the cloudless blue. Mace went to the saddle, again making allowances for his shoulder. It was going to be a rough day for both him and the sorrel. The smart thing to do, he concluded, would be to pull back in the hills and rest for a few hours. It would allow them both to recover their strength.

He pulled about, glanced toward the house. Amanda Fallon, framed in the doorway, lifted her hand to him. He raised his fingers to the brim of his hat, gave her his salute, and hurried on toward the barn and the trail beyond.

The sudden rush of hoofs brought him up short. Riders—Zapf and the posse—had come in from the west, were halting in the front yard. He saw Amanda turn, look into the interior of the house. She stepped back and closed the door quickly. Mace waited no longer. Touching the sorrel with his spurs, he sent the gelding trotting for the corner of the barn. Once on its yonder side he could not be seen by any of the Hashmark crew.

He gained the corner of the bulking structure, rounded it, and again rowelled the sorrel, this time raking him deeply. The danger of hoof beats attracting attention was no longer a factor; the need now was to get out fast. The red leaped ahead, drove hard for the brushy hill. He had just reached the foot of the slope when a yell went up. Seevert flung a hasty glance over his shoulder.

Two men had spotted him. Halted in that area between the house and the barn, they were pointing excitedly and yelling something to others on the crew, already beginning to pour around the side of the main building. By the time he was halfway up the hill, the entire party was again in the saddle and surging across the flat in pursuit.

Mace Seevert grinned tightly. Once more Hashmark was behind him, snapping at his heels. The race this time, however, was on a more equal basis. The posse's horses had been out all night, were tired and no better off than the sorrel. The riders, too, would be saddle-weary, doubtlessly hungry, and in short temper. Zapf could expect little from them. Mace, risking a second look, saw that the sorrel was holding his own, and that now, on the crest of the slope with a lengthy grade falling away below him, he likely would draw away from the others. But where to go?

Evidently they had failed to capture Rosales, since he was not among them. He could, of course, be dead, and that thought had an immediate sobering influence upon Seevert. Yet he doubted if it were true. The old *vaquero* was wily as a fox, and, trapped once by Hashmark riders, he would be no easy mark the second time. Likely he was deep in the *malpais* country, well hidden and beyond their reach.

Perhaps he, too, should head for the rough badland; it was a wild, forsaken area, a world of black, ragged lava flows that formed innumerable caves, sharp cañons, and precipitous buttes. It was ideal for hiding if a man could survive the blistering desolation. Many an outlaw, dodging a peace officer, had buried himself in the vast, unfriendly wasteland until it was again safe to move.

He dismissed the idea; the *malpais* on the far side of the valley was too far; odds were the sorrel would never make it—and there was Chopo Rosales to consider. If he had sought safety there, it would be wrong to lead Hashmark to him; they could, accidentally, run into the Mexican.

He pressed on, riding due east for the buttes that, now near, were taking shape. Zapf and his men still followed, a dozen dark figures in the early light. The breeze was at his back, and now and then he could hear a shout above the steady drumming of their horses. They were not crowding him hard, he realized. They seemed content to hold their distance, hopeful of eventually running him into the ground.

An arroyo, wide, brushy, and sandy-floored, appeared to his right. It struck a familiar chord within him, and he recalled that it led, in a direct line, to the first outthrust of embankments. Guided by impulse, he swung into it and brought the sorrel down to a trot.

A short time later he noticed a decrease in the sound of the pursuit and hope lifted within him. Perhaps the posse had missed his turn-off and swept on by, just as he had planned. Cheered, he urged the sorrel on.

The first, frowning façade of the buttes loomed up ahead, and, beyond it, the brilliant flare of the now climbing sun. For the past mile he had not heard the hammer of hoofs in his wake and he was convinced that he had shaken Zapf and the Hashmark riders. But he could not afford to take any chances. He must climb the bluff to a point where he could look down into the valley, and there lie low for a few hours. In that way he could keep tabs on the trail and on Zapf and his men while he and the sorrel rested. When the chase was called off, as from necessity it surely would be soon, he could return to the flat. Should someone discover his trail and lead the posse to the bluff, it would be a simple matter to mount up and continue on eastward.

He reached the bottom of the cliff, a ragged, overgrown, almost vertical wall, and halted. The trail up, he remembered, lay to the left. Putting the sorrel into motion again, he veered toward that point.

He overrode it the first try, but he finally located the gap, choked with tumbleweeds, and fought his way through to the narrow opening. No one had been over the trail in years. Rain had washed out narrow slashes and small rock slides had filled in at several places. But it could be worse. A quarter of the way up he halted to breathe the sorrel and listen. He could hear nothing of the posse. They were still in the valley, somewhere north along the foot of the buttes. He had managed to throw them off.

Below in the arroyo a stone *clattered*. The sound brought him around quickly. Hand on his gun he waited out the hot, breathless moments. He heard no more, and with a long sigh turned back to the trail. Likely it was a rabbit, or possibly a prowling coyote.

He touched the sorrel with his heels to urge him on. The horse resumed the climb, now growing steeper. A dozen paces higher the gelding stopped. Mace looked ahead. An adjacent arroyo, slicing across the trail at right angles, had at some time in the past run wild with storm water. It had left a gash in its wake.

The barrier was not wide, little more than an arm's length, in fact, but it was deep. Because of the slanting approach the sorrel was reluctant to proceed. Mace studied the ground for several moments and could see no reason why the red should have any fear. He looked upward; they were almost to the summit.

He gave the horse a reassuring pat on the neck, rowelled him lightly. The sorrel moved to the edge of the wash gingerly, tossing his head nervously. He halted at the brink of the gash, bunched himself to leap. Unexpectedly the soil beneath him began to crumble.

Mace, hampered and slowed by his injured shoulder, threw himself from the saddle as the horse began to flounder. The gelding managed to get his footing, drew back, and jammed Mace against the face of the bluff. Seevert, wincing with pain, put his good shoulder against the horse and threw all his weight into a desperate heave. The sorrel shifted. His hoofs went out from under him suddenly and he went down, legs flailing. Seevert tried to get clear but the butte held him prisoner. Lights popped before his eyes as a hoof struck his head, and then a wave of darkness engulfed him.

XX

Someone was close by. Mace Seevert sensed as much as he returned to consciousness. He opened his eyes cautiously and remained entirely still. He was on the trail. He could see the sorrel a short distance below, waiting in the hot sunlight.

A familiar voice said: "Head of yours must be mighty hard stuff."

Yancey Harper!

Mace stirred, rolled to his back. Pain slogged through him with a sullen insistence and the wetness on his shoulder told him the wound had begun to bleed. He sat up, grimacing in agony. Harper was above him on the trail, squatting on his heels near the edge of the wash, back resting against the bluff.

"Had me a hunch about this place," the young lawman said, toying with a heavy ring on his finger. "When we rode by, I remembered how you and me used to come here as kids. Dropped back and took me a look at the sand. Sure enough, there were hoof prints. So I followed."

"Where's Zapf and the rest?"

"Somewhere north, I reckon. Still hunting you."

Seevert frowned, not understanding. Why hadn't Yancey summoned the others? It was what he expected. He studied Yancey thoughtfully.

"Now what?"

"Talk," Harper said promptly. "I figure we've got a few things to hash over . . . for old-time's sake."

"Like what? You figure I killed Fallon, and you've nailed me. What's there to talk about?"

"Plenty. I know you didn't put that bullet in Con."

Seevert's jaw dropped. "You know . . . then why the devil . . . ?"

Yancey Harper shrugged. "Just sort of suited me to let things ride along and see the way they shaped up . . . leastwise until I could get them squared away in my head."

Yancey wasn't making much sense, or else he wasn't thinking straight, Mace decided. After a moment he said: "Who shot Fallon . . . Charlie Zapf?"

The lawman smiled. "Just what I aim to talk about. Now, take Charlie . . . it'd be easy for me to prove he did it."

Seevert, more confused now than ever, simply stared. He shook his head in exasperation. "I don't get this, Yance. What are you driving at?"

"This," Harper said, drawing his pistol and placing it on the ground before him. "You didn't kill Fallon. Neither did Zapf . . . I did."

"You!" the word fairly exploded from Mace Seevert's lips.

Yancey nodded, smiled. He was pleased at Seevert's startled reaction. "That damned Fallon euchred me out of my ranch, plain double-crossed me. I had it in mind to call his hand for quite a spell. Always making me cover up for him and his bunch of hardcases . . . and still he never would come across with what he promised. . . ."

The lawman was rambling. His face was drawn and his eyes glowed with a strange light. Silent, Mace watched and waited.

"When you showed up to take over your place and start ranching again, guess it sort of made me see what a blamed fool I'd been to turn loose of Hashmark. Reckon that's when I decided to settle up."

"I had it figured that Zapf murdered Fallon," Seevert said

when Harper fell quiet. "Everything pointed to him."

"Just what I've got in mind to do . . . make it look like Charlie did it. That is, if you're with me."

Mace considered that, and shook his head. That made no sense, either. Why would Yancey want to shift the blame to Zapf when he already had a pigeon all laid out to take his place on the gallows?

"Why would you do me this big favor, Yance?"

"I need your help, for one thing . . . and maybe I'm thinking about the old days . . . the times when we were plenty close, like brothers. Sure do miss the old days, don't you, Mace?"

"Sure," Seevert replied without thought. Harper's answer gave him no satisfaction, and there was too much he did not understand. "When did you jump Fallon?"

"Caught up with him on his way back to the ranch the other afternoon. He said you and Chopo had just taken him for a ride at the point of a gun. I told him right straight out what I had on my mind . . . that I wanted Hashmark back and for him and his bunch to get off. I told him just like you did, I guess. He got all high and mighty, like he always did, so I shot him."

"He didn't have a gun," Mace said, his voice tightening.

"I found that out afterwards. Didn't know it then. Wouldn't have made no difference. I'd have killed him anyway because he wasn't no great shakes with a six-gun."

Seevert said nothing. He was remembering that day when he and Rosales had ridden out with Con Fallon. Later they had heard an oncoming rider and pulled off the road. It had been Yancey. A few hours later Zapf and the others had found the rancher's body. It all jibed.

"You let them go ahead and think I did it," Mace said. "Still can't understand why you're changing that now."

"I've got to get Zapf out of the way. And like I already said, it'd be same as it was in the old days . . . you on the Circle S,

213

me on Hashmark."

"What about Fallon's stepdaughter?"

"Amanda? No trouble there. She sure can't handle the ranch by herself. I figure I can talk her into getting out . . . one way or another."

"The same way you did Fallon?"

Yancey grinned. "Plenty of ways to skin a cat."

Mace Seevert was finding it hard to believe that such words could be coming from a man he had known almost his entire life. Either something had happened to Yancey—or he had never really known him at all.

"I've got things all worked out," Harper said in a confidential tone. "I picked up a shell casing from Zapf's pistol. It's a Forty-Four. Just sort of thought it might come in handy someday. Been planning on using it. I'll take it to Glyde. He's down there with the posse, looking for you. I'll tell him I found it close to where Fallon was shot."

"He'll wonder why you waited so long to bring it up," Mace said, stalling for time.

"I can explain that, too. I'll say I never did believe you did it, that I kept poking around until I come across the cartridge. The firing pin mark will prove it fits Charlie's pistol. That'll mighty quick clear you."

"I'm in the clear now, far as the murder's concerned . . . because I didn't do it. Just a matter of getting some proof together."

"It'll be hard to do," Harper said, his manner stiffening. "Everybody around's made up their mind you're guilty. Town's getting another posse together right now to help run you down. You don't have a chance unless you throw in with me."

"And if I don't . . . ?"

"I just keep my mouth shut and do my sworn duty. I'll tell them I had a hunch you'd head for the bluffs to hole up. When

I tried to arrest you, you put up a fight and I had to kill you."

"Like you did Fallon."

Yancey Harper picked up his pistol and spun the cylinder absently. "There'd be nothing else I could do. I'd be a fool to turn you loose now. But you ain't loco enough to turn me down. What's Zapf mean to you? Nothing. Neither did Fallon. We're the ones who belong around here, Mace. It's up to us to stick together, hold onto what we got. Only smart we work together . . . like brothers. Ain't that right?"

"Expect so . . . only murder's not the way."

"The only way, sometimes. What's the difference in killing a man on the road and killing a man in war? Ends up the same . . . both dead."

"There's a big difference," Mace said, shifting slightly so that his pistol was more available. Yancey was talking like a fool— like a man half-crazed. He made no sense at all and Mace realized that, if he expected to stay alive, he was going to have to fight. His fingers touched the holster at his hip. Shock and despair rocked through him. The pistol was gone. He saw it then, laying on the trail an arm's reach away. It had fallen from his holster during the accident.

"I'm not so sure you can make this stick with Glyde," he said, covering up his surprise. "He's a smart old man."

"He won't doubt me. I'm the law around here, and lawmen always sort of work together. Showing him that Forty-Four casing will do the trick."

Seevert fought to maintain his composure. He must humor Yancey, keep him talking, make him believe his proposition was being considered—even accepted. It would be suicide to make a move just yet; Harper had all the advantages, and he must take the lawman alive. Yancey was his only proof of innocence.

But Harper was turning edgy. The strange glow in his eyes burned brighter. "What about it?"

"I'm thinking about it, Yance."

"What for? I'm offering you a good deal . . . your own neck, actually."

"I realize that, but we better figure all the angles. A man's got to be sure."

"I've done thought it out. Like I said, it'll be no problem. Then we can have things like they used to be."

Seevert felt his nerves draw tighter. "It would be fine," he murmured, and then as something dawned on him, he said: "Were you in the war, Yance?"

Harper bobbed his head. "Sure. About a year. Joined up right after you did. Got myself all boogered up, though, and they sent me home."

The reason for Yancey Harper's odd behavior and warped line of thought was beginning to break through to Mace. He said: "Sorry to hear it. What happened?"

"Load of canister plowed into my squad. Killed everybody but me. Damned cannon was so close the wind knocked me flat and turned me deaf. It was quite a spell before I could hear anything."

It was suddenly clear in Seevert's mind. Yancey had been badly injured in the war—not so much physically as mentally. Shell shock, he had heard it called. It had addled his brain, left his reasoning twisted and crippled.

"You got your mind made up?" Yancey demanded abruptly. "Boys will be coming back. We got to have things set."

Mace nodded, calculating his next move, his chances. They weren't good.

"Yance, it won't work the way you say. Only one thing I can do . . . turn you over to Glyde, tell him you admitted killing Fallon. The law will treat you right, once they hear all about you."

Harper was staring at him, eyes spread wide, mouth hanging

open. "You're what?"

"Handing you over to Glyde . . . ," Mace said. As he saw Harper's gun come up, he hurled himself to the side and snatched up his pistol.

Mace felt a bullet pluck at his sleeve as he rolled frantically. He fired as he came onto his back and thumbed the hammer for a second shot. There was no need. Yancey Harper was folding forward slowly. His weapon had fallen to the ground and there was a dazed look in his eyes. Suddenly he toppled.

Seevert, a heavy sickness rushing through him, watched in stunned silence. He got to his feet unsteadily, making his way through the coils of smoke to where Harper lay. Kneeling, he rolled the young lawman onto his back and felt for a heartbeat. There was none.

Sweat bathed him and the sickness grew. He rose, his eyes fastened on Harper's face. Yancey once had been his best friend; still was, if you considered what he had offered from the depths of his distorted mind. And then a new realization came to Mace Seevert; he had just slain the one man who could prove him innocent of Con Fallon's death.

XXI

In those three days the world had changed. He had dreamed of returning from war to peace; instead, he had gone from one war to another. Now he could fight no more. Exhausted, desperate, and trapped by the ruthless men who had moved into the valley and become masters over all, he had reached the end of his rope. What was the question Doc Wallace had asked of him? *Are you sure Circle S is worth it?*

He leaned forward, recovered his hat, and walked down the trail to where the horses stood. Taking up the reins of Harper's mount, he led him back to where the lawman lay. Kneeling, ignoring the pain in his shoulder, he slipped his arms under the lifeless figure, prepared to lift.

"Let him be, son."

At the sound of Carl Glyde's voice Seevert sprang back in surprise. The sheriff stood off the path, a few paces below.

"Best we do this according to the book," he said. "Zapf and his boys will be coming soon. They'll have heard them gunshots. I'll name one the coroner. Won't be time to go after the regular man in town."

Seevert, stricken dumb, watched woodenly as the lawman made his way to the trail. Once there, Glyde cocked his head to one side and said: "What was you aiming to do with him?"

The question jarred Mace from his stupor. "Take him down, turn him over to you."

Glyde nodded in satisfaction. "I guessed right. Being an honest man, you'd look at it that way, even though it might put a noose around your neck."

Mace stared at Harper. "Yance was my best friend for a long time. I couldn't just leave him there." He looked up suddenly. "You see anything of Rosales?"

The lawman's eyes held steady. "He's dead, son. Hate telling you that, but it's so."

Chopo dead—gone. The words sank slowly into Seevert's brain. Chopo, who had never harmed a soul in his entire life, who had wanted only to help. Abruptly anger burst with explosive force within Mace.

"Damn Zapf and his murdering bunch! Damn them all to hell! I'll settle . . . somehow . . . with every mother's son of them for what they've done. . . ."

"The law'll do the settling," Glyde said calmly. "I got there right after it happened. Over in the *malpais*. I was hunting for you two. I wish I could have found him *before* the shooting started, like I did you."

The lawman's words registered dully on Seevert's flaming

mind, then gradually took on meaning as the rage cleared away. "I didn't catch what you said, Sheriff. The last."

"That I got here before the shooting. I heard most of what was said, including that deal Harper tried to make you to frame Zapf. Only thing, being down below, I couldn't get up here quick enough to head off the gun play. Real sorry . . . for you . . . it ended up the way it did."

Relief was flowing, swiftly and coolly, through Mace Seevert, but there was no joy, only a deep measure of sadness. He was clear of Fallon's murder, but at the price of Chopo Rosales's life—and Yancey's, too. He looked again at the young lawman's stilled face. "Of all the men who might have thrown down on him, it had to be me."

"You didn't have much choice," Glyde said gently. "He would have killed you."

Mace nodded. "Yancey wasn't quite right in the head. I realized that at the last. How'd you happen to come up here?"

"Didn't just happen. I saw Harper drop out of the posse and backtrack to the arroyo. I sort of had my doubts about him from the start, so I followed. I trailed him here to the bluff. When I got near, I heard you two talking, so I climbed off my horse and worked my way in close as I could."

Glyde checked his words and glanced down into the wash. Riders were moving up.

Mace could see Charlie Zapf in the lead. "He's the one I thought bushwhacked Fallon. I ought to beg his pardon for that. Instead, I feel like putting a bullet in him for Chopo."

"Never you mind," Glyde said. "He's got plenty to answer for . . . the killing of your Mexican friend, and the Cargills, and a few other things. While I'm over this way, I figure to clean up this mess, once and for all. You be around. I'll be needing your testimony."

"I'll be here," Mace replied. He had a ranch to rebuild after all, and a new life to start. "Just you holler and I'll come."

ABOUT THE AUTHOR

Ray Hogan was an author who inspired a loyal following over the years since he published his first Western novel, *Ex-Marshal,* in 1956. Hogan was born in Willow Springs, Missouri, where his father was town marshal. At five the Hogan family moved to Albuquerque where they lived in the foothills of the Sandia and Manzano Mountains. His father was on the Albuquerque police force and, in later years, owned the Overland Hotel. It was while listening to his father and other old-timers tell tales from the past that Ray was inspired to recast these tales in fiction. From the beginning he did exhaustive research into the history and the people of the Old West, and the walls of his study were lined with various firearms, spurs, pictures, books, and memorabilia, about all of which he could talk in dramatic detail. "I've attempted to capture the courage and bravery of those men and women that lived out West and the dangers and problems they had to overcome," Hogan once remarked. If his lawmen protagonists seem sometimes larger than life, it is because they are men of integrity, heroes who through grit of character and common sense are able to overcome the obstacles they encounter despite often overwhelming odds. This same grit of character can also be found in Hogan's heroines, and in *The Vengeance of Fortuna West* (1983) Hogan wrote a gripping and totally believable account of a woman who takes up the badge and tracks the men who killed her lawman husband by ambush. No less intriguing in her way is Nellie Dupray, convicted of rustling in *The Glory Trail* (1978). One of his most popular books, dealing with an earlier period in the West with Kit Carson as its protagonist, is *Soldier in Buckskin* (Five Star Westerns, 1996). Above all, what is most impressive about Hogan's Western novels is the consistent quality with which each is crafted, the compelling depth of his characters, and his ability to juxtapose the complexities of human conflict into narratives always as intensely interesting as they are emotionally involving. *Range Feud* will be his next Five Star Western.